"Readers who enjoyed *Cold Sassy Tree* will be entranced by *A Journey of Choice.* Liddy will live in the reader's memory long after the final page is read. Pat Laster is an author to remember." --Deanna Dismukes, Director, Hemingway-Pfeiffer Creative Writers' Retreat, Hemingway Barn-Studio, Piggott, AR, Arkansas State University Heritage Site

"I am excited to see Pat Laster's *A Journey of Choice* finally in print. Few have anticipated its publication more than I have. I've watched Pat meticulously develop this story over the last three years and the final product is well worth the wait!" --Roland Mann, author of *Buying Time*

"Written with elegance, imagination, and historical savvy, Pat Laster's *A Journey of Choice* grabbed me from the beginning and drew me into the life and travails of Liddy Underhill, an earnest young woman just out of high school, whose goal is to become a newspaper woman. Spanning the years between the Great Depression and World War II, the story derives its power from Laster's unique sense of place and atmosphere, an effective backdrop for the vivid and complex characters which populate the story. *A Journey of Choice* is a finely detailed, original piece of fiction that is well worth the read. --Sandy Raschke, Fiction Editor, *Calliope, A Writer's Workshop by Mail*

Also by Pat Laster

Poetry

delicious fatigue

Variations

windfall persimmons-Oriental forms

Connecting Our Houses

(a flip calendar of haiku)

with Dorothy McLaughlin

2003 series of haiku/ senryu / cinquains:

January Gimcracks, February's Fallout, Measuring March, April Acclaimed, May Day, Jam-Packed June, A Junket Through July, It's August Already? September Cinquains, October's Outlook, November Nuggets, Dynamic December.

2005 series of haiku / senryu:

Listen...the snow, winter's loose ends, along the pasture fence, in the rainy dark, along the creek bank, collecting raindrops, the taste of summer, only sky and sand, a patch of yellow, coffee at twilight, before the frost, a branch of red leaves.

2006-07-08:

hearing puffs of snow, on the same page, just before dawn, at the sound of geese, a bird calls at dusk, lighting a candle (winter)

2010

fishing in the clouds

A JOURNEY OF CHOICE

Pat Laster

iUniverse, Inc.
New York Bloomington

A Journey of Choice

iUniverse books may be ordered through booksellers or by contacting:

iUniverse
1663 Liberty Drive
Bloomington, IN 47403
www.iuniverse.com
1-800-Authors (1-800-288-4677)

ISBN: 978-1-4502-5416-8 (pbk)
ISBN: 978-1-4502-5417-5 (cloth)
ISBN: 978-1-4502-5418-2 (ebk)

Printed in the United States of America

iUniverse rev. date: 9/20/10

For my writer friends- you know who you are

Everybody likes to go their own way––to choose their own time and manner of devotion.

-Jane Austen

—— Acknowledgments ——

Special thanks to Dot Hatfield (soul sister and manuscript advisor), Freeda Nichols, and Rhonda Roberts–– Central Arkansas Writers; Danielle Burch, William White, and Bud Kenny––Hot Springs Writers, Lissa Lord and Eileen Krause, friends and colleagues.

Also, to Cynthia Sabelhaus and Sandy Raschke, editors, *CALLIOPE: A Writer's Workshop by Mail.* Several chapters of this novel were published therein as winners of fiction contests.

To Joan Banks, Shelba Tankersley, Pat Craig, Sue Watson, Joan Hearn, Jeanie Carter, Nina Tillery and the late Ann Kinnaird, who for many years as the Steel Magnolias writing group, fostered the birth, early care and feeding of this book.

To the staff of The Writer's Colony at Dairy Hollow, Eureka Springs AR, especially Vicki who vetted the trial, and Cindy; the staff of the Hemingway-Pfeiffer Museum Educational Center, Piggott AR, especially Deanna, who read the manuscript, and Karen, who loaned me her office for two retreats, and mentors Rob Lamm, Roland Mann and Donna James.

To the BHS-'54 'girls',––Glenda, Barbara, Beverly, Doris, Marie, Mildred and Shirley––who challenged me to 'get this book done so we can read it before our eyes give out.'

To Fred Pfister, editor of *Ozark Mountaineer,* for permission to use recipes from Jewell Fitzhugh's book, *Old Time Recipes for Modern Day Cooks.*

To Steven Cortez, Mara Rockey, Jade Council and George Nedeff of iUniverse.

Lastly, thanks to my family, especially brother Thurman Couch MSW, LCSW, MFT, ACSW, who vetted the chapters about writing therapy, and all who respected my need to write. And no, you are not characters in this story. If you find yourself, it is your own doing––not mine.

— Chapter One —

LIDDY UNDERHILL

Suffocating isn't a strong enough word for the agitation I felt. It was late summer of the year I graduated from high school in Lock Rivers, Missouri. Mother's constant whining about 'Daddy's leaving' and 'what were we going to do?' grated on my nerves. Yet I dared not mention it, or she'd get all sappy and pitiful. She cried a lot. So I spent as much time as possible at the store.

Poor Yvonne and Juliana. But they had each other and their playhouse in the hayloft. They could escape. At least after their chores were finished. And until the next meal.

Instead of showing pluck and determination to make the best of it, Mother stayed on the telephone a great deal with her friends, who, knowing her plight, were loath to tell her they had things to do. They could listen, at least, while polishing silver or shelling peas. More likely, they would lay the receiver down facing their ears, so they could know when to 'ummm' or 'lawsy me, Genese!' at the appropriate times.

At the store, I sorted the mail, hoping to discover a letter from Daddy, but one never came. Then I rearranged the grocery shelves, filled in the blank spots left after yesterday's sales.

One day, after the school term began but before Editor Redd answered my inquiry, the young peddler from St. Luke stopped by again. "Heth Coursey, Esquire, at your service," he introduced himself.

He told me then he would be passing by every two or three weeks. Each day when the third week rolled around, I dressed as carefully as I could. Mother asked once why I spent so much time primping. I plastered my bangs down with some of Daddy's pomade, hoping to cover the slashing scar across my forehead, and ignored her.

The day came when I heard the clop-clop of horses' hooves. Not too eagerly, and with a broom in my hand as if I'd been sweeping, I opened the door and pretended surprise.

"I'd like to fill up my team with some of your gasoline, please," he said, eyes glittering. He tied the horses to the hitching post. "No, I'm kidding. They had a good drink a while back. Any grass hereabouts?"

"Around the back," I said. "There's a small patch they could crop. It'd save me mowing."

"Much obliged." The young salesman unhitched the horses and led them past the gravity pump and around the stone steps. He picketed them so they could munch the paltry patch of Bermuda.

Meantime, I went back inside and opened the rear door, so he could watch the team as we conducted our business. If we had any business. He took the back steps in one leap.

"Would you like a Dr. Pepper?" I asked, opening the top of the box on the north wall. "They're ice cold."

He selected a bottle and pried the lid off with the opener Daddy had attached to a string on the bare stud.

I wasted no time asking my question. "I know you are not a transport service, but could you possibly haul my steamer trunk and sewing machine to St. Luke?"

"If I could sell half the wares in my wagon, I might be able to fit them in."

"Oh, I don't mean today, but maybe by your next time through, I will have the job I've applied for. I could always ship them by train, but––"

We were facing each other in the space between the back door and the counter. Mother would be mortified to see a customer in the area with the shelves of goods.

"No, I think my horses and I can move you––if your mother will sell the goods I have to leave here."

"I could pay you," I blurted, and then felt my face burn.

He moved one step closer. "Could you now?" He smiled and reached out, brushing the shirred bodice of my dress. I couldn't move but I know my eyes widened.

"Uh, I saw a gnat on your clothes," he said, and stepped back.

I stepped back, too. A shiver rippled through me and settled in my lower regions.

He suddenly turned very polite. "Will you or your mother need any of my wares today, Miss?" I hoped he thought Mother was in the back room. "You can look through my merchandise––" His eyes searched for a way past the counter. I quickly raised the panel and stood back, allowing his passage "––while I get the horses."

Once into the front area of the store, he faced me again and locked his blue eyes on mine. Then he turned at the entrance, stepped over the threshold to the porch and pulled the door closed. I followed him out, determined to stay on the opposite side of the wagon from him.

During the time it took to bring the horses around, I surveyed his wares. There were several bottles of salve made of 'buffalo bush berries for burns,' key rings with little horns blown by clowns with 'jolly' on their shirts, a wolf pelt, a May issue of *Saturday Evening Post*, a stern-faced doll with a gray and white outfit that reminded me of a character in *Little Women*.

"We'll take the burn salve," I told him as he hitched the team to the wagon. "How much?"

"All four for a simoleon. A dollar'll do."

I handed him the only bill in my pocket. His fingers touched mine as he took the money. Once more, our eyes locked for a moment. He climbed onto the seat, doffed his cap, smiled, and said, "I'll be back before the month is out. Until then, hubba hubba and hurdy gurdy! " He clucked to his horses and they pulled away from the store and clip-clopped toward the main road.

After the wagon was out of sight, I ran inside and grabbed my journal. *Hubba hubba and hurdy gurdy.* I'll have to look that up before Heth Coursey comes again.

Now where to put these bottles of burn balm that we didn't need?

— Chapter Two —

The morning after Heth Coursey visited, the ten-o'clock freight from Donathan whistled through town right on time. After the long train rumbled past, I skipped over the track to the mail drop and retrieved the canvas sack marked, "Lock Rivers."

Dumping the letters on the counter, I found one addressed to me from Editor Redd in St. Luke. I wanted to rip into it fiercely, like a hungry dog that's just been thrown a bone. Was I prepared for her answer? *Patience, now. Patience.* Hands shaking, I placed letters in the boxes for the Oliver Sloans, the Brian Bishops, the Carroll Tyndalls, the Mack Berrys, Clifton Ferrel and his mother.

By 10:30, if nice weather held, folks would walk over to our store-post office, check their boxes and leave outgoing mail for tomorrow's run.

Finally, my sorting job finished, I used the mother-of-pearl letter opener I'd received for graduation, and carefully slit open the envelope from Editor Redd.

Dear Miss Underhill," I read aloud. *In receipt of your letter and impressed with your credentials. Prepared to offer you the job of reporter for the* St. Luke (Missouri) Banner *beginning October 1. Telephoned Mr. Tom Grindle at the boardinghouse to see if he has a room available. He assured me he did and that he would look forward to meeting you. His address is—"*

"My first job!" I whooped and hollered, dancing through the shelves with the feather duster. "I've got a jo-ob; I've got a jo-ob," I sang the two-toned chant all children use.

I will have to tell Mother and the girls. They'll miss me but they'll survive. Mother will cry and wring her hands and call me ungrateful.

"But," I'll say, "Mother, I'll send you what's left of my paycheck after room and board, and a little pin money." Then she'll turn silent and icy for three days.

The front doorbell sounded and Mrs. Bishop stepped in heavily, followed by a shaggy black and white mongrel with long ears and huge, sad eyes.

"Oh, dear. Where did that ugly creature come from?" she asked, then clapped her hand to her mouth. "I'm sorry, Liddy. Is that your dog? I swear I never saw the sneaky thing behind me."

I laughed. "No, Mrs. Bishop. That's not our dog." I eyed the animal that nosed around every corner, sniffed every bare board it could reach. "Something I can help you with today, ma'am?"

"Just the mail, dear. How's your mother faring, poor thing?"

"She's just fine," I lied, but it was enough to stop any prolonged conversation. The buxom lady fiddled with her too-tight shirtwaist and turned to leave. "What about this dog?" I asked her.

"Someone will come by looking for it today, surely," she said, and lumbered out with her mail.

I continued dusting the shelves. Now that I was leaving home and moving away, I wondered what would reduce the jarring effect on Mother and the girls. I'll have to work steadily to be ready and gone by October 1.

The bell sounded again, startling the pup, which slept in a sunny spot by the corn plant. He was full of Friskies Dry that we happened to have on the shelf. "Oh, hello, Mr. Ferrel. This your dog? He slipped in when Mrs. Bishop came in for her mail."

"Nope. Never seen him. Seems happy enough where he is." He turned from the dog to the counter. "Need a jar of Garrett's Scotch for my old mother." I could see brown oozing from the sides of his mouth. *His old mother indeed.*

"She sits and quilts and listens to her radio stories. Oh, yes, some food for that silly canary of hers. We don't get bird seed down at the feed store."

While I found the items, I decided to ask him a question. Maybe he could give me some ideas. "Mr. Ferrel, has your mother lived with you very long?" The middle-aged man dressed in khaki work clothes had retrieved his mail and strolled back to the counter.

"Oh, she doesn't live with me. I live with her." He picked up two penny suckers and dropped them by the snuff jar. "Once Daddy died, she couldn't bear for me to leave. So I stayed on."

"Were you the only child?"

"Yes. I felt obliged, I guess." He ran his fingers through his thinning hair. "You have a reason for asking, Miss Liddy? Might you be thinking about leaving Lock Rivers now that you're out of school?"

"Sh-h-h!" I put my finger to my lips. "I only got word this morning." I pushed the letter over to the scrawny man. "I haven't even told Mother. She outlawed my applying, but I disobeyed. Now I have three weeks to get to St. Luke. I know she'll be furious. And heartbroken."

He read the letter, then looked straight at me and said, "Don't let that stop you. You're smart, bright as a new penny and pretty as a skinned onion." We both laughed at his comparison.

"Don't do like I did twenty years ago. I'm still selling feed; still living in the same house I was born in."

Raising the counter panel, I walked through to the front of the store. I motioned Mr. Ferrel to a chair and I took the other one. I told him about asking the Nance Mercantile peddler to haul my furniture to St. Luke on his next trip. "It'll be three weeks at the most before he comes again," I said.

"Say!" The man sat up in the chair as if he'd had the greatest idea since the telephone. "Maybe this dog's the ticket. Do you have a dog? Maybe your mother needs a replacement for you." He snapped his fingers and the little animal ran to him and stood as if waiting for an ear scratch. Its tail took to the air like a funeral fan waving in the heat.

"I don't know. We've never had a dog." I bent toward the pooch and it ran to me, licking my outstretched hand. "But anything to help soften the blow of my leaving will be worth a try."

"Tell you what, Miss Liddy. Why don't I pay a call on your mother? We both live alone. Well, we both are single, even if other folks live in our homes. I might be able to help her change her tune. You wouldn't mind that, would you?"

"A dog, a male visitor––whatever it takes to make my leaving easier on her." Mr. Farrel rose to leave and I followed. As he walked out the door with his merchandise, I remembered something.

"Oh, by the way, Mr. Ferrel, do you know what 'hubba hubba and hurdy gurdy' means?" He stopped, cocked his head and laid his finger on his chin. Then, negotiating the stone steps, he shook his head. "Nope," he said. On solid ground, he turned and waved goodbye.

— Chapter Three —

I began telling my story to Heth Coursey, the near stranger on the wooden seat beside me. He had allowed me to ride along on his team-pulled peddler's wagon to St. Luke, where he lived. I had never done such a thing in my life, disobeying my mother for one, hitching a ride with a handsome young man, for another. I never thought my journey into the larger adult world would mean rebelling against Mother and sneaking off like a thief.

"After I told Mother I had a job in St. Luke and waved Editor Redd's letter about, she exploded. 'No, no, no, no, no!' Her voice rose with each syllable. She turned back to the fried potatoes, clacked the pancake turner on the iron skillet and said, 'We've gone over this before, Liddy.'"

We rode in silence for a spell. A late-September breeze scuttled in, blowing the yellow leaves across the road and over the horses' broad rumps. Other leaves settled on us. Had this man heard anything I said?

Heth Coursey finally spoke. "How did you pull it off? Did your mother give you any more trouble? Parents can be such crab patches."

"It took a lot of help from neighbors. Mr. Ferrel had made plans with Mother––without setting a specific day––to drive into Madison so she could check on her legal options to Daddy's desertion. Everything depended on what day *you* came through Lock Rivers."

"Me? You mean I––"

"Yes, you. Mrs. Bishop––she lives south of town––when she saw you coming, she called me at the store. I called Mr. Ferrel, and then he phoned Mother. He told her he wanted to leave early to eat breakfast at a new pancake house between here and Madison."

The road ahead disappeared into mountain fog. I saw a towering pine rising from a rocky ledge. I held onto my hat and looked up. Sometimes eagles clutched the top branches. But the foliage was so thick I couldn't see that far.

"It's a good thing the train station is close to the store and that our house can be seen from both locations. Yesterday at noon, I ran over to the depot to check with Mr. Mashburn about shipping my trunk and sewing machine. I decided they would not fit in—" I motioned to the back of the wagon. "I also made arrangements with Ishmael to bring his cart over to my house as soon as Mr. Ferrel's car pulled away. See what I mean about the neighbors' cooperation?"

Suddenly Heth hollered, "Whoa!" and pulled on the reins. "There's a pecan tree and a persimmon tree. What luck! That'll be some good eating, and maybe mean some sales on up the road. Bring your hat and fill it up."

The horses munched roadside grasses. They seemed happy to rest. Squirrels, interrupted during their meal, skittered up a nearby tree. They watched us steal their dinners. Now and then one would chatter in a voice like a mother's scold.

After we were back on the road, I continued my story. "I had saved a little money from working at the store and put it in the Postal Savings System. Before Daddy left, he let me write out the certificates for the depositors. Afterwards, Mother made me take care of everything."

Heth glanced over occasionally as I talked. Once when I looked, his eyes were fixed on my face. Another time, his eyes rested on the bulges a little lower. Did he even know my name? I don't remember him ever asking or that I ever told him. It didn't matter. I likely wouldn't see him again once I got to St. Luke.

"Let me get this straight," the peddler said. "Your mother is gone for the day. She doesn't know you've run away from home. What if she and Mr. Whoever don't make it back? Or we meet them coming home? Didn't you say you had sisters? What about them?"

The sun had burned off the fog, and in the distance I saw sunlight glint off a tin roof. The higher we climbed, the cooler the breeze but I had packed my shawl deep in my suitcase.

"I thought of that, too," I answered. "Mrs. Bishop agreed to mind the store until time for school to let out. If Mr. Ferrel hasn't brought Mother home by then, at the first sight of the girls, Mrs. B. will go to the street and call them to the store. Otherwise, none of my family will know I've actually left until they go into the house and see the letters."

Heth laughed. "You sound like me. I do as I please as much of the time as I can, given this peach of a job. I only need enough moolah to keep me in hooch and pocket change."

The farther west we traveled on this mountainous, curvy road in the Ozarks, the cloudier it became. I shivered and crossed my arms, rubbing my hands up and down them.

"Here." Heth gave me the reins and then reached back under the bench where we sat. He pulled out a quart jar of something and a yellow oilcloth slicker. "It looks like we're headed into rain. This stuff'll warm your insides and we'll have to share the raincoat as best we can."

"I'll pass on whatever that is in the jar," I said, "but I'll be happy to share your raincoat."   Heth took a slug from the clear liquid, screwed the top back on and replaced the jar. He found the right sleeve of the coat and reached around me.

"Move the reins to your left hand and put your right arm in––"

Pretending to settle me in, he ran his hand across my breasts. "Hmm. Nice bubs. Small, though."

"Hey! Not so fast!" I said and jerked my left hand under his arm to move it off me. When I did, the reins flapped on the horses' backs and they took off in a trot. I had to hold on to the end of the bench. My face was hot and my pulse jumped like the horses' feet.

Heth got the team under control. I scooted as far away from him as possible. No sharing the slicker now. I pushed my other arm into the remaining sleeve and pulled it close.

Not long after that, the sky darkened and lightning flashed farther west. Then rain pelted the slicker.

"There's a tourist court around the next bend," he shouted over the rain. "I did tell you the trip takes two days, didn't I?"

— Chapter Four —

No, he had *not* told me the trip from Lock Rivers to St. Luke took two days! I didn't have enough money for a night in a tourist court. And I certainly would not share a room with *that* cad––not after the liberties he took during the rain.

Sure enough, on the next rise and around a bend in the road, several small weathered cottages sat like water-logged animals. Each one had enough space between for a vehicle.

Heth pulled the wagon between the office and the first cabin. While he released the team, fed and picketed them behind the building, I stepped out on the front wagon wheel and jumped to the ground. Pins and needles ignited fire in my feet and I fell. It took a minute for the feeling to come back.

Neither of us spoke, and even encumbered by the oversize raincoat, I somehow hauled out my cases from the wagon and lugged them under the office overhang.

"Hey!" Heth called when he noticed. "Where you going? We can stay in the same––"

"Not on your 'hubba-hubba and hurdy-gurdy'!" I answered in as scolding a voice as I could muster.

"Aw, go on! I didn't mean nothing. It's just my way."

The owner of the business came out of the office. "Can I help you with those cases, miss? Don't you want me to take them to your cabin? Where's your husband?"

"No, no!" I shouted, shivering. "He's not my husband!" I set the bags down."I hitched a ride from Lock Rivers. He didn't tell me the trip took two days. I don't have extra money for a room." I tucked the smallest case under my arm and lifted the others. "Might I sleep on your sofa tonight? I could work off the cost by doing chores." Inside, I set my luggage down and wriggled out of the slicker. The man reached for it and hung it on a nail by the front door.

A woman stepped out of the office in time to hear my offer. "Poor dear! You're soaked. Horace, bring those bags to the linen room." Turning to me, she said, "Let's get you outta those wet things. Of course, you can stay here with us." As she led me into a hallway, I heard Heth stomp in and speak to the man.

"'Lo, Horace. Nice weather for ducks." I stopped to listen and signaled to the woman, palms toward her, finger to my lips. She caught my drift.

"Coursey, you scoundrel!" was the man's answer. "Gone and got you another woman, have you? She's a looker, even in the rain."

Heth answered. "Oh, she got in a lather because I rubbed on her headlights. She's definitely not a smooch date."

I was shivering so badly my feet would hardly move. The proprietress tiptoed over and wrapped me with her arms to help stop the shaking. We padded to a small room behind the office.

"You can sleep here," she whispered, gesturing to a small bed already made up. "Let me fix us some hot cocoa to warm up your insides. Get yourself dry, Miss––?"

"Liddy. Liddy Underhill from Lock Rivers." I couldn't thank her enough, this aproned and hair-netted matron who looked a little like my Aunt Leacha. I opened the valise, pulled out my flannel gown and chenille robe. The lid flopped down like a tired runner. Peeling off my wet clothes, I hung them on wall pegs, and slipped into my night wear. Pulling my legs under me on the bed, I waited for the cocoa. I looked around––no window, no clock, no lamp, but a slop jar sat under a bench against a wall.

The woman came in with two cups of steaming cocoa and a small pitcher of water. I moved over and she set the tray on the bed. She handed me a flashlight from under one of her arms. "If you have to get up in the night––" and she motioned to the bench.

"Thank you most kindly," I said, and reached for the warm mugs in the tray beside me. I handed her one.

Mrs. Outler pulled the bench over in the middle of the room. "May I sit with you a while?" She leaned toward me. "He didn't try anything, did he?"

"Not much," I said. "He has wandering hands." I peered into my cup at the melting glob of marshmallow white. I'd never mentioned such personal stuff before, even to my mother. Especially to my mother.

"Men! Oh lordy, girl, wait till you're my age. Hands will be the least of your worries." We finished our cocoa in silence, and then she rose, and pushed the bench against the wall. "Goodnight, deary. After what all happened today I hope you get some rest."

I rose, too, set the mug on the tray, handed it over and followed her to the door. "I appreciate this very much. Thank you. Thank you."

— Chapter Five —

I awoke to the blended aromas of coffee and bacon, and to the sound of voices. “You mean he just drove off without her?” the woman asked.

“Yup. Said something about her promising to pay him. But that he hadn’t seen any sign of her keeping her word,” Horace answered. “Said he’d teach her who she could toy with—–”

That low down skunk! It’s a good thing I brought my cases in last night.

I folded the linens from my bed, then snatched them back, wadded and tossed them into the large hamper with other sheets that I might be washing later. I dressed in yesterday’s clothes that had dried, but dug out my shawl. Slamming my bag shut so the owners would know I was up, I heard their voices drop. A dog yipped and scratched on my door.

“No, Muffy, no!” the woman scolded.

I opened the door and the little mutt bared her teeth and backed away. Then she darted past me and onto the bed where I’d slept.

“Did I get your bed, little dog? I’m sorry.”

Horace Outler scraped his chair on the floor as he stood. “Good morning to you, missy. Here, sit and get some breakfast.” He moved to the end of the table and pulled out the chair. “Nell, I’ll serve it up; you sit and visit with our guest.”

The office of the tourist court was adjacent to the Outler’s kitchen. A player piano stood near the front along one kitchen wall.

“Here you go, child,” the man said, placing before me a plate of bacon and scrambled eggs, biscuits and a cup of coffee. “Guess you heard that your ride’s already left.” He moved the sugar and cream, salt and pepper, and butter and jelly closer.

I nodded and took up my fork. "Thank you for this kindness. You're very thoughtful."

Mr. Outler kissed his wife on the top of her head, pulled a hat from a wall peg and left the building. The slicker was gone.

Mrs. Outler bustled about while I finished eating. "Who can you call? You're closer to St. Luke than to Lock Rivers." She looked at the clock over the sink. "It's past nine––time everybody was up and about their business."

"I should call Editor Redd and tell her I'm this far." I took my things to the dish pan and poured another cup of coffee.

My hostess wiped wet hands on her apron and moved to the phone on the counter. Picking up the receiver, she waited. "Hello, Esther? This is Nell Outler at the tourist court on Lightman Road. I need to speak to the newspaper editor in St. Luke." She listened. "Oh, it's not for me, it's for a guest. Okay, I'll wait while you get the operator. Thank you."

She motioned me to the high stool behind the counter and close to the phone. "She's connecting. When she comes on, tell the operator who you want to speak to." She handed me the phone.

I told Nell that I'd never been in such a predicament. "A new job and no way to get there––Hello? Will you please connect me with Editor Redd at *The Banner*?"

The operator's voice had a lilting quality. "One moment, please." I hooked my feet on the rungs of the stool.

"Purcelley Redd here. Who's calling?" Her voice sounded throaty and impatient.

"This is Liddy Underhill from Lock Rivers."

"Who? Oh, yes, the girl starting here next week. Well?"

"I am as far as the Outler's tourist court. My ride left without me this morning."

"Well?"

"No other travelers are registered here. The Outlers' car won't run. I have three cases." Silence. "I suppose I could leave one here and begin walking."

"Well, be careful. This is Friday. I need you here by nine o'clock sharp on Monday. Is there anything else?"

"No, ma'am." The dejection in my voice surely traveled through the wires. I hooked the phone in its cradle.

"What did she say? Didn't she offer to come get you? Or send someone for you?"

I shook my head and wiped tears with the back of my hand.

"What a mean old witch!" Nell Outler said. "She made no suggestions at all? I've a good mind to call back and give her a piece of my mind. The very idea!" She handed me one of Mr. Outler's handkerchiefs from the ironing board.

I took a deep breath, a silent sobbing one, wiped my eyes and laid the cloth on the table. "Let me help you clean the room Mr. Coursey stayed in, and do the wash like I promised. At least I can pay you that way. I'll take care of *his* pay later. After that, I'll start walking. May I leave the large case here until someone can pick it up?"

In the cabin, the sheets and pillow case were jumbled in the middle of the bed. "He stops here often enough that he's learned to strip his linen," Mrs. Outler said.

An empty fruit jar sat on a small table. I smelled it. "This must be the same one he had stashed under the seat of the wagon," I explained. "Let me wash the clothes and then I'd better strike out for St. Luke. I can carry two cases. I'll have to send someone for the other one." I gathered the linens and walked toward the door.

Nell Outler had replaced the sheets, straightened up the room and swept. "Maybe tonight's guests will be headed that way," she said. "Could I send the other one? Where'll you be staying?"

"At the boardinghouse––"

"Let's call there." She interrupted me. "Do you know who––?

"Editor Redd said a Mr. Spindle––Windle––Grindle––that's it, Mr. Grindle––that he would have a room for me."

"Then there's the answer. I'll call Esther and have her connect to the St. Luke operator to call the boardinghouse."

"Let me start these clothes to washing––"

"Nothing doing. I'll poke them in with the others when there's a load." She lifted the receiver and talked to Esther.

I went back to the room I'd slept in to see if all my things had been packed. Satisfied, I moved the large case against the wall, picked up the other two and prepared to leave.

"Liddy," Nell called. "No one answers at the boardinghouse. Esther said she would keep trying. Oh, I hate it that you have to walk the rest of the way. Or even part way. But it's not dangerous, if you keep to the left edge of the road. There's not much traffic."

I dropped my load and hugged her. "Thank you so much. Not all folks are as thoughtful as you."

She returned my embrace and patted me.

As I continued, my throat tightened. "I'll stop by here any time I have a chance. And when you get to St. Luke, be sure to look me up, either at the paper or the boardinghouse. Good-bye. Tell Mr. Outler I said 'thanks.'"

With a bag in each hand, I backed out the front door and started toward the road. Just then, I heard a clack-clack-clacking. A beat-up green truck pulled in and stopped under the overhang.

"You Miss Underhill?" the older, red-haired driver asked me after he dismounted from the truck. "I'm Tom Grindle of Tom's Boardinghouse––at your service, ma'am."

Nell Outler sputtered. "But how?––"

"Oh, we have a very efficient telephone operator." He grinned as he moved gingerly around to the front of the truck. He seemed to be favoring one leg. Limping, in fact. "She makes it her business to know everything about St. Luke and its people. She passed on the word from your operator that Miss Underhill," he gestured toward me, "was walking from Outler's. So here I am. Let me take those cases."

He loaded them, and I ran back for my other one. I returned just in time to hear Nell say, "You don't know how glad I am to see you, Tom Grindle. That witch of a newspaper editor didn't make any effort at all to help this girl get to your town. If I ever get to St. Luke, I'll give her a piece of my mind, I will."

The man with the kind face rumpled his hair with a weathered hand. He laughed. "Oh, yes. She's something else. But the lady puts out a good newspaper." He turned to me. "And it should be even better with Miss Underhill on the staff." He opened the door and held out his hand to boost me up. "Shall we go now? Not a very fancy conveyance for a newcomer, but it'll have to do." His eyes crinkled and he smiled.

— Chapter Six —

TOM GRINDLE

I turned the twelve-year-old Ford––my prized possession––around in the Outler's yard.

"Nice truck," the young woman passenger said. "Sure beats jostling around in a wagon." She turned away and said something I couldn't hear.

"Ma-am?" I looked over and saw a red flush cover the back of her neck. We were strangers, after all, so I waited for her to speak.

In a few moments, she turned to me and said, "Mr. Grindle, do you know anyone on *The Banner* staff? How many work there?" She fiddled with her dark hair. "I hope I fit in. This will be my first real job."

"Please, Miss Underhill, call me Tom. I'm not *that* much older than you are. Wrennetta Fincher works there––she's about your age, but I don't know what she does. Then there's the old man who sets the type and cleans up the place. That's all I know about. Don't worry. You'll do fine."

We rode in silence. Out of the corner of my eye I could see that she twisted her hands and picked at her nails. She appeared to be chewing on the inside of her lip.

"What do you suppose Editor Redd will have me do?" She looked like a frightened child on the first day of school.

The clatter of the car's motor and the hum of the tires as we pulled Pig Snout Hill were music to my ears. And this young woman sitting beside me was a sight for sore eyes. "Could be anything from selling ads and subscriptions to interviewing important people."

"Ooh, not selling ads. I'm not good at asking folks for––" Once again, she stopped short and turned away. In a minute, she continued. "Oh, Mr. Grin––Tom, sir. What I meant was––"

This country-girl-come-to-town was growing up mighty fast. Obviously, the past few days had taken a toll on her stamina. Whoever left her at the Outler's should be horsewhipped. But if she hadn't been left, then I would have missed the pleasure of escorting her to St. Luke.

"My trunk and sewing machine are at the depot. Could you?–– How can I?––" She sighed and laid her head back on the leather padding of the seat.

"I'll take your bags by the boardinghouse to make more room in the back, and then drive you to the depot. It's on the same street."

"They are my most precious possessions." She brightened for the first time since leaving the Outler's. "The trunk was my Gramma Roper's and Mother spent her hard-earned money on the sewing machine for my graduat––"

The last word caught in her throat like a sob. Startled, I turned to see her face crumple. Wracking sobs vibrated her slender body. She covered her face with her hands. How hard it was to keep both *my* hands on the steering wheel. I wanted to reach out, pull her close, smooth her hair and say, 'There, there, child, it'll be all right.' Like Granny said to me many a time.

"I'm sorry," she mumbled.

I reached for my handkerchief, which thankfully was clean, and held it out to her. I hate it when women cry. I never know what to do, what to say. So I didn't say anything. Kept my eyes straight ahead in case a deer or a 'coon took out across the road. I didn't want to risk spoiling my green queen of a truck. Nor add further woes to my pretty passenger.

— Chapter Seven —

HETH COURSEY

Monday morning after I got back from the Lock Rivers run, I hollered out to Pop, "I'm going to Nance's. Need anything from town?" I had to stay on the up and up. My old man'd have a fit when word got out that I was a bad egg and left a passenger stranded between here and there. *Me* leaving any babe behind would seem fishy to my buddies. She should'a been more friendly. But I figure she'll get here in time.

"Just the usual, son. Bring the mail. You know how Mother likes to get mail. Even if it's only a catalogue."

The old Nash Six grunted and gurgled. I hadn't drove 'er in two weeks. I pulled the choke till the motor caught, then throttled till the idle was regular.

In the post office, I asked Jake for the mail.

"Well, well, well!" Jake grinned, handing me a pink envelope. "We have ourselves a lady friend, do we?"

"Can't imagine anyone bothering to write me," I replied, moving over to the outside window, curious. I ripped open the envelope. No return address. Hmm.

Mr. Heth Coursey
Coursey and Sons Farm
Route 1, St. Luke, Missouri
September 28, 1932

Dear Sir,

I didn't have a chance to thank you for allowing me to ride partway to St. Luke with you. If I'd known ahead of time that it took two days, I would have taken the train.

Enclosed is the pay I promised you when we first talked.

I am settled into Tom's Boardinghouse and looking forward to my job at the newspaper beginning Monday. When you are through Lock Rivers again, tell everyone hello for me and that I miss them.

Sincerely,
Liddy L. Underhill

Grinning from ear to ear, I pushed out of the post office door. She doesn't sound *that* mad that I left her. I might have a chance with her after all.

I looked up and there was Miz Myrt gaining on me like a raging tiger in tortoiseshell eyeglasses. "Stop right there, young man!" she ordered. "What kind of a creature are you––leaving a stranger stranded at Outler's? Huh? Huh?" She poked me on the chest.

I was caught. Damn! How'd she find out? The old busybody!

"Your daddy know about this?"

I hung my head at her explosive charge. "What does that say about St. Luke, huh? Huh? Here we are trying to build up our civic pride and reputation around Gillette County. You should be ashamed. Now let me by."

Thoroughly chewed out––like I figured I'd be––and back in the Nash, I drove on to Nance's. Gaith Nance owns my peddling business. I gave him the money I'd collected and the inventory of items––sold and not.

"Sales are down, boy. Anything happen I should know about?" the lumpy old man asked.

"No," I lied, "unless it's getting so close to Christmas that folks are covering their coins until then."

"Speaking of Christmas," he said, shoving the November issue of the Eastern Trading Company catalogue across the counter, "look through here and see if you think you could sell any of this stuff."

I thumbed through the flimsy pages until I spotted just the thing my customers could afford––small enough to fit into an empty salt box, cheap enough to buy several, in enough colors for work or church, strong enough for the heaviest pants or the largest man.

"Here, Gaith. Order me some of these here braces, er, suspenders. Two navy, one khaki, two black, one––port?––looks maroon to me––one cobalt blue, one green, two red and two gray. That's a dozen."

Thinking back to the friendly tone of that girl's letter, I had an idea. "Say, Gaith, you ever thought about taking an ad in *The Banner?* The smallest one possible, of course."

"Never done that," he said. "Might be worth it now Christmas is nearly here."

"How about I go over and check out the"––I nearly said 'new piece'–– "prices right now? Got nothing else to do. You can set out my stock––get ready for the next route."

Gaith doesn't have to know that I have another reason for going to the newspaper. That new girl that I left at Outlers. One Miss Liddy L. Underhill.

— Chapter Eight —

LIDDY

I wrote to Mother and the girls on my first Saturday in St. Luke. That was October 6, 1932. A week later, I received a letter from Yvonne. I ripped it open and sat on the closest street side bench to read.

Beloved sister Liddy,

Juliana and I are so glad you are happy in your new home. A boardinghouse sounds so exciting. Are there lots of men living there? I can't wait till I am old enough to––(don't ever let Mother see this letter).

Mother is still pouting over your leaving. She said to tell you she was too hurt at your disobedience to forgive you like you asked. She said, 'Maybe later.' You can believe she is making every effort to keep the same thing from happening with Juliana and me.

We never know whether to go straight from school to the store or to go home first. If Mother is to be gone when we get home, she hires Mrs. Bishop to mind the store––and us. Mother has started fixing up some. Since Mr. Ferrel comes around so much, she makes herself a little more presentable. On their trips to Madison, she tries to find out from the legal folks if she can consider herself single since Daddy's been gone so long. So far, she's found out nothing.

Thank you for sending the money. Next time, would you please tell Mother it is for mine and Juliana's clothes and shoes and school supplies? Mother took what you sent this time and bought herself a new dress and some jewelry.

Next semester, I will get to take sewing, like you did. Should I buy my fabric from your peddler man? (ha) I can pay for it with the money you might send. Or I could let you pay him when he returns to St.Luke."

Harrumph! I thought. Not on your 'hubba hubba or hurdy gurdy'! Not again.

The dog is with Juliana constantly when she's at home. They take walks behind the house––away from the train tracks. Sport––that's what she named him––is always on a leash outside. Even Mother won't turn him out during the day for fear he might run toward the tracks.

Your trip also sounds like a great adventure. Were you ever scared during that time? And your job! Oh, I can't wait. Except I don't want to be a reporter, I want to be a lawyer. Or marry a lawyer. Juliana and I both like school and our teachers. The boys seem to fancy us well enough. We sometimes share our lunches with them. Juliana plays hopscotch and jacks and the boys play marbles and mumbledy-peg. We older girls and boys sit and talk about what we'll do when we grow up. Sometimes, we'll hold hands walking back to the schoolhouse. Did you ever do that, Liddy? I wish I'd have known to watch what you did, since you were such a good student.

I'd better close this up so Mother can't see what all's in here.

I'll stick it in my history book and mail it at school tomorrow.

Love, Yvonne, Juliana and Sport (and Mother)

* * * *

Saturday, April 1, 1933

Dear Mother, Yvonne, Juliana and Sport. Mr. Farrel, too.

It's been six months to the date that I started my new job at the St. Luke Banner. But it's Saturday, and I have time to write again. Mother, I am thankful you finally found it in your heart to forgive me for leaving while you were gone. You should be proud of me—-I have been promoted. I no longer have to go around St. Luke begging businesses for ads. Nor do I have to write them. I have moved beyond the obituaries, too. Now, I get to report on meetings at the Gillette County Courthouse-South. The jail and all city and county offices are in the same building. It is a step up, for sure.

Yvonne, will you tell my old teachers about my promotion. And that I send my thanks.

I have been going out with Heth Coursey quite a bit lately. I hear that his old girlfriends don't like it, me being a newcomer and all, but that's too bad. He minds his manners. When he is back in town, and after I get off work during the week, we sometimes drive down to the Creel River and talk. Now and then, we go to the movie house here. It's in pretty bad shape, but it's the only one closer than Madison or Bower, and that's too far to drive. It used to be an opera house, but now it's open only on weekends. The last movie we saw was "The Big Broadcast," *with Bing Crosby. It was a musical comedy. Usually the movies are scary ones.* "Frankenstein" *and* "Dracula" *played here during the winter.*

Mother, tell me about Mr. Ferrel. Do you like him? What do you do on your dates? Yvonne, which one of those boys you hold hands with at school is your 'sweetie'? Juliana, write me about Sport and your school subjects. What is the greatest thing you have learned so far? For me, it's to watch out for wolves in sheep's clothing (ask Mother what that means) and not to get carried away too soon by whatever (or whoever) comes along.

Need to close and do my laundry and clean my room. Might even start sewing a little. Do your dolls need new clothes? Send me their sizes and also your sizes. If you see a pattern you wish to have a dress like, send me a picture.

Mr. Walden has a fabric and pattern section in his store. I don't remember what colors you like and don't like. And do you prefer solids or prints? Fitted or loose? You may have to hem them yourselves to your favorite length. Until I get your directions, I'll use what scraps I have and make napkins for Tom's Sunday dining table. He tries to dress things up a little on Sundays.

Until next time, I remain you ever-loving daughter and sister, Liddy.

* * * *

Saturday, August 5, 1933

Dear Mother, Yvonne and Juliana,

It's Saturday again and it's fairly warm but not hot like Gram and Gramps said it was down in northern Arkansas. Before it gets too cool, he said, Heth has planned a picnic for next Saturday. He's in charge. I don't have to do anything but dress according to the weather. And bring a quilt. All the picnics I've been on, I've had to make potato salad or bake cookies.

I wonder if he's planning to 'pop the question'? Girls, if you don't know what that means, ask Mother. He's dropped a few hints lately. You'll be the first to know if he does.

Did the doll clothes fit? Did your dresses fit? Tom likes my napkins so well, he goes to Mr. Walden's fabric bin for end-of-roll pieces that he likes, and brings the material to me. It's nothing to stitch around cotton squares. I even fringed one set of six. Most tables seat four, but the big table needs eight napkins. He doesn't care if they match or not, but I do.

Is the garden stuff all in? Mother, are you teaching the girls to can and make jelly? Girls, have you taken up embroidery yet? It'snot too early to cross-stitch some dresser scarves for your hope chests.

I made one that I am using on Gramma Roper's trunk—my bedside table. On top of it are your latest school pictures. And, Mother, the one of you and Mr. Farrel—hubba hubba and hurdy gurdy! I look at them every day.

Love, Liddy

P. S. I'll let you know if Heth and I become engaged next Saturday during the picnic. Enclosed is some money for Yvonne and Juliana's clothes and school supplies.

— CHAPTER NINE —

What a grand day for a picnic. Even though it was mid-August, the grassy glade Heth selected deep in the woods was cool. How did he know it would be so perfect?

After lunch, we lay on Grandmother's quilt. I felt the lump of a stone under my shoulder blade. I heard the drone of an airplane, the call of a mockingbird, the chitter of a squirrel, and I felt the breeze in my hair. The sky was azure, the color of Heth's eyes.

Warmth from that cider stuff we drank moved from my throat down my body. I closed my eyes, sleepy, relaxed, like when the doctor put that black mask of cool air over my nose before removing my tonsils.

Heth's hand moved over me. No, No, I thought, but I didn't stop him. I'd turned into jelly. Mother perched on my shoulder with her words of caution: "Keep your legs in a gallon jug before you marry." But I just smiled, melting into the tingling pool expanding through me. I rose and soared—–higher—–higher—–then hung there, dancing with the trees and the breeze and the birds, till I flew into heaven, forcefully entangled in Heth's passionate heat.

* * * *

Two months later, I knew I was in trouble. Deep, deep trouble. I must tell Heth and insist that we make plans to marry.

— CHAPTER TEN —

TOM

It was the last Monday of October. Of all nights, why did I have to wipe up spills on the buffet? That's what I paid Xann to do. While I was scrubbing, I banged my funny bone on a warming pan and turned my lame ankle again.

Since Liddy Underhill became a boarder, I'd become preoccupied with cleanliness. I found myself hovering during meals with my crumb brush and damp cloth. If a guest dropped a utensil, I reacted almost before the clang of metal on wood. Diners dared not leave the table without posting lookouts, in case I mistook their intent and swooped in to clear their areas.

The north wind whipped in off Little Trot Mountain barreling through the big oaks and shaking the drafty old house. No one sat on the porch tonight.

At supper, Liddy asked if she could come down later and cut out her wedding dress. I was glad when the diners finally went to their rooms or left for home. For some reason, I felt edgy and anxious. And yet eager, too.

Scrubbing like it was Heth Coursey's hide, I took my polishing cloth to the big table. The chandelier reflected its satiny gloss. I moved the chairs back so Liddy could stand close to the table.

I jerked down the "Dining Room Closed" shade and locked the door. Checked the mirror to be sure my shirt was still clean, no turnip greens stuck between my teeth. Slicked down my hair, and rubbed first one shoe and then the other on the back of my pant legs.

I opened the door to the stairwell. Leaning heavily on the banister, I pulled myself up to the landing, rested a second––my ankle hurt something fierce––and managed the short distance to Liddy's door.

I rapped. "Miss Liddy, the table's ready."

Back downstairs, I busied myself at the buffet, checking for the fourth time that the cloth-covered silverware faced down. Hefted the salt and pepper shakers to see if they needed filling. Checked the pepper sauce bottles to be sure they were full. The diners doused their turnip greens with this specialty of the house that I still cook myself. Granddaddy Grindle––God rest his soul––passed the recipe down to Mother, and she gave it to me.

At the creak of the door to the stairs, I looked up. Liddy, her arms full of sewing goods, managed to close the door with her foot.

Balanced atop the material was a pattern envelope, scissors and a rose-colored cushion, whose pins reflected the light as she glided to the table. Ah, she was beautiful––dark hair against that creamy skin. I could have sworn a halo glistened above her.

"Real nice of you to let me use your table, Tom," she said and flashed that glorious smile. "My bed wouldn't have worked very well, and it was too dark on the floor for close work. Not that it's dark in my room, mind you––"

She needn't have worried that I would take her words as criticism. "Oh, no," I said. "Glad you asked. I'll sit over here at the counter, out of your way and––"

"No," she interrupted. "I'd like it if you sat––" and she motioned me across the table. "That is, if you're not too busy."

Of course, I was eager to be near her, so after I locked the register, I turned a chair around, dragged it closer to the table and sat a-straddle. I crossed my arms over the back and watched. Gazed, actually.

Liddy laid her tools on a chair, and unfolded the shiny ivory material. She opened the envelope and pulled out the directions.

"Let's see," she said. "Should I fold it lengthwise or crossways? Mrs. Evans warned us about how crepe crawls––how hard it is to sew without puckering. Maybe I should have chosen a different fabric," but she kept folding. "Too late, though. I'm bound to do this right, or else."

"Who's Mrs. Evans?" I guessed it was a teacher or a neighbor. The tension in my body lessened. I waited.

While she straightened the cloth, pinned and cut, Liddy told me stories of her home economics classes––how she had scratched the marble table with her and Lewie Cooper's initials––the only time she ever 'got in trouble' at school. I felt a shiver of jealousy.

She described the green-and-white checked material she'd selected for her first dress project as 'a horrid garment with white waffle pique collar and cuffs that I never ever wore.'

I couldn't take my eyes off her face. Her skin glowed under the sparkling light. Like pictures I'd seen of angels.

Liddy gestured with her scissors as she talked about the county fair competition when she and her partner had to test their fashion sense. They were to choose the best blouses for different skirts, and the most suitable accessories for a black dress.

"We lost," she said with a laugh."Anyone who'd make a gored dress out of checkered material––we didn't have a chance against the girls from the bigger schools."

I got lost in the sound of her voice and what could have been if I'd met her before Heth did. When I refocused, Liddy was staring beyond me, her face as white as the cloth covering the silver.

"Could I have a glass of water, Tom?" she asked, and stumbled to the nearest chair. "And a cracker, if you have one."

I moved as fast as I could to the water jug on the counter, grabbed a glass and filled it. I reached into the cracker bin. Her look frightened me, and I hurried back.

In the sudden quiet of the room, I noticed the wind had died, as if it had tucked itself into the treetops with the squirrels and gone to sleep.

Liddy drank a sip or two and devoured the cracker. "Guess I just got hungry," she said."I usually have a snack about now. Sorry to bother you."

"Would you like a cup of tea? It's ginseng."

"I'm finished with the dress," she said. "That crepe wasn't as hard to cut as I thought. Yes, I'll drink a cup if you will." She stood up, swayed for an instant, and then gathered her things. Pushing the stack to the end of the table, she drew the chair close and sat across from me.

"I can't believe I talked so much tonight, Tom. Why didn't you shush me? I don't know why––"

I shook my head and handed her the tea. "Oh no, I enjoyed hearing about your school capers." I flicked fabric lint from the table. Liddy closed her eyes and rubbed the back of her neck.

I spoke first. "So you knew Heth Coursey before you came to St. Luke? I thought you met him after you moved here."

"My mother told me that a skinny, young peddler occasionally dropped by our grocery store when he ran out of something his customers wanted. I guess we always had what he needed."

Her last sentence spun in my ears like a maple seedpod on a March wind. I winced, reflecting on its larger meaning, but I knew this sweet girl did not intend such a message.

Liddy ran her fingers over the polished table. "I remember the first time I saw him." She sipped her tea. "It was early June. My high school days were over. I was restocking the lower shelves and Mother was in the back totting up the ledger."

I had not met her mother. I would, though, when she brought her two other children to Liddy's wedding. Then I could see which parent was responsible for her dark hair, wispy curls and high cheek bones.

She continued. "This deep voice above me said, 'I need some blueing,'. Mought this establishment have some I could bargain for?'" Liddy mimicked, and I grinned.

All at once, she put both hands on the table and bent forward, riveting me with her gold-flecked eyes. "I looked up into the face of this brown-haired Adonis. He doffed his cap, and I knew he was the one Mother had mentioned. Can you imagine how embarrassing it was to be caught gawking at him from a squatting position? Thank goodness, I'd worn my gathered skirt––the one I made from ugly green and orange feed sacks." She grimaced, as if to shake off the memory.

"I felt red running up my neck, and somehow I pulled myself up and stood eye-to-eye with this handsome young man. "'Name's Coursey, Heth Coursey, area peddler of various and sundry necessaries for the discerning lady. Of which I take you to be one, Miss––' He stuck out a long-fingered hand, never taking his blue eyes off me. I know, because I never stopped looking into them."

Liddy suddenly crumpled out of her chair and to the floor. For a split second, I thought she was still playacting. When she didn't move, I knew something was wrong. My chair crashed to the floor as I untangled my gimpy leg from the bottom rung. I hurried around the end of the table. Liddy's eyes were closed.

What to do? What to do? I wrung my hands like Granny had done when I was sick. A wet cloth on her face? A sip of water? Yes, Granny would do that. I ran to the kitchen and brought back a clean wet dishtowel. Somehow, I knelt and laid the cold cloth over her ashen face. What if it doesn't work? Did the tea make her sick?

But Liddy roused and opened her eyes. "What in the world? Tom, what happened? Why am I on the floor?"

"You fainted, I guess. One minute you were describing your meeting with Heth, and the next, you were on the floor."

"I'd better get to my room. It's late. Thanks again for letting me work down here, Tom. And for listening to me carry on. I don't know why I––"

"Glad to. I'll take your stuff," I said, though I desperately wished I had both the strength and boldness to scoop her up and carry her to her room––like Heth would soon get to do. At her door, she took the sewing materials back, said goodnight, and entered her room.

I lingered. "Will you be all right?"

She smiled, nodded and touched my outstretched hand. "Thank you," she whispered, and closed the door.

I floated down the stairs, turned off the hall lights and in the dimness, raised to my warm cheek the hand that Liddy had touched.

I suddenly realized how tired I was. Oh, not tired of mind or of spirit. Not after the warm touch of her hand. But tired in body.

I brewed another cup of tea, turned the chandelier off and the wall lights on. It was dim, but I wasn't going to read. Back at the table with my tea, I could still see Liddy's gestures and smiles and hear the thrum and lilt of her voice. Listening to accounts of her younger years took me back to thoughts of my own childhood.

— Chapter Eleven —

I had seen better days. As a schoolboy, I ran track for the Driftwood Mud Daubers. On short legs, I would fly along the dirt roads of the neighborhood. Some called me Streak. Some called me Whirlwind. Other runners choked on my dust.

But at Cotton Point Tech, the competition was something else. The fastest runners in each school around the area ending up on the Cotton Weevil track team. We held regional meets at Hendrix College in Conway, Arkansas, a three-hour drive southeast. That's where I met Ivell Grove and Skinny Whipple. One or the other was always high point man. I couldn't touch them.

A knock on the front door startled me. "Tom, it's me, Quinn Coursey."

I limped to the door and opened it.

He said, "I saw your light on. Can I sit with you awhile? I can't stop worrying about––"

"Come in. Will you have tea? I can make a fresh pot of coffee. I might find something even stronger in the cupboard back there." I smiled and Heth's father said tea would be fine. I brought in two rockers from the porch. "They'll be a lot more comfortable than those straight chairs."

"Go on about what you were doing," Quinn said. "Tonight, I'd rather listen than talk."

"Earlier tonight," I began, "Liddy came down to cut out her wedding dress." I motioned to the big table, "and she talked about her high school days." I settled into my chair and set it to rocking. "I was sitting here remembering *my* earlier days."

"Go on. I'd like to hear about them if you don't mind," Quinn said.

"I was remembering how good at track I thought I was in high school. But when I got to Cotton Point Tech, I was nothing. I wanted to be something," I said, and sipped the strong tea. "So I tried jumping hurdles. Each day, after practice at the college, I would stay in my runner's shorts for the two-mile walk home. I trained by jumping fences along the route. I pretended I was the foxhunter's horse clearing the hedge windbreaks. Soon, folks called me 'Osprey' or 'Eagle.'"

"Just hearing about that makes me tired," Quinn said.

"Oh, but it encouraged me. I defied gravity and soared higher and higher until I was the best jumper on the team. Our trophies and plaques sat on a glass shelf above the serving area of the dining hall." I drained my cup and motioned to refill his. He handed it over, and I poured each of us another round.

"Then what happened?" Quinn asked after a sip of the steaming liquid.

"Shortly before graduation, my world crashed. My father was laid off. He traveled by train to Kansas City to look for work in the entertainment trade. He was a folk singer of sorts and played the guitar." I leaned back and rocked for a spell. Quinn looked out the window. "He stumbled onto a bank robbery and was shot to death."

"Oh, my lord!" Quinn said. "Oh, my lord!"

"A month later, Grandpa Grindle––he was living with us––walked out of our yard and disappeared into the mountains. To this day his body has never been found." I stopped to take a deep breath, wait for my eyes to dry up and my throat to loosen.

Quinn leaned back this time, muttering, "Unbelieveable!"

"After those two deaths, Mother grieved herself into a sickbed. I dropped out of school and became the breadwinner for her and my three younger sisters. That was the end of sports for me."

We were both quiet for a time. The north wind whistled around the building like a giant diesel engine. I continued. "I worked our farm and hired out to plow the neighbors' fields. My only exercise was plodding behind the horses. Soon, I felt old. And tired. And hopeless. Was this going to be the sum total of my life? I wondered."

Quinn broke in. "I know the feeling. What happened? How did you get to St. Luke?"

"One day, I was backing Sally and Belle into the plow at the edge of a field. A swarm of red wasps came out of nowhere and spooked Sally. She reared and kept backing. I can still hear the eerie sound as my right foot crunched into the black dirt under her weight. I went down like a sawed-off cedar."

"The pain!" Quinn said. "It must have been unbearable."

"It hurt so bad I lost consciousness for awhile. I've never walked right again. Don't think I could run if a bull was chasing me. Say, there's some cake left from supper. How about we move to the table and eat a slice. Talking's made me hungry."

Quinn stood. "I need to be getting home, but yes, I'm always good for cake. How did you come to land here?"

I cut two good-size slices of the double-layer coconut cake and poured more tea. "A few months later, three missionaries came to our house and my life got another twist. Our fatherless family grabbed the hearts of the old man and his wife, who immediately assumed our care and feeding. The third was a single man studying for the ministry. He and my mother soon married."

"Oh, what good cake," Quinn said. "Maybe the wife and I ought to eat at your place now and then." He wiped his mouth on a napkin. "But you're still not at St. Luke."

"Mother and the missionaries gave me leave to go back to school, or to a bigger town where I could make something of myself. The college had declared me a graduate since I was so close to the end, so I chose to move. All they asked was that I send part of my money home for their missionary effort across the mountains."

I drained my cup. "Here I am in St. Luke, the first place I got off the train. Folks have been good to me. I feel needed and wanted. I like running the boardinghouse and repairing cast-off furniture."

Quinn stood. "Thank you for a restful evening, Tom. I didn't realize how much I needed the company of another man."

I saw him to the door and stood on the porch until he drove away.

— Chapter Twelve —

LIDDY

[Saturday, October 28, 1933]

Following the somber director down the aisle, I entered the second pew. The only one not related to the deceased, I preceded Heth, the youngest son, my fiancé. The three older boys with their wives and children sat in order of ages so that the eldest, Lloyd, sat next to his father on the front row. Lloyd's wife Frona Lee and their children came next, then Ozell and Alice, followed by McKinley and Caroline.

Sula Mae Coursey, Heth's mother, who wouldn't have believed what her precious baby boy did to me, lay there old and cold and, to my way of thinking, unkind. The other girls referred to her as Mother Coursey. She had opinions about everything. She would have hated my hat.

The preacher droned on. "Family came first with Sister Sula Mae. She loved her sons equally, and her daughters-in-law called her blessed."

The few times I visited in her home, she said terrible things about her daughters-in-law—how Lloyd's wife let her kids run wild, and Ozell's wife played cards while her house was filthy. And McKinley's woman couldn't cook worth dirt. She probably talked about me to the others: my face was too round. I should have had that ugly scar on my forehead seen to before now. I wasn't good enough for her precious Heth.

My stomach churned, and my mouth filled with saliva. The church was overheated. I wished I could run back out the side aisle, but the old biddies would sure enough grasp at *that* straw. I rummaged in my handbag for the cracker I'd taken to carrying, after someone told me they were good for emergencies. Behind my hand, I bit off one corner, and then another, and the bile receded. My face grew hot and I felt red winding itself up the back of my neck under the lace of my dress. I retrieved my fan also, and it helped.

"Lord," the preacher continued, "thank you for the life of this dear sister. Rock her forever in your loving arms in return for the time spent doing your work on this earth, especially crocheting all those coverlets for the dear old veterans. Amen."

I cut tearless eyes at Heth and followed his stony gaze to the stained glass window near the top of the arched ceiling. The iridescent blue dove seemed stopped in downward flight. At that moment, I identified with the bird.

Is Heth trying not to cry? I hear Frona Lee sniffling. Papa Quinn honked into his handkerchief as the blue-haired pianist began "Abide with Me."

Heth jerked into the present, and I reached for his hand. We would follow his brothers and sisters-in-law and their children past the open casket one last time. I didn't want to, but I knew I would. *I must appear dutiful and sad like Frona Lee, Alice and Caroline.*

At the foot of the gray-blue coffin, before I could look down at the woman who would not now be my mother-in-law, my legs turned liquid and the lights went out. Oblivion swallowed me and I fell into a cool, soft sleep––

My hands are crossed at the wrists just like Sula Mae's
in the coffin. I feel closed in, deep in the darkness of my own box.
I hear voices. That's Frona Lee. She's singing "Amazing Grace."
And there's Heth looking down––smirking. Why is he so dressed up,
his hat at that jaunty angle? Is he taunting me? How could he?
"I'll pour this drink on her," Ozell says. "That'll wake her up."

"No, Ozell! It's me, Liddy!" I struggle to sit up, but fall back
into the darkness and intense heat. I gasp for air. A strong
aroma of cinnamon surrounds me. This must be my wake.
I've died from embarrassment. No, I've been struck down by
God for my part in our fornica––

Suddenly I shuddered and opened my eyes. "I'm not dead?" I took a moment to focus. There was Frona Lee's full-moon face a foot away from mine. She looked like a caricature from a werewolf movie I saw in school assembly one year.

"No, dear, you fainted from the heat," said Frona Lee, the new Coursey matriarch. "Let's take her to my house, Heth. She'll need some rest before we finish planning your wedding."

"No!" I whispered in a raspy voice. "Let me sit here and gather my wits. I'll be okay. Wait for me at the back, Heth, please."

From my front row seat, I could hear Frona Lee's voice drop and drone as she and Heth walked slowly down the center aisle toward the exit.

The pianist kept the hymns coming as though she had been instructed to play until the church was clear. I recognized "When They Ring Those Golden Bells" and "When the Roll is Called up Yonder." Why didn't she just disappear? Did she want to hear something, see something? I sat up. While I felt in my bag for a mirror, our eyes met.

"Are you all right, dear?" she asked. The ladies would clean up later and likely gabble about why Heth's fiancée fainted.

I had to stop Heth before he agreed to go to Frona Lee's. She couldn't have any input into this wedding. No bridal shower, no shopping, no socializing. I fainted often and nausea seemed always just under the surface. Staying out of the sight of the Courseys was vital. What could keep me out of circulation? Seeing to the details of the ceremony––the minister, the place, witnesses?

I gathered my purse and hat, stood up and nodded to the pianist, mouthing a 'thank you' and a small smile. I moved to the center aisle and walked toward Heth.

"Take me home, please, Heth," I said. "Heth?" He's in a daze. I grasped his hand to pull him out the back door of the church. Inertia and grief must have glued him to the floor. I tugged. The same way I tugged Old Sukey's tail before she kicked me in the face.

Heth finally moved. I turned to the front of the church and waved at Frona Lee, who had walked up to chat with the pianist.

"Thanks for the kind offer," I called to her, "but I need to get home." Did I detect a sense of arrogance in the look of my soon-to-be sister-in-law? Perhaps it was disappointment that she could not immediately take over our lives.

The burial service across the road had ended and neighbors were pulling their jackets closer in the cold October wind. Several men detoured to shake Heth's hand and tip their hats to me. I let go of Heth and ran for the Nash. He could dawdle and catch cold, but I could not.

In sullen silence, he drove to the boardinghouse where I had lived since moving from Lock Rivers. He didn't cut the motor or make a move. I pushed on the heavy door and finally hoisted myself out. After shutting it, I leaned into the open window.

"Heth, we've got to get married. Soon! Shall we plan it together, or shall I do it?"

He stared straight ahead.

"Remember, you promised to keep––our secret. You will, won't you? Heth? Answer me, Heth!"

"Yeah, you go ahead––I'll come by tomorrow sometime," he mumbled.

"You won't go peddling before the wedding, will you? Heth, you *can't!"*

He shrugged, raced the motor idling in neutral, then stomped the clutch and threw the gearshift of the old car into low and peeled out.

I jumped back but not soon enough. My legs stung with slung gravel. Before I could climb the five wooden steps to the boardinghouse porch, Tom Grindle opened the door. "Get in out of the wind, Miss Liddy. You'll catch your death."

"If you only knew how much death I'd lived through today," I told him.

I knew from Heth's silence and the way he tore down the road that he was furious. I could almost read his thoughts: *How dare she order me not to make a peddling run! We'll need the money to get married on––The trouble with women is they don't think about money––just themselves, and how it's going to look to everyone else.*

Upstairs, I stripped off my funeral clothes and treated my tired body to a long soak. I hung my mind out some place else, some place free, where the rain could wash out all its complications. For once, I wished to be mindfully unconscious––just for a little while.

What was that line from Mrs. Earheart's senior English class? *Sleep that knits up the raveled sleeve of care?* Or was it *ragged?* Shakespeare? I don't remember. Why didn't I pay more attention?

Come to think of it, I wouldn't be in this predicament if I had paid closer attention to what I drank––especially around Heth. "Smell it before you drink it next time," I said aloud, "if there is a next time." My self-scolding was too late, of course.

The autumn wind creaked and seeped through these wooden walls. The claw-foot tub didn't hold heat very well. Feeling as old as my mother,

I pulled up and dried off. Not much more relaxed than before, I tried to forget Heth and what he might be thinking or doing. "What's done is done," I said to the mirror, "No use worrying. Don't do like Mother and make yourself miserable over it."

After a good supper, I might feel more like tackling the wedding plans. Funny, *the* wedding plans, not *our* wedding plans. Maybe I should be more like Heth: disinterested, objective, disembodied from my teenaged dreams about weddings. And marriage. I chose to make this journey to St. Luke with no idea of its unexpected turn that would force me into a marriage I didn't feel ready for.

What was my parents' wedding like? And why haven't I thought to ask before now? I can't run home to Mother. She couldn't take any more bad news. No, I'll bear this burden alone. And when the baby comes, perhaps the joy, the shared exuberance, the bonding between Heth and me will follow. And maybe, forgiveness. On both sides.

— Chapter Thirteen —

In the dining room, I took the only chair left at the round table in the center. Custom demanded that you fill up one table before opening another. Large bowls of black-eyed peas, turnip greens, pickled beets and mashed potatoes clustered around the platter of pork chops. Biscuits and cornbread hid under a cloth to keep in the heat.

Fresh-brewed iced tea sparkled like jewels. I hadn't realized how thirsty I was, so when Xann Price came around with the pitcher, I raised my glass for a refill. Tom knew how to sweeten it the way I liked it.

Despite the wind, the soft murmur of voices blanketed and warmed the large room. Lamps in sconces flanked each door, and the chandelier from an earlier time glittered with new electric bulbs. Muted music of silver on china accompanied the diners who never seemed to notice, totally intent on their own circumstances of life.

As folks came in to eat, I looked around for someone who might be a preacher. Did they wear collars so people could spot them? I knew the Methodist Episcopal Church, South, had sent a new minister to town last June.

Once when the seat next to me emptied, Tom sat for a minute and visited with the diners. I asked him if the new minister might be eating here tonight.

He looked around. "No, I don't see him. But have you heard his name? Or what the townsfolk call him behind his back?"

I shook my head and said, "No, what?"

"His name is B. R. D. Briley," Tom said. "We call him 'Blind Bird.'" Tom grinned a shy crooked smile.

"Why in the world?—"

"Because there's no "eye" in Bird: his initials are B. R. D. Makes a good nickname, don't you think?"

Tom glanced around at the other diners to see if any needed his attention. No one seemed to, so he turned back to me. "He stayed here a night or two while the church folks fixed up the parsonage. About thirty, I'd say, same age as me."

I just learned something more about my landlord.

"He lives alone," Tom continued. "Answered the call later in life, he told me. Took his studies at Springfield." Tom hailed Xann to bring more tea. "He still has to travel to that Methodist College in Arkansas during the summers for more credit toward his ordination." With his hands, Tom brushed crumbs from the areas he could reach. "I think it's the same place our college track team went for meets. Hendrix, as I recall."

Tom moved on to other tables. People liked his friendliness and the careful way he prepared the food. I stacked my dishes in the pan near the pass-through.

I didn't want to go back upstairs just yet, so I strolled out on the wrap-around porch and turned the rocker nearest the steps toward the sunset. Maybe I could lean my head back and just 'be' for a spell. The wind had died to a comforting breeze. Songs of katydids reminded me of a creaky porch swing. But Tom had only rockers and straight chairs.

Several groups sat together. Across the hills, the sun––a giant tangerine––fell below the horizon, leaving lengths of mare's-tail clouds as pink as freshly filleted fish. The blue sky further north tinged to aqua.

Just then I heard snatches of a female voice, "––fainted––funeral––what he sees in her–– we went out before *she* came to town." I dared not turn toward the sound. Not yet.

I'd known that Heth Coursey had other girlfriends, but he hadn't ravished *them*, had he? When I first came to St. Luke, I saw him occasionally on Sundays in his white suit playing tennis at the park. But after walking the other girls home, he usually came by the boardinghouse to visit with me.

Darkness fell and the new streetlights came on. Townsfolk took their leave. We boarders said our 'goodnights' and retired to our rooms. I never saw who the voice from the funeral was.

Behind my closed door, I changed into a chemise, fluffed a pillow against the headboard and took up my writing box.

'Dear Brother Bird, er Brother Briley,' I wrote, momentarily distracted by the loud clack of a car on the street. I scratched through 'Brother Bird' then wadded the sheet and tossed it toward the wastebasket.

> *Dear Brother Briley,*
>
> *You don't know me, but I need to see you right away. I am new to this town, as you are, and reside presently at Tom's Boardinghouse. Tom gave me your name. It is Saturday night. I will send this note by Xander Price and ask him to wait for your answer. Thank you for your time. Liddy Underhill*

I hoped Xann wouldn't mind being my runner. I'd pay him, of course, with what pin money I'd put back. Tom would do it if Xann couldn't. I folded the paper into an envelope and wrote 'Brother Briley' on the front.

My mind wandered. I stared out the south window toward Little Trot Mountain and saw an occasional light twinkling through the trees. Today's events had drained my strength. I couldn't think any longer.

Maybe that was the way Heth felt when he let me out after the funeral. Today must have been hard on him. He was Sula Mae's baby. Could that be why he was so unresponsive? A semi-orphan at twenty-three. If he needs mothering, he'll likely turn to Frona Lee. Or maybe to me. What if it were *my* mother who was buried today?

— Chapter Fourteen —

LIDDY

A lamppost on Main Street punctured the dusk, but no porch lights lit the deepening blue. A crescent moon didn't help either. I wish I'd thought to bring a flashlight.

The minister took a long time to answer my knock. He opened the parsonage door, covering his mouth with the back of one hand.

"Brother Bird—er, Brother Briley?" I asked. "Liddy Underhill. My letter?"

The short pudgy man had a small head shaped like a pumpkin. Straight dark hair fell onto his forehead in bangs. Bushy brows accented gray eyes. He looked older than I expected.

The parson motioned me inside and gestured toward a wood-framed love seat upholstered in English-hunting-dog fabric. He excused himself and left the room. I heard him over the sound of running water clear his throat, spit and then gargle.

The living room was a combination of mismatched chairs, tables and lamps—a drab, worn, smelly place. A kitchen faucet dripped. I thought Tom said the church had fixed it up in June. Surely they could afford a better place than this for their minister.

I sat on the upholstered dogs. When he returned, the preacher motioned for me to move over and he took the other half of the seat. I hugged the edge, held my knees tightly together and turned toward him.

"Will you marry me?" I asked.

He grabbed a handkerchief from behind him and daubed at his face, which had quickly reddened.

"I know this is sudden," I continued, "but you sound like just the man I want. When Tom described you, I knew you had to be the one."

The reverend's freckles deepened. He sputtered. "Why––why––"

It sounded like 'wye––wye.'

"This is so sudden," he said. "I had no idea. When did you––why did you pick?––We don't even know each other. What would my church members say––if their preacher married someone?––"

"Ministers do marry people, don't they?" I couldn't see his point.

"How do you know I'm not already married?" he asked, raising his eyebrows. His eyes twinkled with mischief. "I'm not, you understand––and yes, I'll marry you." The country cleric reached out and took my hand.

At that moment, I realized my mistake. "Oh, no, sir," I said, pulling away. "I mean will you marry *us*? Heth Coursey––and me? You know, Nance's Mercantile salesman? His mother was buried last week. Perhaps you read about it?" I looked down at my hands and then back at the man's face.

The pastor sputtered. With his handkerchief, he brushed away brown drool escaping his twitching mouth.

So that's why he hurried into another room when I entered. To get rid of his snuff. Or his chewing tobacco.

"Well, Brother Bird, will you? At your earliest convenience? This Saturday perhaps?" When he didn't answer, I continued. "Heth's gone on one last peddling trip, but as soon as he returns––a private wedding? Do we have to have witnesses? A blood test? How long to wait after getting a license? My family lives away––"

"Just a minute, young lady. Why do you keep calling me Brother Bird? My name is Buchanan Robert Deymond Briley. Reverend––Brother."

It was my turn to sputter and redden. "Uh, did I?––I don't know." I stood.

He sprang from the sofa. "Maybe you'd better come back when your sweetie gets home. In the meantime, I'll check my calendar. Good evening, Miss Overdale." He walked me to the door, and as I turned to leave, he squeezed my behind with one fat hand and closed the door with the other.

Cast into complete darkness on the unfamiliar porch, I froze. What does he mean pinching me? Soon, my eyes adjusted and the blackness receded.

Underhill. My name is Underhill. Overdale? At least he has a sense of humor. That's a good play on my name. I deserve it, calling him Brother Bird. But not the pinch. How dare he!

I walked down the steps and out to the road. Nothing moved except the dry leaves that eddied when a breeze blew in. In the distance, the Mo-Pac train chugged along its route from St. Luke to Lock Rivers and on eastward. Its eerie whistle sent shivers down my spine. A sharp pain gouged my stomach. I walked faster.

Somewhere close by, twigs snapped. I began to run toward Main Street and Walden's Corner. A high-pitched voice 'Bo-o-o-o-ed' behind me and then cackled. "Trick or treat! Smell my feet, give me something good to eat," the voice chanted in a distorted sound unlike any I'd ever heard.

I slowed. A stitch in my side added to the cramp in my stomach. I remembered, then, that tonight was Halloween and hoped the sounds were from neighborhood children. For an instant, I imagined Brother Bird chasing me.

Turning the corner, I headed toward town. The boardinghouse was two curvy blocks past the *Banner* office, and the streetlamps gave enough light to spot any moving shadows.

From the darkness, a 'cl-ump, cl-ump, cl-ump,' sound approached. The noise from both directions on the brick-lined street pounded in my ears. The heat of fear exploded. My face became a tinderbox. Walking closer to the storefronts, I noticed a light in an upstairs window.

Just then, Tom rounded the corner. The last thing I remember is shouting his name.

— Chapter Fifteen —

TOM

I could do many things, but even with a rush of adrenaline, I could not carry a dead-weight adult, even a small one like Liddy Underhill. But somehow, I managed to lift her to the porch of MaGriff's Drug Store.

"Ullan! Ullan MaGriff! Quick! Come down!" I pounded on the wooden door. "Emergency!" I hobbled back across the planks and fanned Liddy with my handkerchief. A downstairs light came on and the druggist hurried out.

In his maroon smoking jacket, he bent over Liddy, felt for her pulse, pulled back her eyelids, and then turned to me with questions in his eyes.

"I don't know where she's been or why," I said, "but when she didn't show up for supper, I was worried––her being alone and all." I continued to fan this boarder that I'd become too fond of. "I went by the *Banner* office. Locked up. She'd been asking about the Methodist preacher, so I took out for his place. This is as far as I got. When I saw her, she was wild-eyed. She hollered my name and then fell out. What shall we do?"

"I'll call Doc Everett." MaGriff ran back into his store.

A figure clad in a black cape and wig swept up the dark street astraddle a broom. "Trick or treat, smell my––" it said, and stopped abruptly upon seeing me.

Now it was my turn to go bug-eyed. The witch jerked off its wig and Brother B. R. D. Briley stood there.

The reverend *had* been following Liddy, he said, with the thought of playing a Halloween trick. "She'd just played one on me." But before he could explain, he saw Liddy laid out on the porch. He stepped out of his cape, threw the broom down and joined me.

"Brother Tom. What's wrong?"

"Don't you 'Brother Tom' me. Did you scare Liddy? She was as white as a sheet when I came around the corner, just before she fainted. Had she been to see you? What did you?––" I moved toward him with my cane raised.

"Hey, back off," said the preacher. "Meeting you would turn anyone white, with that crazy 'cl-umping' sound you make."

MaGriff returned. "Let's get her to Doc Everett's office. It's not very far. He'll meet us." The druggist brought out a bottle of smelling salts and a litter. I helped Ullan roll Liddy over onto it. She was as limp as that stalk of old celery in my Frigidaire.

"You, preacher," Ullan said, "you grab one end and I'll carry the other. Tom, get Liddy's pocketbook, and take these salts." He tossed the bottle at me. "Let's go. It's this way."

— Chapter Sixteen —

DOC EVERETT

When Dovie, my wife and also my nurse, heard that Liddy Underhill was down, she insisted on coming to the office with me.

Dovie's friendship with Liddy's mother went back to mining camp days when they were teenagers. Last year, when Dovie learned that her friend's daughter had moved to St. Luke, my sweetie assured Genese she'd keep an eye on Liddy. But she had not.

An urgent-sounding rap at the door let me know that Ullan, Tom and Brother Bird had arrived with the patient. Dovie had barely finished with the examining table. "Come in, fellows," I said.

With Dovie's instructions, the men moved Liddy from the litter. Then Dovie did what nurses do, and I took the men to the records room. They told me everything they knew. Before long, Dovie opened the door and motioned to me.

"Stay here, fellows," I said, "while I go see––Afterwards, we can decide what to do next."

Once inside the examining room, I saw alarm on Dovie's face. Liddy's dark hair made her skin look whiter. She moaned, rolled over on her side and pulled her legs up as far as she could.

"Cramping," Dovie said.

And then we saw the blood. Dovie stripped off Liddy's clothes and wiped the table as much as she could. I wrapped the girl in a coarse-weave blanket. Monthly agonies were worse for some women than others, but we didn't know Liddy's history.

Suddenly her groans became more frequent. They soon erupted into hoarse cries almost like labor pains. I took my seat at the end of the table and adjusted the bare-bulbed light while Dovie rolled Liddy over on her back. She pulled her legs into a tent position.

"Uh-oh," I said. "Look at this." Dovie glided from Liddy's shoulders to my side. A tiny amniotic sac lay on the bloody sheet.

"Oh no," Dovie said. "Oh, no."

* * * *

After Liddy recovered enough to make sense, we learned the whole story. She seemed glad the secret was finally out. We assured her it was all right.

"Thank goodness," she said, looking at Dovie, "you're not judgmental like––"

She stopped before naming anyone and then reached for our hands. "Please, *please* don't tell Heth's family about this," she begged, with tears in her eyes.

Dovie smiled and patted the girl's hand. "Remember the doctor's oath to protect the patient? We're a team on that one."

We discussed with Liddy how she would feel the next few days, and gave her information and supplies for her recovery. When she could walk steadily, Dovie dressed her in a long robe and coat while I excused myself to tell the men what I had found. Anemia, we'll call it.

We drove Liddy to the boardinghouse and the men followed on foot. While Dovie got Liddy ready for bed, Brother Bird, Tom, Ullan and I gathered around the big table in the roominghouse. I had some ideas for the patient upstairs.

"Tom," I shouted. He was in the kitchen making coffee. "Call the *Banner* early tomorrow. Tell Editor Redd that the doctor has ordered bed rest for Miss Underhill for the balance of the week. If she wants to send Liddy's daily assignments, that's fine, as long as it doesn't involve any moving around. Got that?"

"Got that, Doc."

To the rest of the men, I said, "We've got to get hold of Heth Coursey. The best medicine for the young lady up there is for this wedding she's been planning to happen. And the sooner, the better." I stopped while we received and doctored our coffee.

"First thing I'll do is try to locate Quinn Coursey." I looked at Brother Bird. You plan to hold a wedding Saturday morning, either at your house or the church, possibly right here if Liddy isn't any better. Ten o'clock sharp."

Brother Bird nodded.

"Tom, go down to the county clerk's office tomorrow and ask Verna Lue to prepare a marriage license and take it home with her in case we find Heth after hours." Tom signaled his assent. "Tell her to be on call to fill out the paperwork. Let's see, tomorrow is Wednesday. Thursday, Friday, Saturday––three days. Preacher, leave your Sunday afternoon free in case we can't find Heth soon enough."

Bird Briley sat mute. Again, he nodded.

"Ullan, you can stand up with Heth, and Dovie will stand up with Liddy."

The druggist, who was Heth's friend, said, "I'll do it, Doc, I'll do it."

"By the way, Ullan, I'll need plenty of Bayer Aspirin. Maybe some codeine. And iron tablets."

"Yes, Doc, I have those in stock."

"Tom, there's an empty house southwest from you––behind the cedars. While you're at the courthouse, find out who owns it and if it's for sale––or rent. I could talk Quinn into buying it if it's available."

Ullan spoke up. "Heth told me his pop had asked him and Liddy to move back home since Sula Mae died, but Heth wasn't too fond of the idea. With all due respect to Quinn, I can't blame my friend much."

"I'll check once more on Liddy and Dovie. It's late. Good night, all. Thanks for the coffee, Tom. Reverend, can we give you a ride home?" Little did I know it would be the last time I ever offered him anything.

"No thanks," he said. "I'll walk."

— Chapter Seventeen —

After breakfast on the first November Monday, I kissed Dovie and walked down White Halter Road, then crossed the highway into St. Luke proper. My office was two blocks farther. Dovie would bring the car and come later.

The air was brisk, and the leaves rattled under my feet. The indigo sky was so intense that I stopped for a minute and looked up. But I had a lot to do today besides doctoring. Inside, I headed to the telephone.

"Number please."

"Morning, Miz Myrt. Ring Quinn Coursey, please. Thanks. Can't stop to chat. Got a lot to do today. 'Bye."

In a moment, she was back. "No one answers, Doc. You know Quinn and the three oldest went to Madison Friday," Myrt Lambkin said.

"I know, but I thought they might be back by now. While the line's open, will you connect me to Madison's monument companies?"

The veteran telephone operator didn't speak for a second. "Roscoe, I don't think city or county monuments have telephone numbers. Can you be more specific?"

"Gravestones, Miz Myrt. Headstones."

"Pshaw! What *was* I thinking?"

Hearing the lilt in her forty-year-old voice, I imagined how she looked today: auburn hair piled high, held by tortoiseshell combs; rimless half glasses resting on her beak of a nose; thin lips that became more so when she laughed; hazel eyes that grew larger as she talked. A lace-edged white collar atop her dress would sport one of the brooches from her large collection.

"Doc, I have Querry Mortuary and Monuments for you. Go ahead." She clicked off.

"Nathan T. Querry speaking."

"Dr. Roscoe Everett in St. Luke. I'm looking for Quinn Coursey. His wife died last week, and he and his boys were driving to Madison to find a stone. Have they been to your place? It's important that I reach him."

"Let me see." I heard a shuffling of papers. He surely didn't have enough business that he would forget already.

"Ah, here it is. Yes, they were here late Friday. Found a grave marker, they did. Right nice one, too."

"Did Mr. Coursey say what their plans were after they left your place?"

"Why, I believe he indicated that the four of them would go over to the hotel for supper and stay the night. Call the Golden Lake Hotel, Doctor."

"Just a minute. Didn't you mean five of them––four sons and their father?"

"No. Mr. Coursey and his three sons."

"Thank you, sir."

I hung up then lifted the receiver again. "Myrtie Mae, ma' love, connect me with the Golden Lake Hotel, please. Same town."

"Will do, Dockie. You and Dovie going away for a spell, are you?" After a pause, she said, "You're on. 'Bye." Her last word stretched into two syllables.

"Yes, this is Dr. Roscoe Everett calling from St. Luke. Is Quinn Coursey still at the hotel? Checked out early this morning, did they? All right. Thanks for your trouble."

I rang the operator one more time before my first patient.

"Do me a favor, will you, Myrt? Ring Quinn every half hour. He and the boys are headed home, and I need to see Quinn and Heth as soon as possible. If you do connect, tell Quinn I'll call him at noon. Thanks, love, you're a dear. If I weren't married to Dovie––" I teased in my best Irish tenor voice, and then hurried into the examining room with the sound of Myrt's giggle still in my ear.

After the last morning patient, I rang Miz Myrt again to see what she'd found. But before she answered, Quinn Coursey walked through the door. I hung up, and we exchanged greetings. I re-offered condolences, and he nodded.

"Sit down, Quinn. Have you had lunch? Let me call the market and have them send over some sandwiches. I like their roast beef. Coffee do?"

The new widower and I engaged in general conversation––the weather, his trip to Madison––and then I brought him up-to-date on what happened while they were gone. Except for the miscarriage. The jingle of the telephone interrupted.

"'Scuse me, Quinn."

It was Tom with news about the empty house.

"The house is for sale and ready for occupancy," Tom reported. "Though Fletcher Jewell might rent to the right people."

"Thanks, Tom. Mr. Coursey just came in. I'll mention it. 'Bye." A rap on the door meant our lunch had arrived. "Put it on my bill, will you, Landers? And include a tip." The boy nodded and left.

I spread the sandwiches and coffee out on my desk and motioned for Quinn to pull up a chair. Then I began.

"Quinn, do you know where Heth and Liddy are going to live?" I didn't give him a chance to answer. "There's a vacant house on Depot Street, two blocks down from the boardinghouse. The one behind the cedars. It's for sale––possibly for rent."

Quinn slumped wearily in his chair, sloshing coffee on his khaki jacket. This last week had taken a toll. His mouth, usually droll and plum-colored, was pallid. His brow ridges hid dull eyes that ordinarily sparkled.

He finally spoke. "I kept hoping Heth would take charge and work on it himself, but––all he does is run away. Guess he took his mother's death harder than we thought. I don't know where he is and neither does Liddy. She begged him not to take another trip before the wedding, but he did, and that was just after the funeral. Where could he be? Why is he staying away so long this time?" Quinn's voice had risen with the last two sentences.

I had a sneaking suspicion that Heth wasn't too happy at being calf-roped into marrying Liddy, but I didn't say anything.

"Don't be too hard on him––or yourself, either, Quinn. You need time to mourn. That headstone could have waited a while longer." Quinn and I went back a long way. We could say things to each other with no trace of judgment given or taken.

"No," Quinn said. "You know me. I've got to get on living, with or without her. Set a good example for the boys. Winter's coming on. Need to clear more land west of the house if Heth's not going to build there. This Depression––got to make every inch of ground produce as much as it can. Don't know if enough hay's laid by. Got to check the barns and see if they need winterizing. And fences. The cows––"

"Quinn, the house," I interrupted. "This needs to be done now, this week."

"All right. When I leave here, I'll take a look at it. Maybe I'll make arrangements with the realtor in case Heth hasn't made any plans."

He stuck out his hand. "Appreciate your help, Roscoe. I owe you. Oh, and thanks for the lunch."

— Chapter Eighteen —

QUINN COURSEY

"And thanks for the lead on that house, Doc," I remembered to say as I left his office.

Should I strike out looking for Heth or send the sheriff? No, he's not a wanted man. All we can do is hope he'll get back home. It would be a pity if the groom didn't show up for his own wedding.

Questions about the house Doc mentioned formed in rhythm with my gait. Wonder who owns it? *Step-step.* Who lived in it last and why did they leave? *Step-step.* How long's it been empty? How is it heated? *Step-step.* Is there a yard? And is there a fence? *Step-step.* For sale? Or rent? *Step-step.* Space for the horses? Room for the wagon? *Step-step.*

At last, the house was in sight. Well, almost. I neared the cedars. From the other way, Tom joined me.

"Tom, who owns this place?"

"The railroad owns the land. I heard they hauled in lumber and hired someone from Bowers to build houses for the trackmen. This is the only one left. The others were moved––or torn down. One even burned. Mr. Keeling at the bank holds the house key for the railroad. Don't know who lived in this house last. We can check at the courthouse if it's important to you."

"Why'd the people leave?"

"If you'll pardon me, sir, why does anybody leave? Maybe they needed a larger place. Maybe they moved away for a job in Springfield or somewhere. Maybe the man's crops didn't make and he had to join the WPA. The wife and kids could have gone back home to her mama's. If a

Methodist preacher lived there, he was sent to another town. Or called to another pulpit if he was Baptist. Maybe he died." He stopped a second and grinned his crooked grin. "Or maybe it's haunted!"

"Pshaw!" I said. "It could use a coat of paint. That steep-pitched roof shines likes new. But I don't see a chimney.

"The yard needs work," Tom said. "That chinaberry leans too far over the house. Next strong wind might break it off."

"Steps and handrails seem sound enough. Porch is narrow, at least it widens by the door. Test those columns, Tom. Are they strong? That puny stoop. Wonder how well it keeps the rain off." I tried the front door.

"Locked. Threshold's worn down––gaps around the doorframe. It'll need some weather-stripping before winter."

Tom nodded and I kept talking. "Let's walk around. Where's the electric box? Those overhead wires plug in somewhere."

Tom spoke up. "Look how that persimmon's grown into the fence. Those sprouts got a good foothold. They'd need tending to."

"Many's the time I've called my boys 'young sprouts,' " I said. "The others were easy to keep in check. But Heth––he seems dug in for the long haul. You have kids, Tom?" He shook his head.

"Look at this long back porch. Board-and-batten half way up, but the screen'll have to be redone. How sound are these steps? Ah, they'll hold me. Screen door's hanging like Grandma's sagging stockings. Well, no wonder––the spring's not attached. And the top brace's rotted out."

On the back porch sat a washing machine with two tubs. "Wonder why they left it here? And does it work? 'Upton Machine Co.' *That* came from a Sears-Roebuck store, probably the one in Madison."

Tom spied it first. "Look! There's a well in the middle of the porch. All here––rope, pulley and bucket."

I pushed in behind him. "No one's used this wash basin and dipper lately. Full of cobwebs and bugs. But it'll be nice having water so close. We can get it piped in later if Heth and Liddy decide to stay. Tom?"

"Here I am, sir, under the porch." I descended the steps again, knelt and followed his gaze. Flat stones held end posts off the ground. Planks lay crosswise covering the dirt, and gunnysacks were spread here and there over the boards.

"Whoever lived here worked hard," I said. "See those crates of fruit jars? And that chicken brooder?"

Tom spoke. "Wonder if rats and snakes hide under here. Or 'possums and coons?"

"I'm going to try the back door, Tom," I said, and climbed the steps again. "It's locked, but if I cup my hands around my eyes maybe I can see––There's a wooden icebox––and a cook stove. It looks like the eating area is beyond."

"There's a smokehouse and a privy and a garden spot," Tom said, coming around a log building. "But where would Heth keep the horses? Plenty of space here for a barn."

"That's good," I said. And here's the fuse box. See, this in-line was connected to a light pole at the street. There's a swallows' nest there under the eaves."

I walked out to the driveway. "Now I know how I missed seeing this place before. It's that row of cedars along the street. It cuts out the vision of this line of crape myrtles. And this rickety trellis of honeysuckle, these suspension chairs."

Tom was looking toward the railroad tracks. "There's no fence, so the property must go all the way," he said.

Farther back into the yard, hickory, walnut and pecan trees were spaced out evenly. A stack of stove wood looked to be well seasoned. Grape vines twined on a gray pipe. "Whoever worked this place knew about growing things," I said. "I'm impressed."

"Mr. Coursey," Tom called from the front of the house. "Mr. Keeling's here with the key."

"Fletcher Jewell told me you were over here," I heard the banker say from the road. "Looking to buy? Or rent?"

I walked closer to him. "My son and his new bride will need a place to live. Tom, here, and I thought we'd have a look-see. Maybe fix it up as a wedding present. The outside looks pretty good."

"Well, here's the key. You can bring it by the bank when you're done," he said, throwing the key to Tom and edging away. "I sure don't want to go in there."

"What's the asking price?" I turned, but the lanky man had already hurried toward the bank. "If you're still interested," he called over his shoulder, "come by and we'll draw up the papers." Then he broke into a run.

"What––why doesn't he want to go in?" Tom asked.

Now it was my turn to shrug. I unlocked and pushed open the front door. "Listen. That flutter and scraping."

"What was that?" Tom asked. "It's too late for bats. They would've migrated by now."

"No chimney, so it couldn't be swifts," I said. "Swallows, maybe? Mice?" After I raised the shades, the rooms took shape. A living room, dining area and kitchen. I opened a door into a small room.

Tom looked in. "Liddy can put her sewing machine and trunk in here."

"Huh? How do you know she's got a sewing machine and trunk?"

"You've forgotten, have you, that she lives in my boardinghouse? I helped her move in."

"Oh."

"Is there an attic?" Tom asked, looking around for any sign of an opening, or a stairwell.

"With such a high-pitched roof, surely––"

A narrow door in the back hall caught my eye. Opening it, I felt a gust of icy air and heard a high-pitched keening. Feathers and dust descended into the cramped stairway. "Tom, I found the attic." I closed the door after he didn't respond.

We walked outside and sat in the rusted chairs.

"What do you think, Tom? Could we fix this place up? We don't have much time. Who could we get to help? I can give them some furniture now that Sula Mae's gone. Do you have any spare furnishings to sell? Maybe I ought to rent it at first, with the option to buy."

Tom answered, "I can get Xann Price and Brother Bird and Landers Beane to help. I don't think there's much choice––unless Heth wants to rent an apartment in the boardinghouse." He pulled down a branch of crape myrtle and fingered the fading blooms. "Don't you think you ought to bring Miss Liddy down here for a look-round before you go deciding for her?"

"I like Liddy," I said as we walked around the back and onto the porch. "I'm glad Heth found her. Maybe she'll settle him down so he can make something of himself. Let's see how that well water tastes before we go over to the bank. We'll have to wipe out the dipper first. How strong is this rope? It's fraying but I think it'll hold. Here goes."

"Listen to that pulley creak," Tom said.

"There, it hit water. I'll lower it a little more so it'll go under. Hey, let's see how deep the bottom is."

Tom's voice showed more excitement than at any time today. "Hear that 'thunk?'" he said. "There's plenty of water. Pull 'er up. I love that *creak*. Reminds me of my boyhood. Wait. There's another sound––like castanets."

I reached for the bail, pulled the bucket to the well curb and the noise subsided. Dipping the ladle into the bucket, I felt it strike something hard. "Let's see what that is––Bones! Tom, look!"

"That must be why Mr. Keeling didn't want to come closer. He must think this house is haunted!" Tom said.

— Chapter Nineteen —

LIDDY

I felt as gray as the Ozark hillsides in winter. Tears of pain and self-pity had dried my eyes. They felt as raspy as peanut shells, as wrinkled as our skirts on Mother's clothesline. Over and over, I'd scolded myself for this miscarriage. First, I should have been more firm when Heth got too amorous. Next––

Before I could continue, someone rapped on my door. "Knock, knock. It's Dovie. May I come in?"

"Door's open." I answered. Seeing her smile––this nurse and my friend––I shoved my pity under the covers and smiled back.

"Thought I'd give you the once over to see how you're doing." She felt my sore stomach and asked a few questions. Satisfied that I was healing well, Dovie pulled the vanity stool close to my bed. I followed her eyes to my wedding dress hanging on a peg, shapeless as a shroud.

"Well?" she asked, looking back at me. "What have you been thinking about these last few days?"

I might as well tell her. "I was flailing myself over this situation––for not being more forceful in telling Heth 'no.' For expecting him to act the gentleman. When he told me he could find someone who *would* give him what he 'needed,' I should have answered, 'Good, go find her. It won't be me. Not until we're married.' "

She reached for my hand and held it. "Go on."

"If Brother Bird hadn't misunderstood my visit and chased me like a child––"

Dovie spoke. "Either he was embarrassed at his mistake or he's just plain mean."

"My running away from him was the last straw."

We sat in silence for a time. "Why was I so frightened? I felt like a child again, and ran."

Dovie stood and moved over to where my dress was hanging. She held it up to the light and fingered the stitching. "Nice job, my dear," she said, fitting the hanger back on the peg. She took her seat again.

"Now don't get mad and accuse me of being maternal, but––" She looked straight into my eyes. "Why marry Heth now? Break your engagement. Only the four of us know about this, and we're sworn to secrecy."

I gazed back at the nurse, the beautiful blond woman who had somehow kept her figure, this sweet childhood friend of Mother's. Her suggestion went against everything I had ever learned: *Never go back on your word. You made your bed, now lie in it.* "If I did, how would I explain it?"

"Why explain anything? Doc has passed the word that you're anemic. You could say that while you were ill, you thought better of the plan. That you'd decided to go to journalism school at Columbia. Or visit your cousin in Chicago. There are lots of options, Liddy."

"I don't know––He's been inside me. He's a part of me now."

"Bosh!" Dovie said. "That little bit of sperm left your body when the fetus did." She leaned in and took my hand again. "How can you still love Heth after what he did? How can you trust him? Respect him? After he tricked you, giving you that rot-gut. That's as bad as if he'd raped you."

"I did love him. But Dovie, maybe I did or said something to lead him on. Maybe subconsciously, I longed for someone to want me, so I didn't protest enough. Maybe I'm in love with the idea of being a wife and mother. I'm desperate to be part of a perfect, happy family."

"Forgive me, but the perfect part will never happen. And the happy part? We all want that, but we have to work for it. Happiness comes over time. It grows while we're wallowing around in day-to-day living. Happiness takes more than merely wishing for it."

She paused. "Heth's not the only fish in the St. Luke pond, you know."

"What?" It took me a minute to figure out what she meant. "Who else is there?"

"Tom, for one."

I laughed and pointed downstairs. "Tom? The boardinghouse manager? What makes you think Tom would be interested in me?"

"I'm not saying he is, just that he's a possibility. Fletcher Jewell, the realtor––he's single. Any bachelors in your office? Even Heth's dad is available now!"

"Dovie!" We both laughed. It relieved the growing tension, but my stomach hurt terribly.

When we quit our silliness, I realized that my body *had* manufactured more tears after all. We both wiped our eyes.

"No, I insisted that Heth marry me, and if he's still willing––whenever he returns from wherever he is––and when he finds out I've lost the baby––He will *still* marry me, won't he, Dovie?"

"He won't, Liddy!" Dovie spoke with authority. "Not many men would marry if they didn't have to. And Heth Coursey is one of them." She leaned farther in. "I've known him longer than you have. I watched him grow up. At least in age."

"Are you suggesting that I don't tell him about the miscarriage, Dovie? You think he'll not accuse me of keeping secrets, of trapping him?"

"Didn't he trap you first?" She had a point.

Dovie must have realized she hadn't convinced me. A sad look crossed her face. She shook her head and then stood.

"You've forced my hand, Liddy. For one thing, as a friend of your mother who asked me to serve as your absent parent, for another, as your nurse––" She ticked off on her fingers. "The third reason––because I know Heth Coursey better than you do, and finally, because I love you like the daughter I don't have. I forbid you to marry him! I insist that you call off this wedding." She breathed hard and her cheeks reddened. "You think about that, Lydia Louise Underhill."

She kissed the top of my head, turned and left, pulling the door behind her.

I was stunned by her demand.

Call off the wedding, Dovie said. Now that I think about it, I once felt the same way. But I didn't follow through.

Scooting under the covers, I fluffed my pillow and pulled up the quilt. I was suddenly tired. "I'll sleep on it, dear Dovie," I said aloud.

— Chapter Twenty —

HETH

"Ho, there, Frank. Glad your place is still open." I sidled up to the bar, grinning at my old friend. "I'm coming off the longest peddling trip I ever made––all the way to Rakestraw and back."

"Rough trip, huh?"

"The trip west wasn't much, but oh, the trip back––"

"What're you drinking tonight, old boy?"

"Give me a snort of that cider-tasting applejack. Damn, I forgot! No money since my wagon got blown off the ridge."

"On the house, friend, on the house." The owner and bartender of Yancey's Roadhouse obliged me. "So that's why you ain't been by lately."

"Thanks," I said as he handed me a glass. After a long slug of applejack, I continued. "There was this girl at the hotel––"

"Cottoned to 'er, did you?" His eyes twinkled, knowing my weakness for the ladies.

"The other way around, this time," I said, "but I got out before––After the storm and on the way back, we stopped for the night at Ol' Man Lone Wolf's.

"Who's 'we'?" Frank looked at the door. "You brought the lady home with you? Where is she, then?"

"No," I said. "Me and the horses. They bedded down in the old man's barn. He fed them some of last year's oats."

The honky-tonk player piano thumped out, "A Hot Time in the Old Town Tonight." Several tattered books lay on the end of the bar. *Ships That*

Pass in the Night, The Friendship of Women, and *Bicycling World* magazine. Lights flickered from kerosene lamps.

"About noon the next day, we came upon a gypsy camp."

"Gypsies in these parts?" Frank leaned on the counter, nursing a yellow drink. "I ain't seen a band of gypsies since I was a little coot."

"Speaking of gypsies, Frank, you should'a seen that fortuneteller looking at me under those hooded eyes."

"Was she a looker?"

"She definitely was: black shiny hair, olive skin, long eyelashes, bangles on her ears and bracelets on her arms—–It's a good thing I had on my flannel shirt. It hid my crotch."

"You'd'a-been embarrassed, huh? Want another drink?"

I nodded. In the mottled mirror behind the bar I could see my red face. It might have been the sun, but—–Frank knew what loosened my tongue.

"On the way here, I thought about the horses," I continued. "This could be their last peddling trip, the good old sods."

"Hard to find good horses, nowadays." Frank ran his hand through his graying hair and then walked from behind the bar and looked out the open door at my nags.

"Until I find a new wagon, they get to retire. Not me. I gotta get married." I pounded my fist on the counter and the barware rattled. "My work's just starting."

"Barkeep!" someone shouted. Frank looked out over the room and several patrons lifted their glasses for another round. He knew what each was drinking and poured several clean glasses full. Pulling a metal tray from under the bar, he set each glass or bottle on it. He disappeared behind me long enough to deliver, collect his money and return to his post. And long enough for me to finish off my drink.

When he came back, he refilled my glass, and then came around to sit on the stool next to me. He faced me and could also see his customers.

"Frank, the funniest thing happened."

"Oh my lord, what?" he said. "Let me guess. You decided to straighten up and fly right."

"Har har. No. I reined the horses under some shade and considered this: No one knew where I was except the tomato farmer and the gypsies. What if I disappeared?"

Frank must have remembered something. He bolted from his stool and hurried over to the bulletin board full of For Sale signs, a 'Lost hog' sign,

Found signs, and several business cards. He tore off a sheet that looked like a wanted poster and brought it back.

"You won't be going anywhere," he said. "The law's after you. Here's a notice from St. Luke saying you're considered missing and anyone who sees you should tell you to hurry home. Or notify the sheriff of Gillette County-South."

"Wha—?" I snatched it from him and studied it while he refilled drinks for those who came to the bar. He didn't visit, just took their glasses, filled fresh ones and accepted their coins.

"Oh, this is bound to be a hoax. I haven't broken any law. Why should I go back to St. Luke? All I got there is my clothes and that old Nash—it's about ready for the scrap-yard anyhow."

"How about your family? And your fiancee?"

"But my fortune said I should unhook from family."

"Balderdash!"

"And that my future was on a river."

"Bunkum! A bunch of claptrap!" He turned away.

By then it was close to midnight and customers were leaving one by one and two by two. Some couples held on to each other to keep standing and walking. Their 'goodbyes' were slurred and now and then an oath would escape at the same time as a belch.

"Now I've lost my living—" My voice sounded slurred, too, and a headache to beat all headaches pounded my brain. "I can't support Liddy, much less a baby. I'm too young to settle down anyhow, don't you agree, ol' pal, ol' pal?" I flopped my head on the bar without cushioning it with my arms. But I couldn't even say 'Ouch.'

"Let me blow out these lamps and then we can get you prone."

"If Zindi—she's the one at the hotel—and Tew-the-fortune-teller think I'm such a catch, I should maybe find out who else thinks so—"

"Let's go, buddy. You can sleep it off here tonight. I keep a cot handy for fools like you who can't hold their liquor."

"—I know Wrennetta Fincher thinks I'm hunky-dory. So does Isabel Archer—Liddy failed my test of purity that day at the picnic—"

"You dirty rat!" Frank yelled. "You hornswoggled her with that hooch!" He walked me around the room holding on to my shirt back.

"She shudda known I'd try something. She shudda been prepar—" I said before Frank let me fall onto the cot. "That applejack whiskey I bought from ya' shurre came in handy that day. Here, gi' me anuther."

— Chapter Twenty-One —

HETH

"Ho, Ullan," I greeted my best friend at his drug store on the afternoon I slipped back in to St. Luke after sleeping off my hangover at Frank's. I'd been gone for nearly a week.

"Good to see you, Heth," Ullan said. He was busy behind the counter. "You've not been around much lately, have you? You seen Liddy?"

"Naw, I haven't seen her. No one's home over at our place––Dad left a note. He and the boys went to Madison for a gravestone. Don't want anyone to know where I'm at. Not yet, anyhow."

"What can I do for you?"

"I don't need doctoring except pills for courage." I sat in a chair where people wait to get their medicines. "You can listen, I guess. Then maybe give me some advice."

"I've got all the time in the world as long as I can keep working back here. Shoot."

"That Saturday afternoon after Mother's funeral, I was in such a temper that I just dropped Liddy off at the boardinghouse. She practically forbade me to take another peddling trip before the wedding. It hit me wrong. We may be engaged, but we're not married. She doesn't own me."

I looked at the Cardui calendar on the closest wall. "That's when I knew I had to buck her and make that last trip. I never did like being told what I couldn't do. So I hooked the team to the wagon and lit out. I wanted to get as far away from St. Luke as I could by dark."

"You must have run those horses at a pretty good clip," Ullan said without looking up.

"They were fresh and in the crisp air they almost raced. By nightfall, I was at Rakestraw so I stopped at the hotel. Inside, behind the desk were large portraits in fancy frames. *Jakob Rakestraw* and *Jetta Rakestraw* were etched in the nameplates. I hit the bell, and a woman about Liddy's age appeared."

All I could see was Ullan's slicked-down dark hair parted on the side. "I'm listening. Go on," he said.

"Ullan, this woman could'a been straight out of the girlie magazine I keep under the wagon seat.

"'W-e-e-l-l, hel-l-o, handsome,' she said. 'Welcome to the Rakestraw. It's been weeks since anyone pretty as you's brightened our premises. Name's Zintha,' she drawled. 'Zintha Belle Yielding at your service. You can call me Zindi—with an I.' She leaned over the counter and touched my hand." I stopped, remembering every detail.

Ullan looked up and asked, "You like a cup of coffee, Heth?"

"Don't mind if I do. Black." I stood as he handed what looked like a shaving mug through the opening. "Thanks." I walked around the aisles.

"She told me where to lead my team and wagon. Under the backside of the hotel, near the edge of a cliff, stables were built into the limestone. A boy in a black duster pointed me to the two end stalls. I saw to the horses, retrieved my grip and cinched a tarp over the wagon."

Just then Ullan's front door bell tinkled and a customer walked in. Ullan greeted her, and I turned into another aisle and waited until she left.

"And then what?" he asked.

"To guarantee good treatment of Buck and Charlie, I emptied my pockets, and handed the coins to the stupid-looking boy. He grinned through crooked teeth and pointed to rickety-looking stairs leading up to the ground floor of the hotel. I waved him off and walked back up the way I came." I handed Ullan my empty cup and nodded when he asked if I wanted a refill.

"'Ever been to these parts before?' Zindi B. Yielding asked me, when I returned from the stables.

"'Can't say as I have,' I answered. I couldn't take my eyes off her red mouth. 'I'm from St.—over east. Needed to make one more trip before I—' And then I thought, why tell this luscious stranger that I'm engaged?" Ullan looked up but I couldn't read his face.

"She told me I'd just missed supper but she'd lay out some fixings later. 'Let me take you to your room and then I'll show you around,' she said.

The pall of cigar smoke in the ancient foyer reminded me of Granddad Coursey. Do you carry cigars, Ullan?"

He pointed to the far wall.

"At the end of a hall, she unlocked a door and stepped into the darkness. I stood back and she raised a window shade. 'Well, are you coming in? Hand me your things. I want to show you something.' She sidled out, brushing against me. I can tell you––" I moved closer to where Ullan still worked, and whispered, "I felt my blue jeans bulge."

That got a grin out of him.

"I followed her out the end door of the building and down wooden stairs like those to the stables. Every now and then she looked back, and I figured she could see the front of my pants. She told me some stuff about old man Rakestraw and how he was the first to install outside lighting around his place. There was an eerie glow on the damp limestone at the edge of what she called Tully Mountain."

"There," the druggist said. "I'm through compounding that order." He came down and sat across from me.

"When she turned and asked me if I was coming, I almost peed myself. I tried to get control of my lower parts. I finally said, 'Coming,' and my voice broke like a teenager's. I cleared my throat to recover. 'Must be something in the air,' I lied."

The phone rang and Ullan bolted up the one step and answered it before the second ring. When he returned, he had a feather duster in his hand. "You don't mind if I clean a little while you talk, do you?"

I shook my head but kept talking like I might forget a detail of my story if I paused. "It's a good thing I wasn't scared of heights. I looked down once from the swinging bridge––bad idea. I followed Zindi across the narrow span. She could have been Tarzan's woman. What had I gotten myself into?"

I had talked so fast to Ullan I ran out of breath, so I leaned back and sipped the coffee. The early November wind had picked up. Leaves scraped across the wooden porch of the store.

Then I continued. "When I turned to see how far we had come, I couldn't see anything. It was like Mother Nature'd dropped a black parachute over us. I was beginning to doubt my sanity.

"'We're here,' she said. 'Welcome to my humble abode.' But all I saw was a yellowing willow behind her. She laughed. Then, turning, she disappeared into the weeping branches."

The cuckoo clock in Ullan's upstairs room sounded. "Closing time," he said, locking the door and pulling off his smock.

"I'm nearly through," I said. "I just stood there. Before I knew it, Zindi reached through the leaves and pulled me inside. 'Welcome to Willow Eden.' She stroked my hand, and I shivered. I was in a jungle!"

"The Rakestraws were originally from Chicago, Zindi told me. They brought their National Geographic magazines and moved to the Missouri Ozarks, since their dreams of going on safari could never be. Jetta Rakestraw collected exotic plants, and Jakob, who made his money in artificial limbs, retired, and contracted with zoos in the northeast to buy their animal carcasses. These were shipped to a taxidermist in New York, who sent them back by train to Madison. Jakob hired a wagoner for the last leg of their journey to Rakestraw. How he got them this far out in the woods is beyond me. And I didn't ask.

"Ullan, I tell you, I felt like a child at the zoo in Springfield. An elephant-shaped coffee table rested on a bear rug. A giraffe swag light illuminated four stuffed herons standing in a sunken pool."

After locking the register, Ullan pulled up a chair and sat.

"A real parrot squawked from its cage. Palm fronds brushed the ceiling from pots sitting around the large space. I heard a rustle from the floor and half expected to see a tarantula or a snake. The room smelled clayish, fishy, like the Creel River.

"Suddenly I froze. Humidity or pollen or dust––something had clogged up my nose and throat. I began to wheeze.

"Zindi laughed, probably figuring I was overwhelmed by her décor. She tiptoed across the room and pushed a hidden button. The lights dimmed and mountain music, interspersed with loon calls and chirping crickets, played from hidden speakers. She disappeared into a back room, saying, 'I won't be long.'

"While I still could, Ullan, I bolted and ran for my life. I felt in as much danger as if she had been after me with a blowgun. I felt my way along the swinging bridge, gulped the fresh air, and hugged the edge of the mountainside path. I retraced my steps, with help from the lights that had guided me here what seemed like ages ago.

"I high-jumped the wooden hotel stairs two by two, rushed to the room and grabbed my things, sprinted down the hall and out the rancid foyer. Panic drove me faster and faster down the lighted street. When I reached the stable yard, I found a dark corner, gulped in more fresh air, and panted. In between breaths, I listened.

"After a while, I cooled down and my wits returned, but by now my bladder was full, so I peed over the edge of the ravine beyond the stable way.

"I kept listening for footsteps. What if she sent that dull stable boy after me? A spring trickled from rocks at the end of Benton Street and a wooden trough caught the water. I dunked my head first, and then drank. My nose and throat cleared; my breathing slowed.

"Hunger pangs reminded me I'd missed supper. I smelled ripe fruit and found a yellow pear on the ground, glowing like manna. I didn't see any movement in the street, so I picked it up, wiped the wasps and leaf mold on my jeans, and ate it down to the stringy center. A tree branch drooped over a fence and several more pears hung within reach. I pulled them all.

"Just then, a clock chimed twelve. I realized that I was dog-tired. Fear of what Zindi might do vied with my sudden drowsiness. I pulled out my sleeping gear and unrolled it beneath the wagon. Struggling into my bedroll fully clothed, I finally relaxed and slept, but I had the wildest dream––

> *––I walked into my father's yard and heard noises—women's voices.*
>
> *High-pitched, hysterical cries. Near the steps, Zindi Yielding and Mother were arguing.*
>
> *"It's mine. I'm his wife!" Zindi shouted.*
>
> *"No, it's mine. He's my son!" Mother answered in her scolding voice.*
>
> *Zindi grabbed at the velvet purse in Mother's hand. "Thirty-five grand—what I could do with that!" she said. "He owes me! He never gave me a wedding present, no honeymoon––not even a ring!"*
>
> *Mother countered, "Think of all the money Quinn and I spent while he was under our roof."*
>
> *Slowly, Zindi melted into her jungle and Mother into her coffin. On the rise behind, I saw Liddy standing, pregnant and sad.*
>
> *From the road, four men in black came toward me carrying a battering ram. But they passed on, heading for the house. The sky darkened, thunder rumbled and lightning crackled.*

Just then, Liddy flashed a mirror, blinding me. I fell to my knees. A heavy rain began to fall, and everything, including Liddy, crumpled to the ground like wet paper dolls. My brain went black––

"I willed myself awake. In the stable yard, rain fell in gray sheets. Dirt spattered my bedroll before I could scoot further under the wagon. Buck and Charlie neighed from their stall.

"Soon daylight broke, the rain stopped, and I slept. When I woke, Sunday's sun brightened the forest, ridges, and ravines. I smelled the river. "Holy, Holy, Holy," sounded from a bell tower. It was somehow soothing.

"My dream flashed in and out of my head. Only the day before, I'd seen my mother buried and heard my girlfriend warn against a peddling run.

"And Zindi," Ullan said. "Was she real?"

"I considered it might be my imagination. Or lust. Would I have followed her to glory under different circumstances?

"I fed and watered my team. I found some jerky in my knapsack. Maybe the rain had dislodged more pears."

Ullan looked at his watch. I heard his stomach growl.

"Just a mite more, then I'm outta here. It was then I decided to start back to St. Luke, but I would take my time––look for a new route, investigate trails and tracks, find out where the cabins, the farms, and the settlements were in this western part of Gillette County, Missouri.

"While I harnessed the horses to the wagon, it hit me. I could upgrade my peddling operation with a Ford truck like the one I saw in front of the hotel––cover more territory more often. I liked the freedom of peddling, of being my own boss, working at my own speed."

I stood. "There's no way I can get out of marrying Liddy, Ullan, but by god, I can make sure she don't control my comings and goings. I watched my brothers change after they married. Henpecked and thumbscrewed. If Liddy don't like my being gone so much, well, tough potatoes."

Ullan unlocked the door and as I walked out, I continued.

"I suddenly felt as exhilarated as if I had discovered a vein of coal. I heard a clear message. *Go back to St. Luke, buy Liddy an engagement ring, plan your honeymoon and decide where you're going to live.* I had been to the wilderness and gotten jerked around. That day, believe it or not, Ullan, I determined to be a better man and a good husband."

"By the way," he said after I was on the porch, "Doc Everett's put the word out that anyone who sees you is to tell you to come by his office as soon as possible."

— Chapter Twenty-Two —

LIDDY

It was a warm, sunny autumn afternoon in St. Luke. I had been in bed most of the week and needed some fresh air. Tom and I sat in the boardinghouse yard between the porch and Depot Street. Moss Mountain Highway lay just north of St. Luke proper. A grassy field with no fence bordered both routes. Soon, we heard singing and the sounds of horses and wagons heading east along the highway. At the intersection, a man halted the caravan. Seeing us, he rode over, dismounted and spoke.

"Hello. I am Dowan Mondragon, head of this gypsy band. We are heading to Jerome, Georgia. It is supper time. May we pull into this"––he gestured to the field––"area and partake of our meal which we prepared earlier? And perhaps give our children some room to run and play before we continue our journey?" He pointed to the broom straw grasses beyond the road.

I looked at Tom, who had risen to greet the guest. "Yes," Tom answered him, "you can pull in onto the grass. No fires, of course, not this time of year. Not with this breeze."

"Oh, no," Mondragon said. "We know the laws of the forest and the plains. We are part and parcel of it."

He motioned for the drivers to pull into Depot Street and then into the field. Each wagon turned at right angles into the pasture facing west. The gypsies began moving things into place while the children and a dog or two romped and ran farther into the acreage.

Dowan Mondragon led his horse to the campsite, handed the reins off to a young man and spoke to the elders. He drew a cup of coffee from an urn. Then he came over to where we were. Tom brought another chair from the porch. I could sense a story here.

I said, "Have you seen a young peddler around your area lately? One of our––" I looked over at Tom––"men folk has not been seen for a nearly a week."

The swarthy, handsome elder with a red neckerchief brightened. "Yes, by the way, we had a visitor earlier this week."

"Can you tell us about it?" I asked, opening my journal and unclipping my Eversharp. "I'm a reporter for the newspaper. May I take notes?"

He nodded and began.

Dowan's Story

It was nearly noon that day. Our horses suddenly stopped grazing, raised their heads and neighed. From the road, unseen horses whinnied back. Our children scrambled up a grassy knoll and stood at a safe distance.

The rider came in sight and our horses neighed again. As head of the encampment, I left the gathering and joined the children. The rider dismounted from one of his horses.

'Ho, there, you are the first person we have seen today.' We shook hands.

He was young––early-twenties, I'd say––with raggedy sun-bleached hair hanging from under his cap. His handshake was strong and his eyes were friendly.

Again, I looked at Tom and nodded.

'My name is Dowan. Dowan Mondragon.'

'One of the Coursey boys, from over that-a-way,' the traveler said, pointing east.

I trembled with excitement––both for this story and for myself.

'Where've you come from and where you going?' we asked each other at the same time.

I began. 'We headed east from New Mexico just after the Easter season. From around Santa Fe. The Indians have the place sewed up. They are the only ones who can buy permits to sell handmade goods. We have traveled many days and nights. We are going to Georgia,' I told him. 'How much longer must we travel?'

Our weary visitor laughed. 'How long you got? I had a map in my wagon that got blown off the ridge back a piece. How far can you go in a day? You'll have to hurry to get there before winter. And why Georgia?'

'Our clan is not welcome in the west,' I told him, 'even though we are original peoples from Romany and Russia. Our predecessors had traveled before us until they found a place of acceptance—in Jerome, Georgia. So that's why you are riding one horse and walking the other—your wagon disappeared. It is mealtime. Stop and sup with us.'

'I am *mighty hungry,' he said. 'The old farmer down the road invited me in yesterday for supper and the night. Did you see his tomato field?'*

'We did indeed!' I answered. 'No one was around that early. Two of our smallest children squeezed through the fence. The mist was thick. I did not think the people would miss a few fruit since there were so many. We used the gleaning code. The one from the Bible's book of Ruth.'

We led the horses down to the stream, and then tied them to saplings in a grassy patch. 'We missed the bad weather,' I told him. I introduced him to the camp and shared his tale of woe. He looked around at our quilts and blankets spread on the ground and secured with river stones. Our chuck wagon carried iron and enamel pots, a Dutch oven, metal serving-ware, and fold-up canvas chairs and cots. A chuck-box unfolded into a work surface.

Our brightly clad women, their heads covered, chattered as they prepared the noon meal. The men and older boys drew closer to see and hear the visitor. The children soon lost interest and wandered away.

We feasted on squirrel and rabbit stew simmered in stock and tomatoes. Garlic, we brought with us. While we ate, I filled the visitor in on our ways.

The crunchiness and flavor in the meat comes from wild sage and dock seeds. The potatoes are from our New Mexico harvest and were baked in ashes. 'Ladle enough stew over them,' I told the peddler, 'and you can't taste the soot.' He ate like he was starved.

'Everyone has a job here,' I told our traveler. 'The older children scour the creek banks for dandelions, broad-leafs, poke sallet, wild onion, and wild hydrangea—which make a tasty dish of greens, don't you agree?'

Our sweet dish that meal was wild grapes, nuts, dried peaches and pears—with day-old bread mixed in.

One day each week is our rest day. That day, we were resting, and after lunch, the men gathered under the bridge to smoke, study Nostradamus, and plan tomorrow's route. I stayed with our guest that afternoon.

The older girls busied themselves with needlework. The boys gathered twigs and small branches and built birdhouses to sell on the journey. The younger children napped to the lullaby of a young mother. The visitor and I sat on the rise and listened.

Here Dowan stopped his story and said, "Do you mind if I sing. I do love to sing. But imagine a woman's melodious voice."

Of course, Tom and I didn't mind.

> *Soft o'er the mountain falls the southern moon; far o'er the mountain breaks the day too soon. In thy dark eyes' splendor where the warm light loves to dwell, weary looks, yet tender, speak of yonder dell.*
>
> *'Nitya, Tyuaniyta, let me rest here by your side. 'Nitya, Tyuanitya, stay with me, abide.*

A young woman left the camp and crossed the road to where we were sitting. Dowan looked up in surprise.

"Here's Tew! She is the one who sang it that day. She has heard me singing and come to join me. Tew is my sister."

Tom quickly brought another chair and they sang another verse.

> *When in thy dreaming, moons like these shall rise again, shine on our journey down the eastern lane. Rest, for you will need it, once we travel on our way. Dream, dearest children, care not for today.*
>
> *'Niyta, Tyuanitya, let me rest here by your side. 'Nitya, Tyuanitya, stay with me, abide.*

Tew smiled and bowed to us, then went back to the wagon. Dowan continued his story.

I suggested to our young peddler that we take a couple of our horses and see if we could get down in the ravine where his wagon disappeared. I thought we might find something to bring back. Our sorrels could negotiate narrow passes that his plodders couldn't.

I threw on the saddles, passed the latigos through slits and cinched them securely. He hoisted himself up and held on. I wondered if his inexperience with fast horses would be a danger.

'These peg ponies,' I told him, 'will get us where we need to go.' I kicked my mount into a gallop. 'They need the exercise,' I called to Coursey, who appeared surprised at their speed. He held on to the horn as well as the reins, and bounced pretty badly until he figured out how to splay his legs to take the play out of his body. After that, he seemed to enjoy the ride.

Tom and I both smiled at the gypsy's description of Heth's riding a fast horse.

After the first burst of energy, our horses dropped into a trot. I heard him whistle. He had spied the side road with the mailboxes. Turning in, we soon arrived at the place where the wagon disappeared. We dismounted and searched for a downward path.

'Wait,' he said. 'This is the very place I spotted the wagon in the ravine. See these bare branches?'

I scooped the clusters of sumac berries from the ground into my hat. He told me he had whacked them off in a fit of rage. We gazed into the decline and saw nothing.

'Let's take a rope and go down there,' I said. 'Get that potato sack out of your saddlebag in case we find something usable. And let's put these berries in there.'

'We'd better not risk leaving the horses,' Coursey answered. 'I heard a hound baying yesterday. No telling what kind of people live back––' He pointed in the direction he was headed before the storm changed his plans.

'Let's go back to the main road,' I suggested, 'and see if the slope is more gradual.'

The horses stepped carefully down the rocky decline full of scrub and hardwoods. We gave them a slack rein. A vein of water glistened.

'Must be a fork of the Creel River,' he said.

At the bottom, we traveled south until the ravine curved east. Not a splinter of wagon was visible, no axles, no wheels. It was as if vultures had picked it clean. The storm's sudden downpour had surely deepened the stream, but the terrain was level. Brush had piled up against roots and rotten trees, but not a hint of any peddler's wares was visible. Not even his old yellow slicker could be seen among the debris.

'I feel like a dope,' he said. 'Did I dream I'd seen the wagon in the ravine? Did Mom's death and the thought of marriage send me off the edge?'

Again, Tom and I looked at each other.

Just then, a hound bayed and we both stopped. I said quietly, 'We're being watched. I can feel it. Let us get out of here fast, my friend.' We led the horses up to the road. Neither of us was armed. Once on the road, we gave the steeds their heads and raced back to camp.

The women had cleaned up the food area and washed clothes, hanging the bright shirts and skirts on small bushes and low limbs of saplings. The children swam in the creek.

The men had finished their study and investigated the nearby woods. They looked for branches suitable for walking sticks and dowsing rods. And for herbs, mushrooms, ginseng, green horse apples, muscadines, nuts, roots and huckleberries.

Our young Terrian had found a pear cactus and spent several minutes picking the spines out of his hand. Another lad had noticed the orange-spotted front legs of a land terrapin and hauled it home to play with before it became a meal. Lingo sorted the forest harvest into mesh bags for drying.

'I guess I need to be getting back,' Coursey said. 'No one knows where I am. And I have a wedding to—–Thanks for your hospitality and good grub. We can make it now—–'

'Before you go, let Tew tell your fortune,' I urged him. 'You could use some direction now that you have lost your wagon and wares. We rely heavily on predictions. What do you have to lose?'

I told him about my great grandfather who gathered jimson weed and wild mushrooms. After mixing a potion, he would drink it and go into a trance. He never failed to conjure an answer for our immediate situation. Even our children search for four-leaf clovers. They have learned that the raven is unlucky because it refused to enter Noah's ark.

I called Tew to read his fortune. She soon brought her candle and a stool. 'Tell our hapless friend here what to expect in his future.'

While she was centering her candle on the stool, Tew told about other methods of reading the future. 'Laila likes the mirror-gazing technique, but she has to wait until the moon is visible. Yenne reads tea leaves and coffee grounds, and Savana stares into flames and embers for images.'

We removed our shoes and sat on the ground around the stool. A breeze blew up and the flame flickered. We closed the circle to deflect the wind.

This is what she told this peddler. 'Your family and friends will draw your psychic powers from you if you permit it. You would do well to think about freeing yourself from all your previous pledges. Cast them off and let the universe guide you.'

I wrote in shorthand as fast as I could. I didn't want to miss a word of this.

Smoke from the candle soared in a thin spiral. Suddenly the light went out. 'In time, you will end up on a river. So says the shape of the wax.' Tew closed her eyes, and moved her ring-filled fingers in a pattern before our new friend's face. She opened her eyes, touched his temples with her index fingers and smiled at him.

'She's through,' I said. She knew that the man had lost everything, so she did not open her palms for payment.

Our visitor thanked her, bowed to Tew, and smiled broadly for the first time. 'I appreciate it.' To me, he said, 'Better be going. Thanks for everything, especially for your help in looking for the wagon.' We shook hands. Quietly, the group encircled the visitor and his animals. I took off the colored strip holding my hair and tied it loosely around his neck. As we stood together, a soft murmuring emanated from the circle and the group began to sing. This is the song they sang. We changed some of the words to fit our situation.

Again, the gypsy asked to sing. Of course, I was delighted. From the smile on Tom's face, I'm sure he was, too.

> *To the knights in the days of old, keeping watch on the mountain height,*
> *Came a vision of Holy Grail and a voice through the waiting night:*
> *Follow, follow, follow the gleam. Banners unfurled o'er all the world, Follow, follow, follow the gleam of the chalice that is the Grail.*

This time, when Dowan began singing, many of the adults and older children jumped off the wagons, crossed the street and joined him.

> *And we who would travel on toward the place that will be our home,*
> *In the dust and the rain and snow, our eyes ever toward Jerome.*
> *Follow, follow, follow the gleam, peoples of worth, o'er all the earth*
> *Follow, follow, follow your dreams to the city that is Jerome.*

— Chapter Twenty-Three —

HETH

Damn doctor! Who does he think he is ordering me around? Oh, I know he's delivered and doctored everyone in and around St. Luke. Still, does that give him the right to give orders like that? He's worse than Liddy warning me about my last trip.

What happened while I was gone, anyhow? Doc put Liddy to bed––said she had a bad fainting spell with a lot of pain. Well, bushwa! She's expecting, you dumb lug doctor. And what did he mean, my marriage's been planned? Surely he didn't do that, too!

"Before you see Liddy," Doc said, "go over to the courthouse and make arrangements with the county clerk for a marriage license. Drive her to Liddy's and both of you sign it in the presence of the clerk. Now would be a good time."

"But––I don't have any money on me. All my stuff went over the ridge in the storm," I said.

"Tell Mrs. Fincher I'll see that the fee is paid," Doc said. "You were leaving, weren't you?"

I revved up the Nash, and set her toward Toad Road and the courthouse. After parking, I took the steps two at a time, though I wasn't particularly in a hurry to sign away what might be the rest of my born days.

Inside, I paused, remembering what Doc said––the county clerk's office. I didn't come to the courthouse enough to know where anything was located. I walked down the hall. 'Assessor?' No. 'Circuit Clerk?' No. Here it is, 'County Clerk, Gillette-South.' I opened the door and entered.

"Hello, Heth Coursey," said a woman who stood up from her desk. "I haven't seen you in quite a while. Do you know who I am?"

"The county clerk?" She wasn't nearly as attractive as Zindi Yielding behind the counter at the Rakestraw Hotel.

"Yes, but––my name? I'm Verna Lue Fincher." She stopped. And when I didn't respond, she continued. "Wrennetta's mother."

"Oh, yes. Hello, ma'am." I bowed slightly. Wren and I went out a couple of times before Liddy Underhill came to town.

"What brings you to the courthouse?" she asked.

"I need a marriage license––"

"Oh, really?" She seemed surprised. "Well, congratulations. Who's the lucky girl?"

I knew she knew, so I let it pass.

"Doc Everett asked me to take you to the boardinghouse with the license so Liddy and I can sign it. He put her to bed." I must have acted hesitant. "Can you do that––legally?"

Mrs. Fincher pulled open a file drawer and took out a document. Then she leaned through the doorway to an inner office. "Mrs. West, will you come in here and mind the front while I run an errand for Doc Everett?" She fished her pocketbook from a desk drawer, raised the pass-through and we left the office.

I had hoped to see Liddy alone first, in case she had changed her mind about getting married. But after what Doc said, it sounded like she hadn't.

At the boardinghouse, I explained to Tom what Doc Everett had ordered and why Mrs. Fincher was with me.

"I'll go up and tell her she has visitors," Tom said. "Wait here, please."

He acted like a fox guarding the hen house. He wasn't engaged to the woman upstairs, *I* was. Come to think of it, don't I wish now that *he* was engaged to her instead of me? I noticed he managed the stairs pretty nimbly for a cripple.

"She says to come on up," Tom said, holding the door for Mrs. Fincher. As she passed him, he said, 'How-do,' with a nod.

We entered her room. Liddy was sitting primly against a pillow with a pink bed jacket on. "This here's Miz Fincher, the county clerk," I said to Liddy. "Doc Everett sent her up for us to sign a marriage license." I took the paper from the clerk and tossed it across the bed. "Here, you first."

Liddy looked around for something solid to lay the paper on. I couldn't help her none. She finally picked up a journal-looking book and a pencil. She hadn't said a word. Studying the document, she found the place for her name and scribbled it.

Mrs. Fincher reached for the paper. "Now you sign, Mr. Coursey," she said in a flat-sounding voice, very different from the way she first greeted me. I signed, but no one knew how I wished for some of that disappearing ink I had in the wagon.

"Goodbye," the clerk said to Liddy. "I hope you get well soon. Wrennetta didn't tell me you were ill."

Liddy smiled lamely. "I'll be back in a minute," I told her. To Mrs. Fincher I said, "Do you have time for a cup of coffee or tea or a cola? I need to speak to Liddy."

She nodded. "I'll have a glass of Tom's delicious iced tea," she said, as we walked downstairs.

"Tom," I raised my voice a little, "will you give the lady a glass of tea? I need to see Liddy for a minute."

"Will do," he said. "Mrs. Fincher, do you use sugar? Lemon? Have a seat anywhere. I'll be right out."

I bounded back up the stairs. I didn't know how I was going to get out of this marriage, but I was determined to try. A piece of paper didn't mean handcuffs. But Doc Everett might think so.

— Chapter Twenty-Four —

LIDDY

I sat on my bed reviewing the article from the Lone Wolf again. The one that sounded like it could be Heth. And when the gypsies stopped across the road, I knew it was. Where is he? Why hasn't he been by? Surely he's heard that I'm confined. It's been nearly a week since he sped off after his mother's funeral.

I heard a rap at the door. "It's me, Tom. You have visitors downstairs. Heth and Mrs. Fincher from the courthouse. Shall I send them up?"

"Let me brush my hair and put on a fresh bed jacket." After a minute or two, I called to Tom, "Okay, I'm as ready as I'll ever be."

And then the signing of the marriage license. Dumb, acquiescent me—–I dutifully put my name on the proper line. Short and sweet, no emotion, no outburst—–an all's-well-in-love-land scene. Restrained, for the public represented by Mrs. Fincher.

When Heth came back, he seemed nervous. He sat in a straight chair.

"What's wrong with you?" His voice was spare and hollow. "Ullan didn't say anything about you being sick."

"Uh—–Doc Everett thinks I'm anemic. Where have you been this trip?" I wanted to hear his answer and find out if the peddler in Lone Wolf's account and the gypsy's story was indeed Heth. "Did you happen to meet up with a tomato farmer along the way?"

"Are you spying on me?" He raised his voice. "Wasn't it enough that you tried to stop me from going on one last trip? Now, you're trying to tell me where I should go and how long I should stay?" He stood up quickly and the chair fell over.

"No––I just wondered––" Tears, which lay close to the surface for so long, gushed from my eyes, blinding me for a second. He lifted the chair upright and sat again, looking at the shapeless ivory dress hanging across from him.

Silence. At the same moment he said "I lost the wagon," I said, "I lost the baby."

Then I knew. I knew the details of his trip, but he didn't inquire about the miscarriage. Silence again. I looked at him, hoping for some sign of love in his face, or a move to kneel beside me and sympathize.

"Well," he said, standing and hitching his trousers, "since I lost my livelihood, I guess we can't get married. And since you lost your baby––"

"But we signed––"

"That don't mean nothing if we don't want it to. I was hoping you'd changed your mind."

"I considered it," I admitted. I didn't need to tell him that Dovie forbade me to marry him.

"Well, take care of yourself, Liddy. Our engagement's off." He left then, and I heard him whistling and tripping down the stairs like a delighted child.

I thought I would suffocate. Dovie was right. Men look for any reason not to get attached. Breathing deeply, inhaling snufflings through my nose, I made no move. I stared ahead, aware of each breath that propelled my breasts up and down, up and down. A dull ache where the fetus expelled itself surrounded me like a snake, squeezing what blood that remained, as if to eliminate any reminder of the results of my torment.

Suddenly my sadness turned to rage. I raked everything from my bedside table with such a force that the lamp crashed and broke, the letterbox clattered, the journal thudded, and the lotion, pencil and aspirin rolled across the floor and under the bed. On the second pass, I dumped the shelf Tom had rigged to sit solidly atop the curve of the trunk, adding to the commotion.

Tom was at my door in an instant. He knocked repeatedly, calling, "Liddy! Liddy! Are you all right? May I come in?" Surely, he saw Heth leave.

Sweet, sweet Tom, his eyes were wide, as if he expected a terrible accident or a ghost. After he saw I was where I belonged with no blood gushing, he surveyed the room. Then his eyes found the floor.

"What *happened*? I saw Heth leave and then heard this horrible crash."

"He broke our engagement. Said he'd lost his peddler's wagon in a storm and couldn't support me." I stopped without mentioning the other reason.

"Oh!" was all Tom said as he bent down to pick up pieces of the lamp. Then, "I'll get you another lamp, Liddy."

"Put it on my bill, Tom. I shouldn't have reacted so savagely."

With the cleaning rag from his back pocket, he wiped down the shelf. When he moved to replace it, I stopped him. "While the trunk top is empty, Tom, I think I'll look through it before dinner. If you will open it for me––and I'll need to wash that dresser scarf before I put it back ."

He opened the trunk and picked up the scarf. "Can I bring you some tea and crackers?"

"No, thanks. I'll wait till supper. And thank you for cleaning up after me. You are a good man, Tom."

I had a feeling that after he left my room, he went straight to the telephone and called Doc Everett.

Gramma Molly's Saratoga trunk––a large, black one with a rounded top served as the base of my nightstand. Since Gramma died, it had been in Mother's possession. All of us knew it was in the back bedroom piled high with quilts and hatboxes. Mother always said it would be mine when I was ready. That's why I had it shipped to St. Luke. If I hadn't, as angry as Mother was, she'd surely have given it to Yvonne.

Sitting on the side of the bed, I leaned over, careful to obey Doc's instructions not to lift anything heavier than a fork. I reached into the darkness. Touching suede, I grasped the edge of whatever-it-was and lifted it out. That didn't hurt much.

What I pulled out was a photograph album. The old book was wider than it was long, and fastened with faded gold cords. I imagine it was expensive when new. Settling back on my pillow, I hoped to relax and forget the present.

My reporter training kicked in. Why she kept it seemed obvious. But where did Gramma Molly get this? How old was she? What was the occasion? Who gave it to her? The next time I go to Lock Rivers, I must remember to ask Mother if she knows the answers.

I continued my 'what-ifs.' What if my grandparents brought it over on the boat from Armenia? What if a swarthy gypsy sold it to them while they were waiting on the quay for transportation? What if Grampa stole it? What if Gramma had a lover who gave it to her?

Opening the book, I saw––not a photograph, but a square of parchment attached to the black construction-paper page. In a handsome, measured script were these words:

"I am fighting valiantly my daily nemesis, trying first one weapon and then another. Some work for a while, but the search goes on. One day I will emerge victorious because I always get whatever I go after, no matter how long it takes––unless, of course, I change my mind midstream and decide I no longer want it."

Beneath the paragraph were three ornate letters, M-A-R. Molly A. Roper. This had to be written after she and Grampa married. What in the world could she have meant?

— Chapter Twenty-Five —

DOC

"Hello. Doc Everett speaking. Tom––slow down. What is it again?–– He did what?––OK, thanks. I'll get right on it, patients or no patients. 'Bye."

Dovie rapped on the door and came in while I was on the phone.

"That confounded Heth Coursey," I raved. "That no-good-son-of-a––"

Dovie came closer to the desk. "What? What?"

"I sent Heth to the courthouse to have him deliver the county clerk and a blank marriage license to Liddy. According to Tom, they both signed it, then Heth went back up to Liddy and told her he'd lost the wagon. She told him she'd lost the baby, so he pronounced the engagement 'off.' Tom said Heth whistled down the stairs and escorted the clerk out in the most gracious manner he'd ever seen."

"Oh, no!" my lovely wife said, and then she continued. "I mean, thank goodness! Now Liddy won't have any reason to marry that––" Just then, the receptionist knocked, stuck her head in and asked Dovie to come with her. I could tell Dovie didn't want to, but, being a good nurse, she followed the girl.

I had other ideas. Lifting the receiver I said, "Miz Myrt, ring Zed Jasper's office, please." I pulled out a sheet of blank paper and found a pencil with a lead.

"Hello, Zed. Roscoe Everett here. Have a favor to ask. Could you come over to my office as soon as possible. No, scratch that. Go to the courthouse––the county clerk's office. Heth Coursey is returning with

Mrs. Fincher from an errand. Collar him afterwards and bring him to my office. You come in, too."

"What is it, Doc?" The sheriff sounded alarmed. "Nothing wrong with Quinn, I hope."

"No, nothing like that. You'll see what I want when you deliver that peddler boy of ours. See you shortly. And thanks, Zed."

Ten minutes later, Sheriff Jasper led Heth inside the room. I started on him immediately. "What in blazes do you mean by calling off this wedding, you good-for-nothing package of––If I didn't think so much of your father, I'd have you horsewhipped. If this town knew what I know––"

Zed's eyes widened and he coughed. I guess he'd never heard the town doctor in such a state.

I turned back to Heth with fire in my eyes. "I'm acting *in loco parentis* for Liddy Coursey as her doctor and because her mother asked Dovie to watch over her."

Heth stared me down but didn't say anything. There was no indication of relief or celebration in his face now.

"Sheriff, I hereby notify you that this man is liable for Liddy Underhill's mental and physical health for reasons known only to the two of them, Nurse Everett and myself."

"Yes, Doc?" Zed Jasper answered.

"Liddy is expecting––Heth to marry her. I would like for you to see that he sticks around and keeps his side of the bargain. Is there any legal way we can do this?"

Before the lawman could speak, Heth took one step toward the two older men. "But I lost my wagon over near Rabbit Ridge. I don't have any way to support her." He splayed his long hands in a helpless motion.

"Tough. You'll have to figure something out. Between your dad and Gaith Nance and yourself, you'll find a way. After what you did, you are irreversibly obligated to make an honest woman of Liddy Underhill."

I turned to Zed whose eyes told me he'd gotten the picture. "What do you think? Can we see that he stays around for a few more days?"

"I don't see why not, Doc. On the way back to his Nash, we'll talk about it. Won't we, son?" Zed put his beefy arm on Heth's shoulder and guided him out.

"Thank you, Sheriff. If I have my way, it won't be long before our young man will be happily married––like you and me. Goodbye now."

—— Chapter Twenty-Six ——

MIZ MYRT LAMBKIN

"Come in! Come in here, Miz Myrt." Tom greeted me from the front porch of his boardinghouse. He reached out and helped me up the last step. Dropping his voice, he whispered, "I'm all ready for afterwards," he said.

On this second Sunday afternoon in November, Heth and Liddy Coursey's families and friends planned a surprise reception and wedding shower. Though they did not invite us to the wedding, we intended to––whether they liked it or not––share in their special day. This was St. Luke's way of doing things.

Frona Lee Coursey's big-flowered dress was different from the one she wore to her mother-in-law's funeral two weeks ago. Now that she's the oldest Coursey woman, she's playing Mrs. Matriarch to the hilt. Look how she's flouncing from the buffet to the gift table.

Oh, there's Genese Underhill and Liddy's sisters. So rigid and shy in those fall-ish shirtwaists. At least the colors are right. Three of my brooches would have spruced up their dresses a bit. I'll speak to them in a minute. That little man lagging behind must be Genese's driver.

Ignoring everyone, the two other Coursey wives fussed over the bridal chair. As I approached the gift table, they looked up and nodded.

"Wonder why that silly girl didn't invite us to the wedding?" Caroline asked Alice. I placed my box on the taffeta-covered table and lingered nearby, pretending to admire the decorations. Caroline's red hair was upswept into a knot and fastened with gold combs. Her voile dress––the color of ripe persimmons––showed off her still-tiny figure. Hmm, she's been married to McKinley nearly three years now. Still no children in sight, I see.

"I invited everybody I knew to mine, didn't you?' she continued, watching Alice pin crepe paper streamers to the back and sides of an overstuffed armchair. One of Tom's best, I suppose, but I do wish he'd get a matched set––just for times like these.

Alice harrumphed. "Liddy's just a country girl––don't know the customs of this town––or of this family. But I didn't either, and neither did you." Alice wore a blue chiffon gown, more than likely from her trousseau. Not many occasions in St. Luke to wear a frock like that. Too tight for the body that's spread some since she wore it last. And what are those stones dangling from her earbobs? Doesn't she have enough silver clips among those blonde curls?

I moved toward the front of the room and wondered where Heth's three brothers were. And his dad. And then I heard a commotion. Oh, my goodness, will you look at that!

Now I've known Liddy only a short while, and Heth all his life, but I never saw them look like that. For an instant, sound stopped. Every eye in the room noticed their stony stares. No mouths twitched, no eyes blinked. The only movement was the rhythmic in-and-out of breasts and chests.

I couldn't believe it. Liddy's face was as white as the slip I pour into my ceramics molds.

Her lips closed in a straight line, her dark eyes bored into the crowd. No visible pleasure, no surprise, no recognition, no accusation. Her blue coat, its triangular collar overlapping puffed sleeves, was buttoned, hiding her wedding dress.

Heth's demeanor was no less puzzling. For someone who'd just gotten married, he looked more like he did at this mother's funeral. Vacant, hopeless eyes. Pouty lips. His collar and tie weren't binding, and his pasty face accented the dimple in his chin.

Suddenly, one of Lloyd's boys hollered, "Uncle Heth!" and the crowd murmured to life like a stuck movie reel that suddenly clicks back into its sprocket.

"Surprise!" The room erupted like Sunday-morning Methodists after the last 'Amen.' Frona Lee led Liddy toward the frilly chair, but the young bride spied her family and broke away. They hugged, first as a group, then each one lingered over a separate embrace. I wondered how long it had been since she'd seen them.

The rest of the wedding party arrived. Tom greeted Doc and Dovie Everett, and Ullen MaGriff. Brother Bird disappeared into the kitchen. I maneuvered over to the Everetts. "Glad to see you," I said.

"You, too," Dovie answered, with a sliver of a smile.

"What happened?" I asked them. "Why do these young folks look so unhappy?" Doc raised his eyebrows and shook his head. I'll bet he knows something he's not telling. When I turned back to Dovie, she had disappeared.

Frona Lee's sharp voice could be heard above the din. "Liddy's opening her presents. Gather round." Since Sula Mae's death, she'd appointed herself boss. She plopped down next to the guest of honor. Genese and her daughters sat on the bride's other side.

The women and girls found chairs in the circle. Alice and Caroline took turns feeding the gifts to Frona Lee, who snipped off the ribbons and dropped them into a mesh bag. She passed the wrapped package to Liddy, whose mood seemed to have brightened. Everyone 'oohed' and 'aahed' as she opened each gift.

From my standing position behind the circle, I saw that Tom kept close to the older men sitting around the large dining table. He would be making sure each knew his upcoming job. The younger men drifted out to the porch. I hoped they wouldn't let anything slip.

Walking to the windows overlooking the porch, I saw the youngsters playing chase and trying to reach the low limbs of the sassafras saplings near the road. They scampered to the ditches and waved when an occasional Sunday-afternoon driver tootled by, raising dust and scattering leaves.

I returned to the circle and stood so I could see and hear. Frona Lee pointed. "Here's a chair, Miz Myrt."

"No thanks," I answered. "I sit enough behind the switchboard."

Liddy showed each gift to her mother, who passed it to Yvonne and then to Juliana, who handed it on to the next. Candles, a shelf clock––I gave her that––a photograph album, a curio shelf, pillow cases with crocheted edgings, a sampler and matching dresser scarves––quite a nice assortment. Surely, Liddy had a hope chest of dishtowels and kitchen things.

One small, framed picture in the Victorian style fascinated me. I asked Juliana to let me see before she sent it on. A painting of flowers had been done on a silky material, and padded for a dimensional effect. Now, who could have found such a beautiful thing in this part of the Ozarks?

Frona Lee picked up the last box. "It's heavy," she warned. Liddy balanced it on her knees. She had unbuttoned her coat from the waist down. Aha! Her wedding dress was winter white, but I couldn't tell about the fabric. Crepe?

She pulled out a tissue-wrapped gift. Discarding the box, she slowly opened the inner wrapping and pulled out a monstrosity of a plate––thick, like a piece of pottery. The outer edge had a deep green border decorated with gold swirls, but the plate itself was ginger-colored. Hmm.

I took it from Yvonne before she handed it down. The backside revealed a hand-written sign fired into the plate, "Hot Springs Pottery Arkansas," with an inscription, "Mohernsen." With both hands, I handed it to Juliana.

I turned to Frona Lee. "Who is it from?"

"I don't know," she answered.

"There's not a card," Liddy said.

Frona Lee took over. "Anyone know where this plate came from?" she bellowed. But no one took credit for it.

"Was it addressed to you, Liddy?" someone asked. She retrieved the wrappings and searched through them. A small white envelope surfaced from the brown paper. Opening it, Liddy read, *To Liddy. We heard you were marrying. Bless you. Love, The Outlers.*

Liddy's skin turned the same chalky white as when they entered, but no one else seemed to notice. A haunting overcame her and she froze, eyes fixed somewhere outside the window. She reminded me of a moth wanting out but not knowing the escape route.

By then, Frona Lee was back, offering Liddy a slice of cake on a glass plate and a cup of yellow liquid. It was punch, but it resembled the dye children dip their boiled eggs in at Easter.

When Liddy failed to respond, her new sister-in-law cleared her throat and touched Liddy's limp hand with the plate. Its cold surface startled the new bride back into the present.

As soon as the women and girls got their refreshments, I walked over to see if I could serve the old fellows. Bless 'em, they'd kept their church suits on longer than usual. Doc Everett stretched the inside of his collar. Brother Bird's gaudy tie hung slack. Earlier, Quinn Coursey, the groom's father, had shucked his coat and rolled up his shirtsleeves.

As I approached, some made gentlemen-like efforts to stand. Others reached up as if to tip the hats they had left on the rack inside the door. "Miz Myrt," one mumbled.

Gaith Nance––of Nance's Mercantile, where Heth works––answered for the lot. "Aw, we'll wait till the ladies get done. Thanks just the same."

The preacher wiped his mouth with the back of his hand. Was he drooling? Mr. Walden, the dry goods magnate, nailed me with a leer. "Nice brooch you're wearing there, Miz Myrt. I'll bet I know where it came from."

"You have a good memory, Ezra. You and I both know it came from your store."

I took my punch to the porch. The groom, his brothers, Ullan MaGriff and some older boys had moved their chairs into a tight ring. Dapper hats and caps still rested on their heads.

Though I pretended an interest in the children's games and in the early November sky, I detected periodic flashes of sun on glass. Hmm. I set my punch on the railing, opened my purse and took out my compact. Using the guise of powdering my nose, I saw that they were passing around a bottle.

Heth, too, had perked up since joining his friends and family. He leaned toward the center of the circle and said something I couldn't hear. They guffawed like boys peeking in at a girls' bunking party.

Inching along the porch to get closer to the men, I fiddled with the latticed roses still blooming on scraggly canes by the porch. "You should'a seen her," one of them said, and they all snickered. Their eyes shone from the liquor.

I crossed the porch to examine Tom's plants that he should have taken in before now. Only the geraniums love this crisp air.

At that moment, Tom opened the squeaky screen and motioned me over. "Liddy's showing the family her room," he said. "It's time! I've posted a lookout by the stairwell. He'll whistle if they start down before we're ready."

Now it was *my* turn to boss the crowd. I walked inside. "Frona Lee, get Caroline and Alice and box up the presents. Quick! No questions. Just do it. Doc, send your bunch out back with Tom. Then you and Brother Bird go get Heth. Here's the blindfold. McKinley and the boys know what to do. Dovie, take this tape. Get those bows Frona cut off the packages. Tom'll show you the dolly. Decorate it. Verna Lue, you and Omega go help Dovie. Shoo!

"Editor Redd, you and the girls stay here. You see they clean up the dishes. If Liddy and her family come down too soon, you all swarm them and ask plenty of questions. Keep them occupied until I send you word. If Liddy asks where everybody's got to, make up something. Figure it out while you're washing dishes. Oh, and here's some combs. Get waxed paper and tear enough pieces so all the girls can have a kazoo. Make one for yourself, too."

I dashed outside and down the steps. Activity buzzed. Boney Sanner had loaded all the gifts on Tom's wheelbarrow. He would lead the procession, followed by the girls and their kazoos. We'd have to tie Liddy onto the dolly unless Tom had thought ahead and devised a–– Look, he'd not only found a way for her to stand upright, he had attached sidebars for her to hold. That conveyance glowed like an Easter basket.

"Beautiful!" I called to Dovie and her crew. Lloyd and Frona Lee's boys found some tin cans and tied them together. Another kid bleated on an old trumpet he found in Tom's shed.

Tom scooped mounds of rice into the ladies' open handkerchiefs. Heth cursed and kicked, but Doc and Brother Bird had hogtied him to a tree. On the other side of the building, Heth's brothers and Ullan rounded up two cedar fence rails and lashed them into a litter.

"Here they come! Here they come!" I rushed to the porch steps and called back, "Let's go, folks! This is it!"

Liddy still wore her coat. The girls led her out to the porch and her family followed. Smiles erupted on every face but Liddy's. She had gone white again. She jumped when Editor Redd clasped her arm. I took the bride's other arm and we led her down the steps.

"Come on, dear, it won't hurt," I whispered. "It'll be over before you know it. A chivaree's the way we do things in these parts. Our way of showing you we care. You'll get used to it."

Tear's filled Liddy's eyes. She shuddered and went limp.

— Chapter Twenty-Seven —

LIDDY

November 13, 1933

Dear Mother (and Mr. Ferrel),

Writing this letter is one of the hardest things I've ever done. But I must explain why no one was invited to our wedding today. (It is nearly ten o'clock at night.) You've had your share of burdens, what with Eugene's death and Daddy's leaving. Please don't wring your hands and wonder what you did wrong.

You know the letter I wrote in August about the picnic Heth planned? He plied me with what he knew was my favorite drink. But he laced the apple cider with some hard spirits. After we ate, I went limp and––well, you can imagine.

Later, after discovering I was expecting, I made Heth promise to marry me. After that, he was moody and sullen. He blamed me and I cried a lot.

In late October, Heth's mother died suddenly. Over my objections, and without telling anyone where he was going, he left on another peddling trip.

I had to do everything! I'd already made my dress, thank goodness. When I visited one of the preachers here, he thought I was asking him *to marry* me*! It was Halloween, and he followed me home––out of spite, I guess––dressed like a witch. Scared, I ran until I fainted.*

To make a long story short, I lost the baby and Doc Everett put me to bed. I told him and Dovie––she's turned out to be my best friend, too––everything.

Doc finished plans for the wedding. He knew of an empty house two blocks from the boardinghouse and insisted that Heth's dad, Quinn––you met him Sunday––buy it. Doc called in other favors and some of the town men fixed it up. Tom took his extra furnishings over––enough for us to set up housekeeping.

When Heth came home, he'd lost his peddler's wagon in a storm. After I told him I'd miscarried––I had to, Mother. I couldn't deceive him like he did me––he presumed he was a free man. Again, Doc––not knowing that I'd changed my mind, too––interfered and made sure Heth was available.

I'm glad you weren't *at the wedding. Brother Bird agreed to marry us in his church, but pigeons had roosted in the old building and the stench was so bad that services that morning were held under the brush arbor.*

Nothing to do except go to the parsonage, which was nearly as bad. Brother Bird dips snuff and his place reeked. With five extra people in the living room, it was crowded. Doc stood behind Heth with a pistol in his back. You've heard of shotgun weddings!

Brother Bird demanded his fee before the ceremony, but Heth had no money on him, and I hadn't thought to bring my pocketbook. Doc and the preacher had words. The preacher stomped out the back door of his own home!

It turned out that Doc was also a Justice of the Peace. He walked around in front, holstered his gun and picked up Brother Bird's bible. He thrust it at us and we both put our hands on it, and he said his piece. Somehow, we each must have murmured "I do." When Doc looked at Heth and said, 'You may kiss the bride,' Heth just stood there, still as a stone. I wished I could faint, like I often do. But no, I just sobbed into Dovie's arms.

Doc, Ullan and Heth escaped the smelly house immediately. Doc made Heth stand with him as Dovie led me out and down the steps. Doc Everett's glare fell first on Heth and then on me.

"The town is having a party over at the boardinghouse," he said, "Put on your happy faces." He saw me wiping my eyes. "Pretend, if you have to, but you'd better act like the newlyweds you are. Now get in the car." He pointed to his black sedan.

Brother Bird had slunk back into the yard. Mother, you should have heard Doc!

"You sorry excuse for a preacher!" he said. "I'm gonna see you run out of town come June. You can walk, Bird, you need the exercise. Get going and you'll be there by the time we drive over. Git!"

You know about the reception and the chivaree, so I'll close. I'm so glad Mr. Ferrel drove you and the girls over for the reception. And glad that Miz Myrt had the foresight to invite you.

Do what you think is best about showing this letter to the girls. Maybe you could summarize everything. I love you all, Liddy.

— Chapter Twenty-Eight —

LIDDY COURSEY

Blurp, blurp, blurp. I turned down the gas under the burner and reached for the wooden spoon. Oatmeal must be stirred constantly until it thickened to a perfect, gummy consistency. I remembered the comforting feel of oatmeal as I rolled the warm, sugared and raisined goo–– thinned slightly with milk––around in my mouth, chewing only the raisins before each swallow.

Today, my first morning as a bride, I realize I must learn to cook for only two. There's enough in this pan for six or seven! But I have to do it alone, since I left home and Mother's counsel and moved to a larger town to "seek my fortune."

I set two places at the table near the door. Poured tomato juice from the quart jar brought earlier by the Home Demonstration Club. I lowered the heat under the percolator, covered the biscuits with a checkered cloth and got out the butter. I opened a new jar of blackberry jelly.

For dishes, I chose those Papa Quinn gave us after Mom Sula died. Their fall-leaves pattern fit the season, and Heth might appreciate the reminder of his mother.

"Heth! Breakfast!" Calling out the back door, I sounded exactly like my mother, only she would yell, "Children! Woody! Breakfast!" Or dinner or supper.

I saw my new husband in an old straight chair leaned against the smokehouse. He was digging under his fingernails with a blade of his pocket knife. Occasionally, he would look up and stare beyond the field to the railroad tracks.

I know he heard me. There were no trains or wind to muffle my voice. *Now* what should I do? Opening the back door, I tiptoed down the steps, softened my voice and spoke. "Breakfast's ready."

He turned. "Did I tell you I wanted breakfast?"

"No, but––"

"Did you ask me what I wanted for breakfast?"

"No, but––"

He stood then, closed the blade and replaced the knife in his jeans pocket. "How do you know I eat breakfast?"

"I––I––" He started toward me.

"I'll fix my own breakfast when I want it, so don't *you* bother. Just keep the coffee hot."

And he brushed past, stomped up the steps and disappeared. I heard a cupboard door slam and after a few minutes, the front door. I hurried to the side of the house in time to see him sauntering up the street holding a blue metal cup in one hand and a biscuit in the other.

I blinked back tears until Heth turned down the slope on Main Street and vanished. The gurgle of the spring, calls of the ducks and birds and the chatter of squirrels would surround him. Like school children who, on their way to school, forgot whatever happened at home beforehand, he would likely move into his world of work without a thought of what he'd done and how it affected me.

Turning toward the back door, I released the pent-up disappointment and the specter of failure. It was more than I could bear. The 8:05 screamed through St. Luke. I bellowed and cursed both Heth and Doc at the top of my lungs. The grind and grumble of the long train swallowed my oaths, swirling them into the wheels. Wrenching sobs of pity and hopelessness belched and blended with the smoke trailing behind.

What felt like a hammer punch to my stomach, a reminder of what I'd already lost, sent me to my knees. Not twenty-four hours married, and he'd run out again. Dovie was right. He hadn't grown up. And now it was too late.

Sobs subsided into snuffles and I stretched out on my now-empty belly. One arm became a pillow, the other a warm poultice between my empty womb and the hardness of the ground. A mockingbird sang from the crape myrtle and another answered, farther away.

The noon freight woke me and the mid-November breeze had cooled the air. Pushing up, first to my knees, I brushed tiny ants off my dress and stood. My pillow-arm gradually regained its feeling. Nothing to do now but go inside and clean up the kitchen.

And I hadn't even had breakfast.

— Chapter Twenty-Nine —

LIDDY

November 23, 1933

Dear Mother, Yvonne, Juliana and Mr. Ferrel,

Thank goodness, Thanksgiving with the Courseys is over! And before I fall asleep and forget even one detail, I must tell you about it. You know from my last letter that the newest member of the Coursey family always hosts the next Thanksgiving meal.

'Tradition,' Frona Lee informed me in a visit shortly after the chivaree. 'I did it. Alice and Caroline both did, though it won't bear repeating how pathetic their meals were.'

'But that doesn't give me much time!' I said.

'Didn't Editor Redd give you the rest of November off—as a wedding present? Use it wisely. You'll manage somehow. Goodbye.'

She didn't mention anything else about the tradition, and I was too stunned by her lack of friendliness to ask. Do you suppose she was still smarting over not getting any say in our wedding?

Heth had paid no attention, he told me, to earlier Thanksgiving preparations. Only that he appeared when and where he was told.

'You don't remember what you ate?' I asked?

'Dressing,' he said, 'and sometimes a hen from our backyard. But not always. Guess my brothers killed wild turkeys or bought them in Madison. Don't expect me *to cook whatever you get. I've never done that and I don't intend to start now. You'll have to ask the girls,' he said, 'or your mom.'*

Again, I didn't ask why he never cooked, but I could imagine he was out with friends, or looking for work, or on a drummer's route. He was spoiled rotten. So I called Papa Quinn with my questions.

'I hate for you to be saddled with hosting Thanksgiving so soon, but you might as well get it over with. The three other girls did all right, but they had Sula Mae for instructions. All I heard from her afterwards was how pitiful their knowledge of cookery and presentation was. But I imagine they have all learned enough by now.'

Then he changed his tone. 'How about I kill a couple of the biggest hens in the flock. I'll pluck and cut them, and bring them for you to cook. One big dish of chicken and dressing will fill the bill. I'll bring Sula Mae's recipe, too. Do you have a large enough pan? Can you make giblet gravy?'

'Yes,' I said, and 'yes.' When I asked him about the other food, he couldn't remember who brought what. 'But even the men provide something. Ask them what they want to bring. Or make suggestions.'

So I had to call the others. I'd almost rather done everything myself, but I knew that wouldn't do. Frona Lee harrumphed when I told her about the hens.

'He didn't offer to do that for me! My specialty is jam cake. Lloyd usually does something with his green tomatoes—–a relish or a mush.'

On to the next. 'Alice, what do you usually bring to Thanksgiving?'

'Oh, lord, honey, it's your time to host, isn't it? Some dish using sweet potatoes. We grow tons of 'em. Ozell delights in bringing his mock pumpkin pie.'

I asked Caroline last. 'I can't cook for a big crowd, sweetie, but I can make applesauce since our orchard produced so well. Mac makes a great corn light bread. He'll bring enough for everyone. And butter. You poor dear, having to do this so soon after marrying. I'll help you clean up.'

That left Heth. 'Hell, I got left out when it came to cooking. Mom taught the other boys, but I didn't stay home long enough for her to teach me. Maybe I can mooch more of that applejack—–er, cider from Frank—–' He ran out the back door laughing. I yelled after him, 'You'd better not, you, you—–' I slammed the door and cried. I would make tea and coffee, and grape juice for the kids.

That took care of the food. Now, the seating. Nine adults and three children. Our table would seat only eight. I had to figure something out. At first, I thought about asking Tom to help, but when he answered the telephone, I decided against it.

'Tom, what are you doing for Thanksgiving? Why don't you join us if you––' But he was cooking for his boarders and folks who didn't have plans for a big family gathering.

Aha! I'd sit on the sewing machine stool. Now, I considered linens and dishes, silverware and glasses. Just before I called Papa Quinn, he drove up.

'Thought you might need extra plates and things.'

Mother, he'd boxed up a set of Sula Mae's dishes and glasses and flatware. And located some tablecloths and napkins in their buffet. Two baking pans, serving spoons and bowls and two glass pitchers were in another box. He set them on the dining table. 'I didn't know what all you had and I don't need these any longer. You're welcome to them.'

I stuttered my thanks.

'Oh, I nearly forgot,' he said, reaching into his shirt pocket. 'Here's the hen and dressing recipe I promised.'

Things were coming together. All this done during the first week. Not a bad record, if I do say so myself. I still had to sweep and dust and arrange the furniture. The biggest problem now was where to put the extra table and chairs. Between the kitchen and the back porch is an anteroom just large enough to be a throw-it-all place. I would have to squeeze the table and chairs in there.

Thank goodness I had two more weeks. The last Thursday would fall on November 30. How unusual––end the month with Thanksgiving, and begin on Christmas the next day. Things were going well.

Late on Tuesday, the twenty-first, I answered a knock at the door. Papa Quinn stood there with a big container of meat and a gallon jar of stock.

'I knew you'd need to get this ready tomorrow and cook it Thursday morning. In case no one has told you, we gather about twelve-thirty and eat a half-hour later.'

'But––but––Thanksgiving's not until next week,' I said. 'It's on the last Thursday, isn't it?'

'Oh, my goodness,' he said. 'The Courseys always consider the fourth Thursday as Thanksgiving.'

— Chapter Thirty —

Dear Mother,
Finally, I have time and energy to finish this letter I started yesterday. After I discovered the Courseys had Thanksgiving on the fourth Thursday, all I had time to do was mop the floor and dust the furniture. Oh, I washed the windows close to the table, but couldn't get curtains hung.

I prepared the anteroom for the children. Nosing around the smoke house, I found a milking stool, a canvas chair and a small tub I could turn upside down. A square of roofing tin leaned against one wall and two milk buckets hung from nails. Aha! There was my children's table, but I had to cover the tin with towels and fold a bedspread over it to hide the underpinnings. I overlaid the stools with bright wrappings from the wedding shower. It worked out fine.

I made sure all the wedding gifts from the Courseys were in plain sight—the Philco from Frona and Lloyd on the lamp table in the front room. I draped Sula Mae's 'nicest' quilt—from Papa Quinn—over the back of the sofa.

I leaned Caroline's gift—The Joy of Cooking by Irma Rombauer—into one of the dining room windows. I used her recipe for Roasted Spanish Onions, *and cooked them in one of the Pyrex dishes from Alice.*

I was so glad you and the girls gave me all those kitchen staples. Before the day was over, I'd used the olive oil, vinegar, sage, salt and pepper and the onions.

Dovie's Home Demonstration Club pounded us with canned goods and garden produce, so I had all the ingredients for Red Vegetable Salad. *I served it in a footed crystal bowl placed in the center of the table. But I'm getting ahead.*

Wednesday, I baked cornbread for the dressing and laid leftover biscuits out to dry. Following Sula Mae's hen-and-dressing recipe was no problem. And Papa Quinn's linens and dishes saved the day.

By mid morning Thursday, the weather had turned mild and wood smoke flavored the air. The Courseys traipsed through the front room, and placed their food on the table. Except for Frona Lee's jam cake and Ozell's mock pumpkin (sweet potato!) pie––they went on the sideboard.

'Ooh,' Frona Lee said. 'Where'd you get such pretty china?' She fingered the tablecloth. 'Who gave you this?'

I opened my mouth, but caught Papa Quinn's eye and his slight head shake.

'Must have been wedding presents,' he said. Relieved, I nodded. Thank goodness, she didn't ask, 'From whom?'

I had place cards as I'd learned in Home Ec––man, woman, man, woman––but Frona Lee had other ideas.

'We mothers need to sit closer to the children. Let the fellows sit together so they can talk.' She traded her card with Ozell and––pointing––instructed Lloyd (her Jack-Sprat of a husband) to trade places with Alice.

I glanced at Papa Quinn and he shrugged. Frona Lee pushed her chair to the inside wall and plopped down, blocking any passage. Everyone else sat quietly, turning to me for the next move. But Frona Lee never looked up. She flipped her napkin into position and yelled toward the kitchen, 'Now you kids just wait a minute––'

When she looked up, the entire table was eyeballing her as if to say, Please be quiet! In the second of silence before we ate, I asked Papa Quinn to say the blessing. I didn't know what their tradition was but this was my party.

'Lord, make us thankful for all that we are about to receive. Bless the food and we who prepared it.' He paused. 'We remember Sula Mae who is absent from our circle for the first time, and Liddy who is present for the first time. Bless, forgive and keep us, now and forever.' He stopped, and the Courseys said, 'Amen.'

Mother, I don't remember ever hearing anyone pray for me. Tears came to my eyes.

Frona Lee's snippy comments were the only downside of the meal. 'The dressing's a little on the sage-y side,' she said, but I noticed she ate two helpings.

'Where's Heth?' she asked later between bites. As if choreographed, everyone stopped chewing, some with forks in midair, and all eyes turned on me.

'Oh, you know Heth.' I felt my face getting hot. 'Since his wagon blew off Rabbit Ridge, he's been over at Nance's trying to work off the cost of the wares he lost. He'll be home directly.'

(What I didn't tell them was that Gaith Nance had Miz Myrt ring me Wednesday morning to ask where Heth was. The merchant had Thanksgiving orders to deliver and needed help. I told him I hadn't seen Heth since he left for work on Tuesday morning. Two weeks married and Heth is more unpredictable than ever.)

During the lull that followed, Papa Quinn said, 'Liddy, no one could ever tell you pulled all this together in only a day and a half.'

Pretty, petite Caroline piped up, 'But she's known since right after she and Heth––'

'No, no,' Papa Quinn broke in. 'Her family celebrates Thanksgiving the last Thursday of November. She was planning it for next week.' Everyone but Frona Lee murmured their admiration. I blushed and attempted a smile.

That's about it, Mother. Christmas is right around the corner. Oh, but you haven't had Thanksgiving yet. I can't wait till we're together again. Hello to Yvonne and Juliana. And Mr. Ferrel. And Sport.

Love, Liddy

P.S. Everyone wrote down the recipes for the dishes they brought. I may write a column for The Banner *using them. If I do, I'll send you a copy.*

— Chapter Thirty-One —

LIDDY

November 25, 1933

105 Depot Street
St. Luke, Missouri
Dear Dovie,

It was so good to see you last week when the Home Demonstration Club 'pounded' us with canned goods and fresh produce. You will see later how I used some of them.

My first Thanksgiving as a bride meant hosting the large number of Courseys. All of the adults (but Heth) contributed something to the meal, and they brought along copies of their recipes. In turn, I had to make four copies of what I prepared. As you requested, the recipes follow.

Baked Chicken and Dressing

The name of the cook who gave Sula Mae this recipe was smudged, but the town was 'Ozark.' It had been used in that family for four generations. Papa Quinn brought the chicken already cooked, and the recipe. How could I fail?

*'Cut a **3 pound broiler** into desired pieces, add **1 teaspoon salt,** and stew until tender. Remove bones, and set chicken aside until dressing is prepared.*

*'For the dressing, combine **3 cups crumbled cornbread, 1-1/2 cups toasted biscuit crumbs,** and **1 medium sized onion** chopped fine. Mix with **chicken broth.** Be sure to use enough to keep dressing moist. Stir in **4 raw eggs** and mix thoroughly. Add **2 chopped hard-boiled eggs.** Last, add*

rubbed sage, black pepper, *and* ***salt*** *to suit taste. Combine stewed chicken with dressing and bake about 30 minutes.'*

Of course, Frona Lee had to ask about Heth again after the meal. I mumbled something, and then she shot me a glance that would wither a wedge.

'What did you do to make him leave, Liddy?' I was dumbfounded. I opened my mouth to answer, but she kept on.

'Heth knew this was his family's Thanksgiving. He's never missed one that I can remember. You must have––'

Dovie, I don't know why she hates me so. I've felt it from the first time I met her. Finally, Papa Quinn spoke up. 'Heth's helping Gaith Nance deliver groceries to the Barts and Ponders on Little Trot. The old folks are too sick to ride into town,' he said. That satisfied her for the moment.

Sweet Potatoes and Apples

This is the note from Alice. 'For Thanksgiving, 1933. This recipe has a lot of personality. I prefer it because it is tart (I'm using Caroline and Mac's apples). It doesn't use those awful marshmallows that overpower the taste.'

'Cook covered until nearly done in boiling water to cover: ***6 (scrubbed) medium-to-large sweet potatoes.*** *Peel, cut into one-half inch slices.*

'Cook ***1 and 1/2 to 2 cups sliced apples*** *covered until nearly done in a very small amount of boiling water. If they are not tart, add a little* ***lemon juice.***

'Place in a greased baking dish a layer of potatoes, then apples. Repeat if necessary, but scatter each layer with parts of a mixture consisting of ***3/4-cup brown sugar,*** *and* ***two shakes of cinnamon.***

'Dot them with ***4 tablespoons butter.*** *Pour over the entire contents* ***one-half cup of the water*** *the apples were cooked in. Bake at 350 degrees (or a moderately hot oven) for one hour.'*

For some reason, Lloyd's green tomato mush reminded me of how different Papa Quinn is from my own father. A year after Daddy left the gate open and Eugene toddled under the train, Mother was still silent. Blame oozed from her like smoke when he was present. He responded in kind, except for the perfunctory blessing before meals. I tried to help the younger ones behave during those meals and not cause an uproar.

Surely Papa Quinn never treated his family like this. Do you know whether their marriage was a good one? And why Heth is so different from his brothers?

Lloyd's Green Tomato Mush

*'Chop **6 green tomatoes;** slice **6 medium-sized potatoes;** slice **4 carrots** crosswise and chop **1 green sweet pepper.** Place in saucepan with **1 tablespoon bacon grease** and **salt and pepper** to taste. Cover with cold water and cook until vegetables are tender. While vegetable pot is still boiling, stir in––a little at a time––about **one-half cup corn meal**. Continue cooking until mixture thickens.'*

I can't tell about Lloyd, but I can see why he doesn't say much with Frona Lee around––he doesn't get a chance. What do you know about him that will help me to show that I will be an asset to the family?

The next recipe is where I used your club's gifts.

Red Vegetable Salad

This recipe came from an old cookbook I discovered in my Gramma Roper's trunk.

*'Cut **2 cups cold boiled potatoes** in thin slices. Chop fine **2 cups cold pickled beets**; slice thin enough uncooked **red cabbage to make 2 cups.** Mix the vegetables and add **6 tablespoons pure olive oil, 8 tablespoons beet juice, 1 teaspoon salt,** and **one-half teaspoon pepper**. Mix well and let stand in a cold place 1 hour before serving.'*

This letter has gotten too long, so come by when you're not busy for the other recipes. Maybe you could include them in your next cookbook fundraising project.

Your friend, Liddy Coursey

— Chapter Thirty-Two —

Oh, my! I just remembered. The deadline for the spring issue of the *Mountain District Historical Newsletter* is next week. I'd better get busy. Editor Redd gave me that job as my first promotion at *The Banner.* Two weeks ago Friday, she handed me a sheaf of old papers. "Here, use these for your research. There's a lot of information in the obituaries, too," she said.

I hoisted the Royal onto the dining table, gathered my supplies. As I rolled in a sheet of clean paper, for some reason, I thought of Heth. He's never been gone this long before––fourteen days so far. The weather's nice––maybe that accounts for it.

I leaned back and watched the gnats flying around the overhead light. He had plenty of provisions––onions and potatoes from Papa Quinn's harvest, jars of beans and tomatoes Sula Mae had canned. Muscadine jelly Dovie helped me make last fall. Salt, flour and meal from Nance's, as well as summer sausages and hams from last year's butchering.

I picked up the last issue of the newsletter and thumbed through it. Even in the late evening, the aroma of daffodils wafted through the open window.

Heth had oats for the horses, hog lard and molasses. He could trade ribbons, feathers and buttons for eggs. Ol' Blue could make good his breeding and tree a raccoon.

I finally put my hands on the keys and typed:

> *What's In A Name?* ***The Ozark District Historical Society Newsletter*** -- *by Liddy Coursey,* St. Luke Banner, *St. Luke, Missouri*

Heth couldn't just disappear into the mountains, could he? While we were courting, he told me that sometimes he searched for catalpa seedlings and healing herbs. And that several of his customers wanted any smartweed, crowfoot and caper bush he could gather.

Another time, he tried to frighten me by saying that panthers were always a threat. "You'd better kiss me now before some 'painter' gets me first," he'd said. Of course, I did.

The image of panthers brought goose bumps to my arms. Then I remembered the wire that came through the newsroom last week. An alligator crawled out of the Creel River and attacked a fisherman. Could that happen to Heth? Would anyone be close enough to find him and get help?

The longer I sat, the more I fretted. Too much of this and I wouldn't be able to go to bed, much less sleep. I imagined a log truck overturning on a sharp curve, with flying timber crushing horses, wagon and man.

Heth never learned to swim well, he told me once. What if he fell searching a creek bank for ferns, phlox or hedge apples? What if the water-logged ground dropped away where he was standing? He might drown and never be found.

I closed the window against the cooling temperature. If Heth ran out of money, he might hop a freight, leaving the team and wagon standing unattended. Or he might join a crew plying the Creel River. I've never heard him wish for those kinds of adventures, but he's been so ill-tempered lately––and he's been gone so long.

No more typing tonight. Not after these disturbing thoughts. I'll get back to it tomorrow. For now, this tired newswoman––I like the way that sounds––will curl up on the sofa and read about Jo March and her sisters. Again.

— Chapter Thirty-Three —

The History of a Few Area Surnames:
The Mountain District, Missouri
By Liddy L. Coursey,
St. Luke Banner, *St. Luke, Missouri*

Now that it's springtime in Missouri, let us investigate the origins and meaning of a few surnames found in area newspapers during the past three months. Most all English and continental surnames fall into four categories: Place names (Hill, Dale), patronyms (based on personal names, i.e. Robertson= Robert's son), occupational names (Smith, Wright) and descriptive names (Long, Smart). Here are a few names of people in this District.

Surname	***Category***	***Origin***
Anderson -	*patronym: 'Anders' son'*	*Scandinavian*
With variants, a very common name, one often adopted by freed slaves.		
Banks -	*place: river banks*	*Slavic, S & E. Europe*
Variants: Banasiak, Banneker – Benjamin, 1731; Bannister – 1876		
Coleman -	*occupation: coal miner*	*Irish, English or Scottish*
Ellis - *(Alice)*	*descendant of Ellis';*	*Wales – 1860s*
10,000 or more Ellises on the Mayflower manifest		

Hall - *'dweller in the manor'* *British*

One of the most common names in 1623. Perhaps O'Hallahan was shortened to Hall.

Hanninen - *Han* *Dutch*

Many variants: Hancock, Handlen, Handy, Hanson, Hansen. Could have had a "Mc" before it at one time, i.e. McClenaghan. Monaghan, which in America, lost the 'g.'

Jones - *'son of John'* *Welsh*

In Jamestown there were nine Joneses. Jones is in the top four or five most common names. (Smith being first.)

Keil- *Short for Kielbasa (sausage maker); also Keel* *Polish*

Kelley - *'grandson of Ceallach'* *Irish*

Kennedy - *he with a misshapen head' Irish, English or Scottish*

Lee - *'plums'* *Either Chinese or Caucasian*

May have been changed/ mutated through the years from Levy, Levi, Levin, Levine, Levitt—Jewish names.

Schultz - *'overseer or sheriff'* *German*

Many variants, Shilt, Shiltz, Sholes, Shotts, Sholtz, Shoults, Shoultz, Shults and Shulz

CONCLUSION: The settlers to the Mountain District of Missouri form a melting-pot of identities—but hail primarily from Europe and the British Isles.

Sources:

**Mencken, H.L.* The American Language: an inquiry into the development of English in the United States, *New York: Alfred A. Knopf, 1921.*

**Missouri newspaper archives available through the* St. Luke Banner *office.*

— Chapter Thirty-Four —

LIDDY

It was only late May, but the sun––cool for so long––suddenly exploded with fire and brimstone. *No, that's too trite. Try again.* It's hot enough to fry a fence post.

At the mailbox, I was checking to see that my petunias hadn't died. Also, I was composing in my head a column for next week's *Banner*. Editor Redd had me working on similes and hyperbole. Now, there's a word I'd never heard before.

Just then, I caught the sound of footsteps in the street. Tom appeared from behind the cedars. On his gimpy leg, he listed like a leaky rowboat. Everyone knew he carried a walking stick, just in case.

"Hello, Tom. Why are you out on such a hot day? And a Saturday, at that? How about a glass of cold water?"

"Don't mind if I do." He walked up the path. "But don't go to any trouble." He doffed his hat and wiped his ruddy face with a handkerchief.

"It won't take but a second. Here, sit in the shade next to the house." I pointed to the metal suspension chair I'd brought around from the side yard. It was so old the red paint barely showed. I'd made a pillow for the seat.

Hurrying inside, I grabbed a server from the buffet, pulled an ice tray from the new Coldspot that Papa Quinn bought us for a wedding present, and yanked the middle piece that loosened the cubes. I turned two clean glasses right side up from the drainer onto the tray, filled them with ice, then poured water from the pitcher on the counter. Two minutes flat.

"Here we are, Tom. I was needing a drink myself. Working in the yard––"

"Without a sun bonnet, I notice," Tom teased. "Don't you know you'll get freckles? Like mine?" He laughed and drank heartily, as did I.

I sat in the other chair, the straight-back wooden one that someone had painted white. Not the one Heth sits in by the smokehouse.

"Nice chair you've got there. Sturdy. Strong," Tom said. "How'd you come by it? I've never seen one around here like that."

"Oh, this old thing? Papa Quinn gave each of the boys one after Sula Mae died. Said they brought them down when they moved from South Dakota." I stood up to show him the seat. "It's not very comfortable. The center must have once been cane, but someone nailed a square of thin board over it. I use a pillow if I sit very long."

"And this table. What a clever way to––" He looked at the makeshift shelf I put together with a sandstone slab as the post and a square of metal I found in the smokehouse for the tray.

Tom leaned closer. "That looks like what concrete masons use to mold squares for sidewalks and things." He glanced back at the path leading to the porch. "Look it! Those blocks buried to their tops––they're the very same size as this."

When I offered more water, Tom shook his head.

"I needed to rest," I said. "There's so much work around here. The cedars block the morning sun, so nothing but crab grass and sand burs grow in that part." I gestured toward the fence on the north. "And look at those hackberry roots. Crawling above ground and into the yard like Gramma Molly's varicose veins."

"You haven't lived here long enough to see all four seasons yet," Tom said. "It'll come. Besides, who said every yard had to have grass?" He picked up a stick and scraped the ground by his chair. "How deep is the topsoil? You could sprig some ground cover. Or ivy."

"Good idea. Where'd you learn so much about?––" I couldn't think of that long 'h' word that meant working with plants.

"Horticulture? Oh, here and there. I took one class in college. Except for keeping up the boardinghouse grounds, I don't do much with it."

Tom broke the stick and threw it toward the street. "Heth's not home much to help, is he?"

I shook my head. "No, not often. When he is here, he––he has to go to Nance's and settle up. Then restock his wagon. I usually don't know when he's coming until he gets here." I didn't tell him that Heth hadn't touched me since that one fatal time that got us into this––union.

Tom stood and turned the metal chair to face east and Little Trot Mountain. I stood, too, thinking he was leaving. But he sat down again. I moved my chair, too, and sat.

"Changing the subject, but have you ever climbed that mountain, Liddy?"

"No. Have you?"

"I haven't either, not ever. Always meant to. Heard others talk about doing it. They say it's easy, what with a trail cleared by the timber and park people." He pulled his bad leg up and crossed it over his good one. "Guess I've used my lame leg as an excuse."

"I don't have any reason not to," I said. "I could walk it after work any time. Or on weekends. I just haven't."

Tom stood. "If I could start over, Liddy, I'd do things differently. I'd get up early every morning and hike, just to get my blood moving. Just to feel the wind or the rain––maybe even the snow––in my face. Just to smell the honeysuckle and the wild roses."

"Why, Tom Grindle, you old softie," I said, moving with him toward the walk.

He pointed. "Did you know there are folks living up there? Not many, I'm told, but now and then people come to town for supplies. Sometimes, they stop to eat at the boardinghouse." He turned. "Thanks for the water. Don't you get too hot in this weather. Put on your bonnet, you hear?"

We laughed over his mother-hennishness.

"Yes, sir." I curtsied. "Come again. Any time." I waved as he headed back to the boardinghouse. What a nice man. I'm lucky to have him as a neighbor. Come to think of it, he never said why he was out today. But it's too late to run after him and ask.

— Chapter Thirty-Five —

TOM

After the visit with Liddy, I strolled back to the boardinghouse sure of two things. I needed to help around her place. And, I must climb Little Trot Mountain. I'm not a boy any longer. My mother's not telling me what to do and what not to do. I'm probably the only man in St. Luke who hasn't had that experience.

"Oh, hello, Xann." My kitchen help sat in one of the new porch swings. "Is it already time for us to start tonight's cooking? I completely lost track of the hour. Let's go in here and set to work." Xann is one of the town boys, and he's made a pretty good assistant.

Once inside, washed and aproned, I asked him if he'd ever climbed Little Trot.

"Sure. Lotsa' times. Haven't you? Oh––" He looked at my bum leg. "I guess not, huh?"

"Not yet, but today I decided that's not gonna be an excuse any longer." As we worked, I began my story.

"When I was a little tot back in the hills south of here, Grandpa Gilley wandered off the porch, followed the dog into the woods. The dog came back, but Grandpa was never seen again. A bear, authorities figured. And as long as we lived near Finn Mountain, Mama never gave us kids leave to climb it. In fact, she told us not to ever, ever even think about it."

Xann looked up from peeling potatoes. "Gee, Tom, a bear? That must'a been scary."

"I still remember the tremor in her voice and the dark dread in her eyes. That convinced me not to disobey." I lit the oven and got out the makings for a cake.

"What made it so bad for Mama was that Grandpa was the only man on the place. Papa had gone to Kansas City and got himself killed. And now, it was just her and us three kids." I opened all the lower cabinets. "Have you seen the sifter?" Xann shook his head.

"Then there was old Crazy Bait Dover. He lived on Finn Mountain with his wife and four young'uns. They didn't come down but once a year. Crazy Bait would shoot at anything moving and shout at it later." I found the sifter in the storage room.

"He operated a still deep in the woods. He and his townie customers shared a code that no neighbor or sheriff could ever crack."

Xann emptied the potatoes into the pot and set it on the burner. He poured the peelings he would feed to his pigs into a bucket outside the back door. "I've heard," he said, "there's a still on Little Trot. Have you?"

I didn't want to get into that now, so I continued the story that I hadn't told anyone in St. Luke. "Let me finish my story. Then you can see why I decided to climb that mountain."

Xann put the lid on the potatoes and turned the burner on low.

"I was small and sickly as a boy. I had asthma, and I was anemic. I couldn't even walk down the hill to the mailbox without coming back so winded I had to stop and rest before I hit the steps to the porch."

Xann washed a sink full of mixed greens I'd picked last night.

"I spent most of the summers of my early years on a pallet in the front porch shade. I learned to weave rugs from rags. During the cold weather, I studied and slept in the glassed-in sun porch at the back of the house. I was seventeen before I weighed a hundred pounds."

"Gee, I've weighed a hundred pounds since I was twelve," Xann said, and laughed.

"The Pecan Grove doctor wondered at the time if I might be allergic to cockroaches and crickets, but we never found out."

"How'd you get well?" Xann asked. "You're healthy enough now." He filled the other sink with clean water and rinsed the greens for a second time.

"It's the funniest thing. All of a sudden, when I turned thirteen, I got over whatever it was. In high school and college I was able to run track."

"Is that when you got crippled?" the boy asked.

"Yeah, but that's another story. I believe I can climb Little Trot even with a gimpy leg. And my walking stick." We worked for while in silence until the alarm for the cake sounded. I pulled the pan out along with its delicious aroma.

"Whatever happened to that crazy fellow back—-?"

"Oh, he's in the pen for killing his wife and kids. Mama's not in my head anymore so I'm gonna do it. I've made up my mind. I'm gonna climb Little Trot.

"And now for the cornbread."

— Chapter Thirty-Six —

LIDDY

Dear Yvonne,

You wanted news about our house that I whispered to you when you visited the last time: It's haunted. A child ghost lives in the attic. We get along fine. Neither Doc, Dovie nor Heth knows about him, though the real estate agent must have had some inkling. Papa Quinn told me that Glenn Keeling refused to come any closer than the yard when he brought the house key over.

I can imagine you saying, 'But why? How? Who?' We all wondered that. Papa Quinn called the county coroner, who came over from Madison––the Gillette-North county seat––to see the bones himself. And to find out if there were more in the well. After that, he went to the courthouse (Gillette-South) here in town and asked for reports of missing children during the past several years. At The Banner, *I ransacked back issues.*

Between us, we discovered––Sis, I hate to bring this up because of Eugene. The news clipping and the courthouse report both said a young boy had been separated from his parents during a tornado. His body was never found. No one involved can fathom how his bones ended up in this well.

The missing boy's name was Carlis Shade Lamb. His ghost plays with the swallows in the eaves and he cries, especially when the wind blows. He stays with me a lot––I feel his coolness. He is like a kitten, always wanting to play. He is like the child I so want and don't have. When he gets too rambunctious––he knocked a wedding gift vase off a table once––I scold and open the door to the attic. He goes to his room but not always willingly––or quietly.

Carlis is a comfort against loneliness when Heth is gone, which is most of the time. Heth worked around Mr. Nance's place until he finally earned enough for Gaith to forgive his debt and provide him another wagon. Carlis will snuggle beside me on the sofa. His soft keening sometimes lulls me to sleep.

Write when you can. I'm all right. Tom checks on me every day. Dovie visits, so does Papa Quinn. I listen to the Fleischmann's Yeast variety show and the Chase and Sanborn Coffee hour on Sunday nights and Lux Radio Theater when I can.

Dovie and I sometimes go to the movies. She's crazy about Jean Harlow—folks tell her she looks like the actress. And I adore Clark Gable. We have seen "Chained" and "It Happened One Night."

Other nights, I write in the evenings and read before bed. And I always love to receive letters. You know the song, "I'm Gonna Sit Right Down and Write Myself a Letter"? I've memorized all the words.

When I'm feeling blue, I listen to "Red Sails in the Sunset." What movies have you seen lately? Who is your favorite movie star? What's your favorite song?

You can tell Juliana about Carlis, but Mother would probably think I was losing my mind, so you decide whether or not to tell her. Are she and Mr. Farrel still seeing each other?

Write soon, love Liddy.

— Chapter Thirty-Seven —

LIDDY

"Come on, Heth." I was annoyed at the grown man who hung back like a child dreading a shot. "You know we both have to attend this meeting." I reached out and pulled open the heavy outside door to the agency. "I wish you would at least act like you want to adopt."

"I don't see why you're so intent on raisin' someone else's kid," he mumbled, stumbling on the rubber mat inside the door. "Who says we need a kid, anyway."

"But it's been seven years," I answered, aware of the quietness of the waiting room. I looked around. The burnished metal arms and legs of the theater seat squeaked as I sat in the one closest to the lamp table.

Heth walked past me and sat on the other side of the table. All the lamps in the room flickered once in the growing darkness of the approaching storm.

"Maybe if we get a baby, we'll—" I wanted to say, 'be happier.' I'd never spoken like that to Heth before. I stared at my hands, then tried to press the wrinkles out of my cotton skirt.

"For one thing, I want a child to keep me company. You're gone so much." I rubbed one dusty patent shoe against the back of my bare leg and then the other.

My peddler husband didn't reply right away. He fussed through the magazines and picked up an old *McClure's* with a deer staring off the cover. "I don't know why you don't look for a *real* job? Or a second job. Then I could buy that red roadster Ol' Man Lincoln's got on his lot over there." He motioned out the window.

I whirled on him. I could feel my eyes widen and my face flush. "Why should I help you? You got us into this predicament that day at the picnic. Or have you forgotten?"

He slammed the magazine down. "How *can* I forget? You figure out a different way to throw it up to me every time I come home. You knew how bad I wanted you. You didn't have to drink that stuff. Couldn't you smell it? Why'd you agree to go in the first place?"

"I loved you. I trusted you," I said, leaning toward him in supplication. "I wanted to *be* with you. I wanted to please you. And you cheated, bringing that rotgut. That's what started––and ended––our only baby––" I crumpled back into the seat and cried a little.

"For God's sake! That was seven years ago. Let it go, will you?"

"I'm trying to. That's why I want us to adopt. But you've got to want it, too. Don't I deserve some happiness after?––"

I was getting a headache. "When I see a baby, I think about how old ours would be, and whether it would be a boy or a girl. When I buy a baby gift for a shower, I feel sad that I've never given birth." I shifted in my seat, but didn't stop. "When I see a woman who is carrying a baby, I get angry. It's not fair that your brothers have children and we don't."

A tremendous clap of thunder at that moment seemed to punctuate my speech. Then a lightning flash darkened the room for an instant. Heth sat stoically, staring at the door as if it could feel his hesitancy.

"I've never told you this," I continued, saying more to him than I had for a long time, "but some mornings I don't want to get up. I can't eat. I don't want to go to the paper. I'm tired and I cry a lot." I stopped to catch my breath, hoping Heth would say something, anything. He just sat there. "I don't know if I'm missing you or the baby that died. I can't sort it out. It never goes away, the wondering."

"Mr. and Mrs. Coursey?" The adoption agent opened the door from the inner office and smiled. We both stood.

That put a stop to the other things I intended to say to Heth. He cut in behind me and bolted for the outside door. "You'll have to do this alone, Liddy. I'll be over at Lincoln's." And he was gone into the storm.

Tears that had lain so close to the surface during our argument erupted. Sobs wracked my body and spilled from my mouth. As if in sympathy, rain descended in torrents, a continuo below the counterpoint of my sobs.

Mrs. Renah held out her hand, and we sat down in chairs close to her door. She held me until I cried myself out. "I'm sorry," she said, "but both parents––"

We stood. "I know," I said. "So sorry to have taken up your time." I breathed deeply, trying to compose myself. But I was angrier than I had ever been in my life. At the door, I turned and waved to Mrs. Renah.

— Chapter Thirty-Eight —

HETH

I wakened at dawn, while the July sun was not yet visible. I needed to drive the team to Nance's and reload my wagon. No need to stick around and make up with Liddy after yesterday's episode at the adoption agency. No reason to think that because she never spoke a word on the drive home she would be any less angry today.

At the store, I automatically checked my wares. I'd been at this routine long enough to almost do it blindfolded: bolts of calico, gingham, percale and muslin always went in first. They had to be covered with burlap because the women on my routes would not buy faded goods.

Just then, I heard the 'splish, splish' of gravel and when I turned, there was Ullan on his morning run. "Ho! Ullan!" I called.

He slowed his pace as he loped into the yard and stopped. "Going out again, I see," he said, and leaned over, panting until his breaths became regular. He raised up and wiped sweat off his forehead and his hairy arms.

"Yeah, I wanted to get an early start, seeing how hot it'll be by noon. Say, you out early for the same reason?"

Ullan, the druggist, had been my friend for as long as I can remember. He nodded. "I'm glad you hailed me. I've always wanted to see what you carry in your wagon."

I showed him what I had just loaded. "On top of the fabrics go Swiss laces, rick-rack, bias tape and threads. Then there's these cards of buttons from the mussel factory between here and Madison. Papers of pins and needles—–everything a body needs to sew with."

"Where's the scissors?" Ullan asked."I don't see any scissors."

"Oh, they're down here somewhere." I held up three sheer drawstring bags. "Guess what's in these babies, Ullan." I teased him by swinging them back and forth. "Ladies' unmentionables––silk mysteries that make me go hard just by thinking about 'em."

"You old scoundrel!" Ullan said. "Married these seven years and still––"

I didn't mention the latest incident with Liddy. "Here's quinine, turpentine, Black Draught, castor oil, bluing, lye soap, unslacked lime, and mutton tallow."

"What else?" He stood closer.

"There's blocks of paraffin, alum, camphor––any high-class peddler would offer these necessaries for folks living in the hills and valleys of Gillette County." Everybody comments on my variety of wares. 'Course I have Gaith Nance to thank for that."

"And look under these feather pillows and ticking straw. See these fancy chamber pots? They're porcelain coated. And these here are retrofits for whale oil lamps. Oh, you'd be surprised what some folks still use from the olden days."

"I need a drink of water," Ullan said. I pointed to the faucet at the end of the store.

"Use your hands, I guess," I said. "Least ways, that's what I do." I continued my inventory. "Let's see, candle sockets and candles, charcoal, actual envelopes and––I've gotta be sure these shelf clocks are packed in tight."

"What you peddle for the men folks, Heth?" Ullan asked when he had quenched his thirst. He seemed in no hurry to continue his running.

"Oh, there's galluses, denim, linsey and striped cotton for overalls. And there's one more pair of those rare Levi jeans from Kentucky."

I poked around a little and found something that would get Ullan's goat. "Say, Ullan, looky here." I showed him a kaleidoscope with girlie pictures. He looked, but not for long.

"Yeah, what else?"

I showed him a key ring with a naked man and woman that had a lever to manipulate them into lewd positions. And a set of business cards with Proverbs on one side––some Biblical and some suggestive. On the other side, an advertisement, *Free Advice Cards––Compliments of Heth Coursey, St. Luke, Missouri.*

"Then underneath, I have a box with girlie magazines, horse feed, a knapsack and dress clothes. Wouldn't want to be caught in a situation with no way to dress up, now would I?"

Ullan raised his eyebrows and 'tsk-tsked.'

"On the very bottom are long boards to use if we have to cross a muddy spot. They've come in handy, too. Soon as I cover these wares with canvas, me and the boys here'll be ready to head out. Today's my day to go southeast. Glad you stopped by, Ullan. So long."

We waved goodbye and took off in opposite directions. Except for missing Pop and Ullan, I might decide to––Just then, I remembered what the gypsy lady said about my fortune––on a river. Hmm.

— Chapter Thirty-Nine —

LIDDY

It was Christmas Eve. In the peacefulness of dusk, I could hear the children from the Methodist church singing as they came closer and closer. I watched them through the sheer curtain panel in the door. They finished the song, walked up the sidewalk, and stopped between the street and the house. I could hear the leader giving quiet directions about what to sing.

"*O, come, all ye faithful, joyful and triumphant!*" they began.

I opened the door, went back and gathered the baby into my arms, walked out and leaned against the screen to hear the final phrase, "*O, come let us adore Hi-im, Christ, the Lord.*"

Someone in the dimness of the yard whispered, 'One, two, three, sing,' and the small group began "We Three Kings." I looked beyond the children to Little Trot Mountain. A star twinkled above the black tree line.

"*Star of wonder, star of light,*" I heard myself sing, joining the children. "Bring our Daddy home tonight." The carolers had quit singing. Had no one ever sung with them before? The children took a step back.

"Lead him homeward, always homeward, star above me, star so bright," I continued and walked down the steps toward the singers.

They fled down the path between the cedars and peeked out from behind them. I stared at the darkening sky, clutched my baby closer and sang the chorus again. I heard one of them say, "Did you see Miss Liddy shaking that old doll and squalling at the sky?"

"Go get the preacher! Quick!" one of the women said. "Xander Price, if that's you under that streetlight, go tell Tom he'd better get down here fast. Move it, boys!"

In an instant, everyone scattered. What had I done? "Let's get you back into the house, child. I have this feeling that your daddy's coming home tonight."

"Liddy! Liddy!" A man's voice called. At the door, I turned to see Tom half-hobbling, half-running up the steps to the path. When he saw me, he stopped. "You okay, Liddy? What happened?"

"I don't know what came over me, Tom. My favorite carols––the crisp air––Christmas Eve––Heth's coming home tonight, Tom, I just know it." I opened the screen. "I'd better get Eliza inside before she gets a chill. Thanks for coming by. Merry Christmas!" And waving the doll's arm to Tom, I said, "Wish the nice man 'Merry Christmas,' Eliza."

Once again, I turned to go inside, but I noticed someone running toward the house from the other end of the street. Could it be? Oh, I was right! "Heth! Heth, is that you? I knew you'd come home tonight!"

But it was only the Methodist preacher. When he reached Tom, he was wheezing. He could only nod to me. I padded inside and stood beside the door. The men talked quietly a minute before moving toward the boardinghouse.

I realized then how tired I was. Bringing a pillow and quilt from the bedroom, I turned off all the lights but the hall sconce, and lay down on the sofa to wait. What a wonderful Christmas present Heth's homecoming would be. And on the same night Jesus was born. I curled up on my side and, with Eliza in my arms, fell asleep.

* * * *

What's that noise? I threw off the quilt and sat up. It sounded like something hit the front door. Breaking glass followed a second crash. "Is it your daddy? Sh-h-h. Don't make a sound. Let's stand by the door and surprise him."

But I laid Eliza back on the sofa. "No, I'd better go alone," I said. "If it were Heth, Ol' Blue'd be barking. The thuds were too muffled to be rocks or gunshots. It's way too late for the boys to be playing ball."

I trembled with anticipation. Or was it dread? From the door pane, I could see the gibbous moon. It shed enough light for me to see that no one was there. I dropped to my knees and opened the door a crack. No sound. Slowly–– slowly, I pushed open the creaky screen door. Two brown oxfords––like Heth's––tied together, and a lumpy drawstring bag lay near the door.

I still wasn't sure whether anyone lurked out there, but I reached gingerly for the shoes. They were too heavy to lift, so I dragged them through the small opening. Odd. The cloth bag was light but bulky. A Christmas present, perhaps?

Still on my knees, I closed and latched the screen, inched over and lit the lamp. "Concrete!" I said to Eliza. "These shoes are full of concrete!" I sat on the cold floor and grabbed the bag. On closer look, I realized it was like those Heth used for storing women's underthings in his wagon.

I ripped open the drawstring and poured out the contents. A kaleidoscope. I looked through it, and even with the lens broken, I saw the awful picture. A key ring with a naked woman on it, and one of Heth's business cards lay there. I turned over the card to search for a clue. Only a suggestive message! "He told me they contained Proverbs!"

I looked in the bag once more and found a sheet of torn brown paper. A note was scrawled in blunt pencil. It read:

You'll find the peddler of these disgusting items in the Creel River. You can have his shoes, but his feet are cemented inside two of those fancy chamber pots. Can't let some dandy get away with what he did to an innocent young girl.

It was signed, *Vengeance.*

"Damn you, Heth Coursey! All you've done for seven years is run out on me. But I'll get myself a baby—–even without you. The Blessed Mary did."

— Chapter Forty —

LIDDY

"But I don't want to get up. Go away," I called to the voice at the front door. Or was it a dream? Sunlight invaded the room and the sofa where I must have slept all night––in the clothes I was wearing yesterday.

"Liddy, it's Dovie. Let me in. Please."

I sat up and the fogginess of sleep gradually melted, shoving me back to reality. I knew I must move again, but my lower back hurt. The sofa was not good to sleep on. And my head felt like a cabbage.

"Coming." Somehow, I managed the few steps to the door.

"Liddy, it's noon!" Dovie, my nurse and best friend, said. "When you didn't show up for Tom's Christmas meal, I offered to come get you. Wha?––You look like a train wreck!"

All I could do was point to the sack in the corner by the door. I fell back on my deathbed. Or what I hoped was my deathbed. Each time a pickup or trailer jostled by, my head pounded. Roosters across the street sounded like they were on the porch. A jay called, as loud as a grackle. How did that bird get inside?

"Oh my Blessed Lord, Liddy." Dovie pulled a rocker to the sofa. "You poor dear. Why didn't you call me last night?" As quickly as she sat down, she jumped up. "I'll make us some coffee. Let me phone Tom and tell them we won't be coming to lunch."

"No, no," I called behind her, half rising. "Dovie, you go back to Tom's. I'll be fine, though I could use some Bayer and a hot water bottle." I tried standing up, but the floor met me and darkness returned.

When I awoke this time, I was in my own bed dressed in my nightclothes. The lamplight helped me focus. I saw Doc Everett sitting close, Dovie standing behind him, Quinn and Tom farther back. I felt like Beth in *Little Women*.

"Am I going to die?" was the first thing I could get my mind and tongue around. "How long have I been lying here?"

Doc leaned in and smiled. "No, you're not going to die. I'll see to that."

I tried to make eye contact with each of my friends, and smiled as best I could while waving weakly. "Quinn's going to sit with you until bedtime, then Dovie's coming back to spend the night. Just in case."

"But it's Christmas. You all have families to be with. I'll be okay. I'll promise to stay in bed."

Doc shushed me with his hand. He had spoken and that was that. Tom came close, leaned down and kissed my forehead. His eyes glistened, and he touched my cheek as he stood to go.

"I'll stop by tomorrow to check on you," he said softly and turned away.

Dovie kissed me, too, before she and Doc left the room. I heard Quinn talking as he let them out. He closed and locked the door.

While I was alone, I straightened the chenille robe around my neck and glanced at myself in the mirror on the vanity. *What a mess. I could at least brush my hair before Papa Quinn comes back.*

"You don't have to stay––" I began, but he pulled the rocker up and sat.

"How about some hot tea? Weak, hot tea. I seem to remember you drink yours with sugar and lemon."

I nodded, and tried to smile, pushing myself higher to make a lap. *This man is as calm after hearing that his youngest son drowned, as he appeared to be when his wife died suddenly. Is he made of steel?*

"Here we are," Papa Quinn said, bringing in the tea things on a blue-onion tray that was a wedding gift those many years ago. He set it on the vanity stool that he pulled close to the bed. Close enough to pour from Sula Mae's china tea set he gave me after she died. Neither of us spoke while he doctored my cup and then his to our preferences. He handed me mine and I drank.

"Now, doesn't that hit the spot?" he said, leaning back in the rocker that sat parallel to the bed and faced me and the tea tray "This seems like a good time to tell you about Sula Mae's death. I've never told anyone––not even the boys, and probably won't. At least for a long time."

This devoted husband, father, father-in-law and grandfather whom I adored, sipped his tea gently, tenderly caressing the fragile cup.

"It was the last week of October. She was helping the girls get ready for a family party after you'd announced your engagement. She'd gone up to the orchard to gather apples for a brown betty, a pie and a fresh apple cake. Lord, that woman loved to bake."

Quinn leaned his head back on the chair and rocked for a minute, as if remembering everything about what happened those seven years ago. His head bobbed up and he went on.

"Suddenly, I heard her screaming. I looked out the window. She was running toward the house and flailing her arms around her head. I opened the door and she fell in. Gasping and holding her throat, she lost consciousness."

Quinn poured himself another cup, stirred in sugar, then stood and walked around the end of the bed. He looked out the window. After a minute, he turned back and continued.

"I lifted her to the bed and rang Doc Everett. I wet a cloth, knelt and put it over her forehead like I'd seen her do with the boys so many times. She jerked and twisted. I talked to her. 'Sula Mae, honey, it's me, Quinn. Wake up and tell me what happened.'"

Quinn steadied his cup and saucer with one hand and pulled a handkerchief from his back pocket with the other. After turning away again and blowing his nose, he stuffed the wadded square back in its place. Then, he returned to his chair.

"Liddy, in the thirty minutes it took for Doc to arrive, she had quit breathing. I couldn't believe it! I laid my head on her motionless chest and bawled like a baby."

I felt like I should say something, but no words formed. I held out my cup and Papa Quinn refilled and tempered it. Handing it back, he looked intently at me, and continued. "Doc Everett said it looked to him like a heart attack. She'd never ever had any symptoms of heart disease. Later, when Caroline was combing her hair, a red wasp fell to the floor. When the girls looked at Sula Mae's scalp, they discovered many swollen red spots."

By now, the tea had energized me and I felt whole again, sensible, real. The kitchen clock chimed, the only sound in the house.

"So she was allergic to wasp stings?" I finally had the sense to ask. "Had she not ever been stung before?"

He shook his head. "Not that we knew of. Doc Everett asked other doctors and consulted his medical journals. He found that allergic reactions could show the symptoms of heart attacks.

"But here's what is different between Sula Mae's death and Heth's." Papa Quinn leaned in. "I had a body I could bury. You don't. Not yet. Not until the river patrol discovers it. Or a fisherman. He's my son. It will be hard to accept his death. Especially if there's no body. It's only natural to keep hoping that the note was a ruse, and Heth will walk in the door one of these days."

Now, for the first time, I cried. Sobs wracked my body. This wonderful man brought me a box of tissues. He didn't try to hush me. He must have known what a release weeping can be. He closed his eyes and rocked as my body finally quieted into spasmodic inhalations. Here was another twisted leg of my journey.

Gathering the tea things, he took them to the kitchen. I could hear him washing the cups and putting the sugar bowl away. I thought about getting up to help, but when I moved my feet to the floor, I felt dizzy, so I piled back under the covers.

Just then, Dovie knocked and Papa Quinn let her in. I heard them talk in low tones and then they both came into the room.

"You're in good hands now, Liddy," my father-in-law said. He bent down and kissed me on the forehead. "Thanks for listening to this old fool. I was trying to make Heth's death easier for you. If that's even possible."

I answered quickly before he left the room, "Thank *you* for sharing your story. I am forever in your debt." And he was out of the room and out the door.

"Well," Dovie said brightly, "that's the second man I've seen kiss you today."

— Chapter Forty-One —

Journal entry––early February––1940

Despite the cold of a February winter in the Ozarks, I sat on the cedar-slabbed south porch at the Jacobi *Haus* that, according to the brochure on the entry table, was constructed

> *—in a wooded spot where the serenity of nature, the absence of daily responsibilities of home and family, away from the artifacts of disturbing scenarios from which our clients come, will aid in each one's recovery. The staff will help clients get from inside the mind to outside it; show them how to balance the things they can touch with those further away––things they can feel but not see.*

—and write as many details as I could remember of our first meeting. The crisp, winter air must have affected my lethargy and depression, for I felt obligated to report everything.

At the first session, we new clients learned that the Rakestraws––the older couple who built the Rakestraw Hotel––were Dr. Jacobi's parents. "My wife, Greta"––he gestured toward her; she nodded disdainfully–– "suffered from an undiagnosable disorder. Finding no suitable treatment in the Chicago area––" he turned his head and stifled a sneeze that sounded like a cat's spitting at an intruder. *P-s-s-f-t.*

"Excuse me––I enrolled in homeopathy and psychiatry courses, and we followed my parents to Rakestraw, which we call this mountain on which our building rests."

As he paused, smells from the room caught my attention. Coffee mingled with disinfectant, perfumes, and aftershaves. The man beside me must not have bathed in a month.

"Greta––Mrs. Jacobi"––again, he bowed slightly toward her and she nodded, waving her hand like she was the Queen of England–– "and I moved from the coal furnace and locomotive smoke that impaled Chicago. Away from the confinement and smelliness of the electric company where she worked. Out of the din and smog of Chicago into the clean air of this Ozark Eden." This expensive-suited doctor sounded like a robot. How many times had he given this exact spiel?

Doctor J––as we were allowed to call him––visited each client as often as possible––sometimes daily. On my first one-on-one encounter, he tried to draw out those emotions that he said were hidden and keeping me a slave to depression.

"Whom do you love?" was his first question. After I didn't answer immediately, he asked again, "Liddy, whom do you love?"

"My family. Doc and Dovie, Papa Quinn, Tom."

"Why?" He insisted I verbalize my answer. "Why do you love your family?"

"Because that's what the Commandment says." I was being dutiful.

"No, the commandment says, 'Honor your father and mother.'"

"I honor my mother. Well, except for the time seven years ago when I left home without her permission." I hung my head. "She's always been available for me."

"And your father?" Doctor J leaned back in his captain's chair so that the front two legs were off the floor.

"He's gone." Only the breeze through the tiny opening of the window in the consulting room broke the silence.

He knew what I meant by 'gone.' "Was he always gone? Wasn't he available when he was home?"

"Uh––"

"Yes? Go on."

I hated to admit this, but I said, "After Eugene died, he was home in body. He rarely spoke except to answer a question or to threaten one of us." The silence was deafening.

The doctor rested one elbow on the chair arm, lowered his head to his fingers and massaged his forehead. His eyes were closed.

"But did he love you––and the others? Did he ever say, 'I love you'? Did he and your mother ever kiss in front of you children?"

Now it was my turn to stall. I leaned back on the upholstered chair. My neck ached. I wanted to sleep. But I sat back up and answered. "I guess he loved us––in his way. He brought home the bacon, as he often said. He saw that we had a roof over our heads and clothes on our backs."

"But did he ever say, 'I love you'?"

"Not that I can remember."

"Did your parents ever show any affection to each other?"

"Not in my memory. Perhaps when they were alone––when I was younger and don't remember."

"Did you or your sisters or your mother ever tell your father that you loved him?" I was ashamed to answer, "Not that I recall."

The doctor poured himself another cup of coffee. He offered me some, but I shook my head.

"Liddy, I'm going to ask you a hard question. But it's important. Did you love your husband?"

"What do you mean, doctor?" I asked, hoping he would go on to another subject.

"Just what I said. Did you love your husband?"

I laid one arm on my waist and rested the other elbow on it with my fist on my mouth. Then I put both hands on the chair arms and leaned toward him. "How could I continue to love him––if I ever did? After he seduced me at the picnic, after we were forced to marry, he never made another move towards me. He only wanted the conquest.

"For seven years, I endured his stoic silence, his obvious disdain. I ached with desire to be part of a happy family. I pretended when I was around his folks. He did the same. But then *he* could go off peddling. And no telling what else!"

I was spent with the rush of words. I leaned back, took a deep breath, and said to the doctor, "You tell *me* why I went off the deep end when I discovered he wasn't ever coming home? I can't yet get my mind around it."

* * * *

Journal entry––February 28, 1940 (leap year)––10AM

I followed the four others to the ground floor sun porch and took my usual seat for a two-hour stint of "writing therapy." The other interest group was needlework with Greta Jacobi, and the alcoholics were cutting wood for the fireplaces, digging up the gardens, hanging bird houses and edging the grounds. The weather was brisk in these mountains but warm inside this glass-walled room. Still too early and too cold for the sarvisberry and wild plums' white blossoms, but soon––

"Good morning, writers," Dr. J chirped (again today). "I trust you slept well, had a healthy breakfast, and are ready to get back on the road to recovery. Today's assignment: *Five traits I admire in a friend.* Make your list," he crooned, "then begin writing in any direction you choose. Remember, to get better, (as he reminds us often) you must dredge up all your feelings and begin to deal with them."

Today, the graybearded, pipe-smoking doctor took a chair under the overhang of the fake wisteria in the corner. He would drink his coffee and finish the newspaper. "I'm always available if you get stuck or have a question," he called to us.

I'm sleepy, but the man says I should fight it. I'll close my eyes for just a minute––and if I'm caught, my alibi: thinking how to begin. (Mustn't snore or pitch forward.)

I could smell Dr. J before I heard his 'Ahem.' I swear his toilet water was a mixture of castor oil and cinnamon.

I opened my eyes, popped my head back and whispered loudly, "I've got it!" and began writing. Dr. J didn't speak, nor move away (eerie feeling). I began writing with a fury, and like a teenager, covered my paper.

The traits I admire in friends are different from those in husbands. As a friend, H. was kind, considerate—except during the picnic—persistent; loyal—well, I don't know about loyalty–– he was gone for weeks (and later, months) at a time. When he came home, he allowed me to choose something left in his wagon––a scarf or a jeweled comb. Looking back, was this his penance for misbehaviors? The note on Christmas Eve makes it seem so.

11AM Break.

Stretched, sharpened pencil, drank lemonade, looked out the south and east windows of this 'rest home.'

Dark clouds had moved in, hanging low and threatening. Lanterns on wooden posts stood like eyes guarding the estate. Make a note: When weather warms, explore footpaths into the trees. Red haw, ferns, tansy, and wild iris––look for 'good' reminders, Doctor J says, of home and happier days.

Break over, 11:15

After that fiasco of a wedding, former-friend-turned-husband Heth became aloof, preoccupied with selling enough to repay Gaith Nance for the lost wagon. Doc Everett, Papa Quinn, and Tom all tried to convince Mr. Nance that the storm was an act of God, and that Heth should not have to pay. Heth *was* at fault, Mr. Nance said, for parking on the edge of a cliff. By working at the main store, Heth eventually worked off the debt and Gaith Nance bought him another wagon.

Friends. Who is my friend? No, who *are* my friends?

**Tom. Dear Tom. Neighbor, former landlord, handyman, packrat, scavenger. Watched out for me when Heth was away for longer than usual. Read to me, brought meals when I was abed and out of my head, they told me.*

**Dovie. My nurse and confidant. Older, but feels like a sister. Not like my former friend, six-time mother, LilaMaude—with her snooty attitude. (I'm sure you displeased God and that's why you didn't conceive, she said.)* Little did she know!

**Papa Quinn, Heth's father––treated me like a daughter––more than my father ever did.*

Here are the answers for Dr. J's assignment. *"Five traits I admire in a friend: Loyalty. Sympathy. Acceptance. Assistance. Attention."*

> *Put pencil down (as directed from the first day); others whispered together.*

"Liddy's through. Let's go in for lunch," Dr. Jakobi called. "Two o'clock, conference room––group session. Eat heartily and enjoy a restful nap."

"Teacher's pet!" one of the four hissed, passing my desk. I'm always the last to finish when it comes to reading or writing. Is that not a good thing?

> *2:00PM––Despicable mid-afternoon group sessions.*

Many interrupt with stories. They don't care about new ways to heal, just need to share their own experiences (is that a good thing?). They jabber; I doodle, describe each one in code. Look up occasionally so Dr. J won't ask me a question. *This too shall pass. This too shall pass. This too shall pass.* (My own internal refrain chanted silently during exercise classes at Lock Rivers High.)

> *7:30 – in my room after ~~supper~~ dinner.*

Dinner (a Chicago term) at a two-person table meant that the fourteen clients would get acquainted. Dr. J expected us to find a place each evening with someone we didn't know. It's like asking a stranger to dance. I didn't like it, but I did it. Dutifully.

Tonight, I sat with Zindi. (None of our last names or hometowns are known). We were about the same age, but beyond that, nothing similar.

Zindi always wore colorful, stylish clothes and lots of makeup. Tonight, her long hair was piled on top. Pins and combs held it in place.

During the meal, she talked about working at the hotel across the road from here. (Dr. J's writing sessions had worked on her pent-up feelings, too.) The only thing I said was, "My late husband was a peddler," and the floodgates opened. This is what she told me. I corrected––in this account––her misuse of the language.

Zindi's Story

Peddlers and traveling salesmen were always stopping at the hotel when I was desk clerk. (Her eyes sparkled then, and she became more animated.) *I was quite a flirt back then––well, only seven or so years ago––but as a child I was a poor mountain lass. My parents were what people called gypsies, vagabonds, transients. Papa once killed a man who 'squatted' on what Papa said was our government land grant. He changed our names and we fled north, finally stopping in these mountains. The Ozarks.*

Mother loved to design playhouses. She could see places in the forest––ravines, cliffs and caves––that provided good hideouts and homes. She put together a grand house hidden even from the old couple—Dr. Jacobi's parents—who had come from Chicago to build the hotel.

I would set off from Mother's latest hideout to the hotel to buy books and supplies and frills from the traveling salesmen. I learned to read from those books. Old Man Jakob let me work dusting and sweeping, and later I washed windows and dishes. I called myself Rhomie and told them I lived in the backwoods. They didn't inquire further.

When I was old enough to live on my own in Mother's latest playhouse, my parents decided to move on. They'd proved that living off even mountainous land was possible, and struck out for St. Louis.

You said your late husband was a peddler. I have a story about a traveling salesman. They are the same, aren't they? I mean, the terms 'peddler' and 'traveling salesman'?

Several years later when I was desk clerk, such a man came to the hotel. Two horses and a wagon. He was a fine looking specimen. I flirted unmercifully.

He was reserved and hesitant, but I finally promised him some food and we went to my place.

He was in a state. Someone close to him had died, he said, but then he clammed up. I offered him whiskey, and while he rested, I changed into my most seductive robe. I couldn't get a response––if you know what I mean. After several more drinks, he did let me help him into my bed where he passed out and slept off his tiredness. And my liquor.

Lean in, Liddy, so I can whisper. By morning, he came to––there I was––and––you can guess the rest.

I certainly *did not* want to guess the rest. I could hardly believe my ears. It sounded so familiar. Surely Heth had not come this far from St. Luke. I can't bear to even consider it. Maybe Zindi is a pathological liar. Maybe that's why she's here! Maybe later, I will have the nerve to figure out what was happening during that leg of my journey those long years ago. But not now.

— Chapter Forty-Two —

MIZ MYRT

"Esther? Myrt Lambkin here. My switchboard's been dark as pitch most of the day. You got time to chat? I'll have to interrupt, though, when I get a call. Yes, I know you will, too.

"A strange thing happened on the way to the Blue Plate one day last week—Tuesday, it was, because the special that day was meatloaf, and I love meatloaf. I'm as predictable as sin about lunch. If someone had a mind to, Esther, they could kidnap me, shoot me, photograph me—anything. I walk the same route, the same time five days a week, every week of the year. Have done it since I began working in St. Luke all those years ago.

"But this day was different. Oh, not in my schedule, but what happened before I got to the diner. I heard this voice from the street. 'Myrtle Jean Lambkin?' I stopped, knowing that it was someone from my past, because no one here knows my childhood name.

"I looked around. But all I could see was a mountaineer leaning on a spiffy red Reo. He tipped his tattered straw. Now, I have no truck with scruffy fellows from the woods, so I turned back and continued walking.

"'Webb Underhill,' the man said. 'From Madison.' I stopped in my tracks and turned again. But not before I surveyed the street to see if anyone was within earshot.

"'Pardon me,' I said to the man, 'but—' It finally dawned on me. This was Webb Underhill, Liddy's father, who walked off one day and was never heard from again. Mother had sent me the clipping from the *Madison Gazette* when it happened. I moved one step closer, but he didn't budge.

His eyes and size and voice were the only things I could see that might prove he was who he said he was. Finally, he grinned.

"Wait a minute, Esther, I've got a call. 'Number please—'

"I'm back. Are you still there? It was Webb Underhill in the flesh. I didn't know what to do. He wasn't going away. Should I invite him to the diner with me, or should we stand there and talk in the street? And if he did come in, what would people say about my eating with a backwoodsman? We stood there looking at each other.

"'I'd be much obliged if you would let me buy you lunch,' he said, moving to stand by the car instead of lean on it. He waved toward the diner. Oh, what the hell, I thought. Who cares about an old spinster and who she's seen with. I nodded, he stepped up to the sidewalk and we proceeded to the eatery.

"Janelle, the waitress, looked momentarily stunned by my companion. 'Your usual place, Miz Myrt?' I nodded. Should I introduce her to Webb now or later? Or never?

"After she took our meatloaf special orders and was gone, I leaned in. 'Whatever are you doing here?' I asked. 'Is that your car?'

"He deposited his hat in the chair next to him and glanced around the room. 'I'm driving for Boss Lincoln from Springfield. He rode the train to Bower, while a salesman from his dealership drove the Reo to the depot. Then I brought him to St. Luke. I work for the depot manager running errands, cleaning the place, things like that. Boss thought it would be good to show off one of the machines he sells. He's at the bank now to see about opening a business here.'

"'So you live in Bower now?' Wait again, Esther.

'Number please. Oh, hello, Doc. Here you go.'

"Now, Esther, where was I? Webb and I went to school together in Madison. Our families were neighbors. We owned the Lambkin Mortuary and his father was in the lumber business. In school, I thought Webb was cute, but I was a year ahead of him. Sometimes, before the first bell, we would sit on the grass and talk. He dropped out to work in the lumber mill and learn the construction trade.

'Number, please—'

"Esther, he opened up like a beaver dam dynamited in the Osage River. 'You remember how I hated school,' he said. 'I spent more time at the lumber mill than at school *or* at home. That sweet-smelling sawdust drew me like a magnet.'

"Our orders came. In between bites and sips, he kept talking. 'My uncle worked in the planing mill and persuaded his boss to make me an errand boy. I worked hard and moved up the ladder. When I was eighteen, they moved me to Lock Rivers to run a branch mill there.'

"Esther, you should have seen the looks we got from the other diners. But, thank goodness, no one came over and interrupted us. We must have appeared too intent in our conversation. After we'd finished, Janelle poured more coffee.

"I kept at him. 'How did you get to Bower?' He wrapped his rough hands around the coffee mug and gazed into it. His eyes softened and actually misted. Esther, can you imagine a hulking mountain man about to cry? An old issue of *The Banner* lay rumpled at the next table. As if he were stalling for time, he reached over, picked it up and turned through it.

"'Oh my lord,' he shouted. 'Here's someone who looks like Liddy! But her name's not Underhill. Is this my little girl?'

"I nodded, and he shouted, 'Liddy's in St. Luke?' The other patrons turned as one to see who'd spoken and then went back to their meals. He lowered his voice to a whisper. 'Look, her name's in this paper.' The newsprint rustled as he raced through each page.

"'When were you going to tell me, woman? Where does she live?' His skin was weathered and his hair turned from black to salt-and-pepper.

"'She lives on Depot Street. She came here in late 1932, and married the next year. You haven't been keeping up with your family for the past dozen years, have you?'

"'How'd you know about that?'

"'I have my ways. You might want to know that after seven years, Liddy's husband was reported drowned in the Creel River. She had a nervous breakdown and is in a sanitarium somewhere west of here.'

"Esther, he was dumfounded. And sad. 'Tell you what,' I told him, 'give me a way to get in touch with you, and if you like, I can keep you up on Liddy. She will be coming back to St. Luke when she's healed, or cured, or however that doctor judges sanity. Otherwise, I need to get back to work.'

"He agreed, wrote out a telephone number and the hours he would be available. He asked for my number, too, and I––I gave it to him. I guess for old time's sake.

"Mercy, Esther, my board's lighting up like a Christmas tree. I'll have to get back to you. 'Bye."

* * *

"Esther? Can you talk––er, listen a minute? Remember last week when I told you about Webb Underhill coming to town?

"Well, you'll never guess who called me this week?––Yes, it was him. And this was the conversation––word for word, I swear. I'll change the sound of my voice when he's speaking.

"'Hello?––Myrt? Can we talk?' I mimicked in a low voice.

"'Pardon me?––Who is this?––Webb?'

"'Yeah. Ever since––lunch last week,––I've wondered––er––if––'

"'Webb, for heaven's sake, spit it out. I have a telephone board to operate.'

"'Is there any chance I could squire you to the pictures this Saturday night?' Esther, he said 'pitchers.'

"'Uh––'

"'It'd make me––happy as a pig in mud––if you would––'

"'Webb Underhill, the last time I heard, you had a wife in Lock Rivers. Has she died?'

"'Why, I––don't know––if I'm still married or not––been gone so long––'

"'I'm not in the habit of being seen in the company of married men––at the pictures––or anywhere else. I have my reputation to think about. And what do you mean, you don't know if you're still married or not? You haven't been served with papers?'

"'No. Nobody knows where I am. Besides, I don't––do legal stuff––Maybe you could––inquire at the––courthouse?'

"'You bumbling clod; you smelly piece of fish! How dare you ask me to take care of your personal business. First, you abandon your family, then you turn into a grizzly mountain man, get a job driving for a rich man, and expect *me,* a respectable member of society, to––'

"'Okay, okay––You don't have to––fly into a rage. I, uh, just––thought––since we met––by chance––last week––maybe it was––fate––you know––meeting again––after all these years. Wha'duh yuh say, Miss Myrtle Jean Lampkin?'

"'Not on your Mama's best sweet potatoes, buster! Not until I see a certificate of divorce in your hands or in the newspaper." *C-l-i-c-k.*

— Chapter Forty-Three —

LIDDY

"Liddy, what is missing from your life?" Dr. Jacobi asked. We were seated on the porch of the convalescent home for what turned out to be our last conference.

Dusk settled into the valley below. A frog mimicked rings of a telephone. Three––four––five. Silence, then again: one––two––three, on and on.

"My husband––my father––my job, my self respect––my baby. Seven years of marriage."

"What do you hope for? What are your dreams?"

"I hope these midges don't bite––I hope I don't go crazy while I'm here––I hope to find out who killed Heth––I hope I get well enough to go back home and start over––I hope my family and friends forgive me––"

"Forgive you? For what?"

I answered with silence, and then continued. "For causing this disruption in their lives."

"Can you be more specific?"

"Well––for being selfish and head-strong. For wanting to move away from home, even though Daddy and Eugene were both gone. I should have stayed and helped Mother with the girls."

"Who told you that?"

"No one. My conscience. Maybe none of this bad stuff would have happened."

"Is it your fault that Eugene toddled under the train?"

"No."

"Is it your fault your Daddy walked off?"

"Maybe I could have been a better daughter."

"How?"

"I don't know. More obedient. More helpful."

"Didn't you help in the store? Didn't you help around the house? See to the little ones?"

"Yes, but––"

By now, it was fully dark. Beetles and moths gathered around the porch light. Frogs croaked in the distance. Insects hummed close by and we both made shooing motions. The doctor continued.

"You know what I think? Forgive me, but I think you need to realize that intimate relations between two people outside of marriage have gone on as long as humans have existed. And you are only human. Leaving home after school was a natural thing to do. Yvonne and Juliana filled the void of your leaving. Changes come. Call them passages, journeys, growth––"

"I journeyed all right, and look where it got me. I had no idea of what lay ahead––the temptations, wolves in sheep's clothing, overbearing self-righteous women––I wasn't prepared for this. I'm not a leader like you talked about yesterday. I let my heart take over my head and look what happened."

"My dear Liddy, willingness to change indicates leadership, and leadership often leads to broader horizons, things you never dreamed of. Didn't some good things arise out of this move? Have you forgotten the good things? Remember writing about your friends? You seem to home in on the negatives and forget the positives."

The night air had cooled considerably, but no breeze stirred. A dog barked in the distance. Night bugs sang.

"You haven't responded. Did I hit a nerve perhaps?"

Silence. I daubed at my eyes with the back of my hand.

"You've got to get past this, Liddy. You trusted Heth, and he betrayed you. We are taught to believe that people are fair and honest and loving. You spent seven years as a dutiful wife. He's the one who never settled in. Now that he is dead––yes, Liddy, you must reconcile yourself with the obvious: *he is dead*. Even if he faked his death, he is dead to you. Don't try to find out who killed him. It's time for you to take charge of *you* from here on out. Concentrate on *you*."

I nodded, and then shook my head like a horse with flies in its eyes, as if to toss away all the feelings of failure clinging to me.

"What are your choices when you leave here? What do you feel like you are becoming?"

My rocker squeaked. "Uh––"

"What do you want now? Have your goals changed? What about your job at *The Banner*? You'll need some way to earn money. Who can you fall back on? You can answer any time, Liddy."

"I could move back to Lock Rivers––I'd like to study journalism––I could bum off the Courseys." I giggled at the idea. "I might trade a room at Tom's for being his housekeeper, cook and gardener. I have a big backyard. Maybe someone could plow it and we could plant vegetables for the community. The grapevine should be bearing."

"Keep going, my dear. This is good."

But I felt wrung out, empty, used up. Venus was visible and I locked onto the light, hoping I could summon its energy, its purpose, its steadfastness for myself.

Doctor Jacobi stood and reached for my hand. As I rose, he hugged me close. "You're about ready to go home."

I sobbed in his arms. How long I had waited to hear those words. And how good it felt to be held again.

— Chapter Forty-Four —

DOC

The telephone rang just as I opened the door to my office. "Doc? There's a Doctor Jacobi on the line."

"Thanks, Myrt. I've got it." I pushed the door closed, swiveled my chair around, sat and pulled out the top drawer of my desk. Surely there was one cigar left. "Hello."

"Liddy Coursey is ready to come home," Jacobi told me. I could barely hear him for the dogs barking outside my building. "Let me know when to have her ready."

"Glad to hear it, Doctor." Oh, dear, now I have this to think of on top of all the other things brewing around St. Luke. "Do I have to sign her out? Can someone else—a friend, say, or her father-in-law pick her up?"

"You can authorize her release," he said. I stuck the cigar between my teeth. "Let me know ahead of time whom to expect and when. The day and hour, if possible."

"Thank you kindly, Doctor," I said, and rolled the Havana across my tongue. "Send me the bill. You have my address." I inhaled the satisfying smell of the hand-rolled corona. "Oh, and Doctor," I said, "we all appreciate what you've done for Liddy." I'd better keep myself in the doctor's good graces. I might need him again. "If ever there's anything I can do for you, please let me know."

"I will," said the man who moved down from Chicago claiming the skills to cure depression and despondency. "Liddy is still fragile. See that no one pushes her too far or too fast," he said. I thought: who around here could possibly cause her anxiety, now that Heth's out of the picture.

Jacobi continued, "Liddy has been a cooperative patient. She seems willing to live once more."

"Thank you, doctor, and goodbye," I said, and replaced the receiver to break the connection. Keeping my hand on it, I raised it again.

"Miz Myrt, ring Tom and Quinn, please. Ask them to drop by at twelve-thirty." It was nearly time for my ten-o'clock patient. "Tell them I'll have sandwiches brought to my office. Thanks, dearie."

If one or both of these men can fetch Liddy, it'll free Dovie and me to stay here in case Isabell Nance has any more trouble. Keener'd go crazy if I wasn't around when his new wife needed me. Too bad Liddy's pregnancy didn't get this far along. Has it actually been seven years since her miscarriage?

But how to get Liddy home? Would Genese be well enough to make the long trip to Rakestraw? Probably not, but I'll call her just to be polite.

"Miz Myrt? Connect me with Genese Underhill in Lock Rivers, please." It's nearly time for my patients.

"Hello? Mrs. Underhill? Roscoe Everett here. From St. Luke. Dr. Jacobi just called with the good news that Liddy is ready to come home. I have to authorize someone to get her. Unless you object, or have a better suggestion, I will ask Quinn Coursey and Tom Grindle to fetch her. It will take the better part of three days, given this unsettled March weather––All right, and thank you very much. How are things with you and yours?––Glad to hear it. I'll send word to Liddy that you will write her at home. Goodbye."

* * * *

"Hello, fellows. Come in. Thanks for stopping by. Tom, I hope I didn't inconvenience you too badly." I motioned them to sit. "Mind my cigar?" They both shook their heads. "What I called you here for is this: Dr. Jacobi called saying he was ready to release Liddy. I'd go myself, or send Dovie, except that Isabel Keener's first pregnancy is giving her a hard time." On second thought, I stubbed out the stogie and pushed the ashtray away. "I thought that one or both of you might be able to get away for at least three days. What about it?"

Neither of them spoke. "We can't let her come home alone, can we?" I asked. Still not a trace of emotion in their faces. "I guess Dr. Jacobi would arrange it if we couldn't." Still no word from either. "Do you think Frona Lee would go?"

A sudden commotion and the door to the hallway burst open. Bird Briley stumbled in, the receptionist behind him, looking helpless. "He overpowered me."

Bird, obviously out-of-his-head drunk, muttered something and pulled a pistol.

I protested, "Now see here, Bird," but he turned on me. Tom and Quinn bolted out of their chairs and stood against the wall. The plates clattered to the floor and spattered food everywhere.

"You see here," the interloper yelled, "you––you quack of a doctor. Now, who's got the gun, huh? Now who's in control? Where's Liddy? I've come to fetch her now that her husband's gone off and got himself killed. She once asked me to marry her––the night I pinched her duff––so now I can. Where is she, huh? Where is she?"

During Bird's outburst, Tom and Quinn had maneuvered like shadows around the wall until they flanked the gunman. Each grabbed an arm and Tom knocked the gun out of his hand. I grabbed it and turned it on the intruder.

Sheriff Jasper appeared just then and handcuffed the former pastor. "We've had nothing but trouble out of this man since the church sent him away from St. Luke. He quit preaching, and has been bothering us ever since. Let's go, Bird. I have a nice, quiet place for you near my office. Let's leave the doctor to his doctoring."

That little fracas shook Tom and Quinn out of their muteness. "I'll go, I'll go," they both said, still standing. They admitted to waiting for the other to speak first.

"I'd do anything for Liddy," Tom said. "Except let––" He pointed to the door.

Quinn wiped his mouth. "I would, too." He turned to Tom. "How about we go together?" They both bent down and cleaned up what was left of their lunches.

My afternoon patients would be signing in soon. "Good. Now, there's the matter of travel. You could drive, take the train or ride the Trailways." They looked at each other. Tom motioned for Quinn to speak first.

He did. "Do we want the fastest way, the safest way or the cheapest way? And it's March. The weather could change in an instant. I prefer the train myself. It's more comfortable. Not as confining as a car or a bus. Tom?"

"Train's fine by me. That's how I got to St. Luke."

"Good," I said. "I'll call the depot and see about schedules. Quinn, can you pay your own way? Tom? Any preference as to the days you're gone?"

Tom answered quickly. "I can pay. The weekend would be easier for me. Then I could put up signs that the dining room would be closed on those days. Or let Xann have a go at it alone."

"Quinn?"

"Any day is okay. I'll stop whatever I'm doing and go."

"It's settled then. I'll get back to you as soon as I know something. Time for my appointments. Goodbye."

Once more, I called Miz Myrt. "I hope you don't mind being my secretary of sorts, dearie. But I need you to call Glenn Keeling and reserve two coach seats to Rakestraw and three back. During the weekend." She started to say something, but I cut her off. "I need all the details––boarding the train here, and the arrival time there. The sooner we know, the quicker we can have Liddy back in St. Luke. Thanks, love." I hung up gently, but abruptly.

Just then Dovie opened the door. She was frowning and motioning for me to hurry. I was already late for my first appointment.

— Chapter Forty-Five —

TOM

At 10AM on Friday, the Ides of March, 1940, Quinn Coursey and I boarded the Missouri-Pacific combine Number 21 headed to Omaha. The combine was a new addition since I rode in to St. Luke ten years ago. It was part baggage car, part smoking car, and part coach.

We would detrain at Rakestraw where a vehicle from the Jacobi *Haus* would meet us and take us to guest quarters. The next morning, with Liddy in tow, we would await the next train home.

Our precious cargo, bound back to St. Luke after a six-week stay in the mountains, was the youngest of Quinn's four daughters-in-law. When Liddy's husband Heth went missing after seven years, she had a nervous breakdown.

Since the recent incident with Bird Briley, Quinn and I had some sorting out to do. After we were seated on the train, I decided to bring it up. "Quinn, won't it be too dangerous for Liddy to live alone now that Bird Briley's back?"

"I've been thinking about that, Tom. As crazy as he is now, locked doors wouldn't stop him."

"So, what are the choices? Let's work out something while we're riding." The train car wasn't crowded so I sat opposite Quinn. "We can at least have some suggestions for Liddy. What a terrible thing for her to face after all this." I leaned in so no one would hear. "Could we get rid of Briley somehow?"

"Tom! Are you suggesting?—That's funny coming from you. You who won't kill a cockroach in your own kitchen."

"Briley's lower than a cockroach. Besides, I don't have roaches in my kitchen."

"Just teasing, Tom, just teasing. What about her moving in with me? I have lots of room now that I'm alone."

I didn't like his idea at all. She would be too far away. "Or," I put in, "she could move back into the boarding house." I paused to see how Liddy's father-in-law would react. He's approaching fifty, I'd wager.

Quinn's slouch vanished, his eyes widened. Then he grinned. "Why, you young rascal. You've had your cap set for Liddy since she first came to this town, haven't you?"

I'd never admit such a thing to the father of Liddy's late husband. "What about her going back to Lock Rivers?" I asked. "She might want to take care of her mother, the poor woman."

"Not a thing Liddy should do, in my opinion," Quinn answered. "Not since our girl's had six weeks of treatment to regain her sense of reality."

The train slowed. "Bowers!" the conductor said, after it came to a halt. "Lunch stop. Local diner's open." The well-fed man waddled down the aisle. "Other side of the depot. Train pulls out in one hour. Watch your step."

After stretching our cramped bodies, we checked out the small depot. A wooden plaque on a near wall read, "Constructed in 1910." We traipsed across the polished floor to the steps.

The diner, an old railroad car anchored by wood pilings, stood between the riverbank and the depot. The building's red paint had faded to old-barn color, but the owner had planted ferns, wild irises and wild geraniums around the front. In the leaf mold, woods violets were putting up their green heart-shapes.

Quinn entered first and selected a booth with a river view.

"Look at that, Tom," he said. "Wouldn't it be nice to be fishing out there—–if it weren't so cold, of course? Not a care in the world." The likable widower gazed out the window. "Like making crops for next year. No children or grandchildren to fret over." His intense eyes under those thick brows looked into mine. "Just sit back, hold a cane pole and let the world swirl by—–like a moving picture show."

"Sounds like you really didn't want to make this trip," I said

"Oh, yes, yes I did. I was just feeling sorry for myself. Liddy's safety and well-being are not a worry, Tom, they're a challenge." Again, he stared out across the river. "Us against the world. Especially Bird Briley." Quinn drank from his glass of water. "You noticed how much bigger he's gotten? Wonder if he eats raw meat."

We ate the only thing on today's menu – brown beans, turnip greens, cornbread, peach cobbler and coffee. "Taste the pepper sauce, Quinn. It's not as good as mine, is it?"

We still had a few minutes before the train pulled out. As we left the diner, a mountain man approached us. Black hair with a tinge of gray fell pell-mell to his cheekbones––except for two jagged holes where eyes looked out. His beard took over then, stopping at his chest.

"Mr. Grindle, Mr. Coursey?" he said through an untrimmed mustache. "Could I interest you in some unusual items for your homes, for your wives?"

I opened my mouth to protest, to ask how he knew our names, but Quinn put a hand on my arm. The man pointed to his cart and without turning, walked backwards toward it. Quinn looked puzzled, but took the first step to follow him. I trailed at his side like a scared puppy.

"Usually people want to know how I know their names," he said. "I make it my business to find out who rides the trains. Now let me show you what I have."

Neither of us spoke, but I followed Quinn's lead and acted interested. While he looked at the rag-tag lot of wares, I studied the cart. Two full-sized wagon wheels with a half-width and half-length bed. The sides were low and the boards looked patched together. Handles like those on cement barrows were attached high on one end. On the other, a pole rested on the ground, stabilizing the bed.

"Where do you get your?––" Quinn gestured across the bed at squared lengths of faded fabrics, a tattered box of sewing notions, cakes of lye soap, tallow and paraffin. Not much at all.

"Left to me by me sainted old mother when she passed, lord rest her soul."

"All aboard!" the conductor bellowed.

"I'll be here when you come back through. Maybe you'll have more time and we can get better acquainted."

Back in our seats, we were silent until the train picked up speed. It would be a good long time before Rakestraw and Liddy. I turned to Quinn "How did he know our names? That's scary."

"He would have to be privy to the passenger list. Let's find out if he called other passengers by name. If not, there's something rotten in Denmark, as they say, only it might be in Bower. Or St. Luke."

I surveyed the passengers in the front of the car and Quinn questioned those in the back.

"See," he said after we'd returned, "no one else was buttonholed like we were. Let's go back over what's happened since that day in Doc's office. Who knew we were going?" He waited for me to answer.

"Doc Everett. Maybe Dovie. Glenn Keeling. Doctor Jacobi." I stopped, stymied.

"Aha!" Quinn smiled. "You haven't lived in St. Luke as long as I have. You've forgotten a very important link."

"Who? Who could it be? Tell me, tell me!"

"Who called the stationmaster?" His eyes flashed and his lips curled. "Think, man, think." When I didn't respond, he continued. "What person has access to every phone conversation in St. Luke?"

Together, we answered, "Miz Myrt."

— Chapter Forty-Six —

QUINN

A snowfall during the night had whitened the Ozark evergreens into mid-March Christmas trees. Tom and I took Liddy in tow and one of the drunks who had dried out at Dr. Jacobi's drove us to the depot at Rakestraw. It was still snowing as we boarded.

"'Take notes; write your feelings,'" Liddy began as soon as we were seated. "Those were Dr. J's––Doctor Jacobi's––last words as we left for our four-day Close Quarters Camp Out."

The train lurched as we began our trip back to St. Luke.

"He gave us our leadership roles and our goals," she continued before we could inquire into her wellbeing. "Each of us took one day as leader. We had to call group sessions and present an exercise––a 'what if.'

"Mine was, 'What if—when you get back home, the person you despise most or your worst enemy, is the first one to visit.' I immediately thought of Frona Lee––sorry, Papa Quinn––not so much because of how I feel about her, but how she feels about me.

"She thinks I had something to do with Heth's disappearance. In my mind, I imagined her saying, 'Well?–– Well?––' You know how her voice rises at the end?

"'Hello, Frona Lee,' I would say, 'how are things around St. Luke?'

"'Fine, fine,' she would answer, 'but I want to hear about––'

"'All in good time,'" I would say. 'All in good time. Here, I've made us some tea.'

"I would no longer be concerned with what she thought about me, or stop a split second to wonder what she wanted me to say. Like I used to. If she cried and whined that I never did like her, and she didn't know why—I could now see it as her trying to twist me into doing what she wanted.

"'I have a lot of catching up to do,'" I would say. Then, I would stand, take her teacup and retrieve her wrap. I'd guide her to the door. "'Thanks for dropping by.'"

I listened in awe at this new person, born during her short stay away from us. Confident, smiling, animated. Talking ninety to nothing.

Abruptly, Liddy stopped her story and yawned. "Papa Quinn, Tom, why did you come all this way to get me? I could have managed the journey home by myself. But thank you," and her head fell onto my shoulder. She slept, poor girl.

How could we tell her that Bird Briley was back in town, changed for the worst, if that were possible, and that he was determined to make her *his* bride now that Heth is dead?

The farther east we traveled, the heavier it snowed. White flakes closed us in. The car was warm and the rhythmic hum of the wheels on tracks became a lullaby. I looked over at Tom and his eyes were closed. I rested mine, too.

No telling how long we slept. But we were awakened by a jolt, a rumble and screams. Our car suddenly headed down like a roller coaster and Tom and I both threw one hand across Liddy and held on for dear life with the other. Soon, we leveled off, then rose again and continued, eventually slowing to a stop. Tom's wide and questioning eyes turned on me. Liddy stirred from his shoulder where she'd leaned on a previous curve.

"Wha?—"

"Felt like the ground gave way," I answered before she could ask the rest of her question.

Soon, the conductor walked through. With every frightened eye upon him, he addressed the entire car. "Unbeknownst to us, the top tier of the bridge over Gaddy Fork collapsed yesterday with the weight of the snow. The track somehow held together and came to rest on the trestle's second decking.

"After the train cleared the dip, we stopped. We've checked the couplings and underpinnings and everything's okay. I wired the depot at Rakestraw to hold up any more trains, and for them to notify the track department."

The three of us exhaled as one. "Thank goodness," I said.

"Next stop, Bower." He pulled his watch from his pocket and looked down. "In thirty minutes," he said, and then proceeded to inform those in the car behind us. Liddy, still drowsy after the excitement ended, snuggled between us and slept again.

"Bower?" Tom whispered over her head. "Isn't that where we met that mountaineer who knew us?"

Before we had time to talk to Liddy about Bird Briley, the whistle blew and the train slowed. "Bower! A thirty minute stop. Then on to St. Luke, Lock Rivers and points east. Watch your step, please."

Liddy awakened, looked around as if to get her bearings, and then beamed us a smile. "It's good to stand up again." She opened her handbag, retrieved an enameled mirror. She surveyed her face and grimaced.

"Zindi showed me how to use face powder and rouge and eye shadow. Norie talked me into trying a pageboy hairstyle with longer bangs." She touched her forehead. "To cover my scar." Liddy searched in her handbag for a minute. "Did I ever tell you that when I was five, I opened the gate to the animal yard––we called it "the lot"––by myself and and walked over to Old Sukey, our mule. She stopped munching weeds and turned to look at me. I reached up and pulled her tail. In a split second, she kicked me in the face and ran away."

She pulled out a blue vial, opened it, placed her index finger on the top, dipped the bottle, straightened it and rubbed the fragrance behind her ear.

Tom's eyes crinkled. "Getting ready for company?"

Our eyes met over her head once again. "Speaking of company," I ventured, "on the way out when we stopped here, this mountaineer fellow hailed us. Called us by name. We have no idea who he is. Still don't. You'd better stay close to us."

"What did he look like?" she asked, as the brakes screeched against the rails and the train stopped.

— Chapter Forty-Seven —

LIDDY

At Bower, a railroad stop between Rakestraw and St. Luke, Tom offered his hand as we stepped out of the train. We joined the other passengers walking across the packed-earth courtyard to the diner. A dusting of snow nestled in uneven places.

"Stay close to us, Liddy," Papa Quinn said. "There may be some odd folks around here. You know, river rats, hobos, people out of work." He pointed to a mountaineer at the edge of the woods. Dark hair covered his face, and only his nose and lips, as brown as walnut oil, could be seen. A black patch shielded one eye and the triangular brim of his floppy hat almost covered the other. Wire glasses rimmed his nose. As he raised his hand to his hat and nodded, he seemed familiar.

I turned to Tom and Quinn. "I feel as if I've been here before, and that I am somehow connected to that man! Could he be one of the gardeners from The *Haus*?"

"That must be it," Tom said. I saw that he glanced at Quinn.

A chill wind eddied through the courtyard and the Creel River rippled. Snow from the trees fell like fairy dust as we headed for the diner. "After we eat," I said, "I must go over and find out who he is."

What did I eat? You'd think that since it was my first food away from The *Haus*, I would have remembered. I was eager to go outside, but I waited for the men to finish. So I watched the Creel River flow by.

Papa Quinn paid the bill, and we finally left the eatery. Each man grasped one of my arms as if I might run away. On solid ground, I turned to the woods where the man had been. He had vanished.

"Did I really see him?" Neither man answered, but they guided me back to the train. The seat of the passenger who sat across from us was empty, so Papa Quinn sat there. "Aha!" he said. "More room."

"Tell us about––" Tom began, but I interrupted––something I would never have done before my stay at The Jacobi *Haus.*

"For some reason, I'm thinking of Daddy today," I said. "Is it the train? The river? The snow? The homecoming?" I directed my query to Quinn, who looked at Tom with raised eyebrows.

"When he worked at the mill, Daddy always smelled like sawdust. He had sawdust in his hair, his pant cuffs, and his shirt pockets."

"How's that?" Tom asked. "I thought you told me he ran a market."

"That was later, when he and Mother took over my grandparents' store."

"Before he and Mother married––and for a few years after––he was foreman at the lumberyard on the northeast side of Lock Rivers––between the river and the tracks."

Papa Quinn seemed to sit taller. "Tell us more," he said.

"After Gramma and Grandpa left to operate a hotel down on the Arkansas border, Mother and Daddy took over the store. It was the only market in town."

"Like Moody's in St. Luke?" Tom asked.

I nodded. "Anyway, Daddy had one blue eye and one brown eye. Only we kids who occasionally sat in his lap and played our favorite game knew. Daddy would say in a deep, playful voice, 'Look deep into my eyes, my children. What do you think you see?'" I felt a lump building in my throat, so I rummaged in my handbag for a handkerchief, in case I teared up.

"'Blue marble, brown marble looking at me,' we'd answer, laughing. He tried to get us to sing 'a blue and brown agate looking at me,' but we didn't know what agate meant until he told us: marble. And 'agate' didn't seem to flow as well as 'marble."

The conductor pulled three long blasts as we neared a farm road crossing. Horses close to the track bolted away, then turned and watched the train pass.

"Daddy made up funny stories about how marbles became eyeballs. He told us that when God made Adam, God checked to see if the man could smell the fruit trees, feel the breezes blowing through Eden, taste the olives, and hear the river gurgling by." In recalling the story, I forgot about myself. We all smiled as we jiggled homeward in our wooden seats.

"'God noticed,' Daddy continued, 'that Adam couldn't see all the beauty and greatness around him, so He knelt and dug some clay, rolled it between His palms into two marbles, then stuck them in Adam's face. *Now*, God said, *you can see. Go and rule the land*. Daddy told us that ever since, children have had marbles for eyeballs."

"But that didn't explain why he had different colored eyes," Papa Quinn said, with a gleam in his own.

"We would ask him why one of his eyes was blue and one brown, when ours are the same color.' He would always answer the same thing. 'I guess God had some blue clay left over when he ran out of brown, and being a God of the land, He didn't want to waste anything. Now get down and let me rest before supper.'"

"Speaking of rest," Tom said, "why don't we snatch a nap before we get home?"

I agreed and laid my head between the car window and the seat back. When I awoke, I was leaning on Tom's shoulder. He and Papa Quinn had not slept, they said.

Later that day, I would find out why.

— Chapter Forty-Eight —

TOM

Quinn, Liddy and I stepped down from the train at St. Luke onto the packed dirt of the depot yard.

Liddy had a spring in her step. "I'm so glad to be home," she said, stretching her arms overhead. She twirled around once, and then snuggled into her coat. "I can't wait to get started on the rest of my life. So much to do."

Quinn picked up her suitcase and I carried her rucksack. It was only a quarter mile from the depot to the boardinghouse, and Liddy's house was in between.

"Whoa!" Quinn said, as we turned into the north wind. All three of us had our coats on, but right there in the middle of the road, Quinn and I set the cases down and pulled mufflers from inside our coats and wound them around our necks. Our gloves went from pockets to hands. Opening her handbag, we watched Liddy pull out a plaid woolen square that she quickly unfolded into a triangle. Holding it by the ends, she covered her shortened hair and tied the scarf under her chin.

"Since you are so kind as to carry my things, I'll keep my hands in my pockets instead of fishing for my gloves," she said, and took off at a fast clip. Her house was visible through the leafless trees and I half expected her to break into a run.

"What are we going to do?" I asked Quinn as we walked behind her. "About Briley, I mean? We didn't decide anything."

"When she gets in the house––who has the key, Tom? Do you?––we'll have to set her down and talk about safety. We don't want her new attitude and excitement to be ruined by a ruffian who can't stay out of a bucket shop."

"You'll do that, won't you? Being older, and all?"

Quinn nodded and continued, "Remember, Doctor Jacobi said not to push her too far or too fast. I don't see any sign of fragility, but still––"

By this time, Liddy was on the porch, rubbing her fingers across the new paint I'd put on the wicker chairs. It was something I could do. I handed her the key she'd left with me.

"Look at that!" she exclaimed. Hung over the front windows, a construction paper banner with each letter printed on a separate sheet had been fastened to a string.

W E L C O M E H O M E A U N T L I D D Y.

"How sweet," she said, and I saw her eyes suddenly glisten. She wiped them on her coat sleeve, and unlocked the door.

"Oh, look!" She opened and read aloud a note propped on the entry table. *Welcome home, sister-in-law. We missed you. Caroline and I cleaned and dusted. Frona Lee left soup in the icebox, and a coconut cake. Dovie is coming after work today. Take very good care of yourself. We'll see you soon. Alice.*

Quinn and I walked in and put down the luggage.

"Thanks again, fellows," Liddy said. "It was good of you to take time out of your life to see me home safely. I'll walk you to the stree––"

"We have something to tell you," Quinn butted in. "Can we sit down?"

Liddy looked puzzled, but motioned us to chairs. The room was comfortably warm. Alice must have turned on the stove against the March wind.

"What in the world?" Liddy asked, sitting on the edge of her chair. "Did someone else die while I was gone? Is Mother sick? Was there a fire? What?"

"No, no. Nothing like that." Quinn motioned for her to sit back.

"Don't get excited," I added, feeling like a dope.

Liddy sat back and took a deep breath. At first, she twisted her hands in her lap, and then, as if on cue, she relaxed and placed them on the chair arms.

As Quinn related the incident in Doc's office with Bird Briley, I watched her face change expressions––from surprise to fear and then to anger.

"This is why we couldn't sleep on the train," I said. "We knew what we had to tell you but hadn't figured out how." Now I was twisting my own hands, but I sat forward and continued. "We agreed that you should not stay alone at night. Leastways, not until Briley is out of the picture––either in jail or run out of town."

Quinn said, "I can make you an apartment in my house."

I had to put in my two-cent's worth. "I'll give you my rooms in the boardinghouse. At least at night, Liddy," I begged. "Until Briley is no threat."

"Oh, you will, will you?" And with that, we saw another side of the 'new' Liddy. "What gives you the right to tell me what I should and should not do?" She was out of her chair like a flash, and her dark eyes blazed, first at Quinn, then at me.

"I have been gone from home six weeks. For the last two of those, I've thought of nothing else but getting back and picking up my life. Right now, I could whip Bird Briley's weight in wild cats. Yours, too, if you get in my way." She pointed to the door.

Quinn and I stood mute after Liddy's stinging reproach. "But we are only interested in your safety," Quinn said.

I stuttered agreement and nodded.

"I can take care of myself, thank you very much," Liddy shot back. "While I appreciate what you've done for me, neither one of you is my daddy. I'm not a child you can order around." She marched to the door and opened it. "Good day, gentlemen."

We walked in silence out the door, down the path, past the row of cedars and into Depot Street. Dusk clouded the stark brittleness of March. Bare branches cast dark shadows and the few oak leaves left hanging rustled in the breeze like tiny ghosts.

"Well," Quinn finally spoke as we headed toward the boardinghouse. "Looks like we have *two* folks to contend with now––Briley *and* Liddy. Let's take my car and go see Doc Everett," he said, when we reached the entry. "He needs to know about this, but I don't want to telephone him."

"I'll call Xann," I said, "and have him open up the dining room for evening coffee and leftovers. Give me a minute."

"I'll warm up the car," Quinn said.

— Chapter Forty-Nine —

LIDDY

"I'm coming! I'm coming!" Who could be visiting at this hour? Who even knows I'm home? I flung open the door. "Oh, hello, Dovie!" I said, greeting my best friend.

"Don't 'hello Dovie' me!" she shouted. She hugged me with one arm, and cradled a covered dish in the other. "You didn't even ask, 'Who's there?' What if Bird Briley had been standing out on your porch? You've got to be careful!"

While she fussed, I helped her off with her coat and gloves. "I guess you've seen Tom and Quinn," I said. "I should have known they'd run straight to Doc."

"Nope. But I did know that Briley's back in town. I knew you would be home today, so last night I made you a welcome-back-to-St.-Luke gift." She held it out with one hand and pulled the cloth off with a magician's flourish.

"A Karo-nut pie," she said. "Some people call it a pecan pie. I knew you'd never make one for yourself."

"What a pretty pie plate," I said, taking the dish. "You're right. I've never tried to make a pecan pie. Thank you kindly. Does it need to be kept cold? I can make us some coffee. Or tea?"

Dovie shook her head. "No, but I want to know how you plan to protect yourself from that awful Bird. He scared us silly the day he burst into the office with that gun."

Dovie looked all around the windows and doors of the living room. She rapped on the glass, and pulled the curtains aside.

"Wha?––" I asked her.

"Testing the thickness of the panes. And the tightness. How good are your screens? Your screen door?" She was nervous as a caged cat.

"I'll think about that tomorrow," I said.

She whirled on me like I had turned on Tom and Quinn earlier. "Tomorrow might be too late! You need to think about it tonight," she almost shouted. "Bird Briley could be out there right now! Go get a dining room chair and a case knife. While you're in the kitchen, get a table fork and a meat fork."

I did as I was told. Dovie had aged a little in the six weeks I'd been gone. Gray tendrils escaped the blond––almost platinum––hair she wore high on top and behind her ears. When I returned with what she'd ordered, I noticed she was rubbing her arms while she paced.

"I feel this odd coolness in your house, Liddy. I wish I had a cigarette!" She grabbed the chair and the knife from my hands. "Here, let me show you how my grandmother taught Mother and me to protect ourselves."

She wedged the back of the straight chair under the doorknob. Then she slid the knife blade into the facing at eye level so that the handle, horizontal, spanned the space between the wall and the door. "That'll at least keep Bird from forcing it open. You keep these forks here on the entry table where you can reach them in a hurry. Go for his eyes first."

Did Mother secure our house after Daddy left? I wondered. Was she afraid? I don't remember her showing it.

By now, darkness had settled in. I turned up the flame in the heater. Just then, something sounding like gravel hit the front windows.

"See there! He's already on the prowl!" Dovie said, her eyes as large as quarters.

"Oh, Dovie, don't be so nervous. What in the world happened today to put you in such a state?"

"*You* came home!" Her hand flew to her mouth. "Oh, Liddy, I didn't mean it in a bad way. I've missed you like crazy. But I've seen Bird Briley up close––with a gun."

A stone hit the tin roof and rattled as it rolled down the steep incline. A horrid laugh––the same one that I remembered on Halloween all those years ago––pierced the air. I jumped at the sound. "He *is* out there." I shivered, and moved closer to my friend.

"I'll call Doc," Dovie said, moving over to the phone. She stood and waited for Miz Myrt's, 'Number please.' Then Dovie blanched and fell into the nearest chair. "The phone's dead! Bird's cut the phone line!"

Though Dovie was twenty years older, and she had helped me through the miscarriage, I realized that I might have to be the strong one tonight. Something had put her in a state of near panic, and I hated to think it was that pudgy little man outside. I ran for a glass of water, and she gulped it. Pulling a chair close, I reached for her hand.

"Dovie, listen to me. We're safe. We are two strong women inside, and Bird is one crazy man outside. Let's suppose he has no gun or he would have opened fire by now." I was surprised at my own calmness. "We can't cower in this house like frightened chickens and wait for the men to discover a dead phone and rush to our rescue."

Dovie was shaking. She sat on her legs and hugged her bare arms. I grabbed a quilt off the sofa, covered her up and kept talking.

"Those three men drinking coffee not two blocks away are most likely discussing my safety and how to get me to change my mind about staying at the boardinghouse at night. By the way, does Doc know where you are?"

She nodded.

"I'll brew us a pot of tea. If we're in for a standoff, we'll need some caffeine." Dovie threw off the quilt and followed close behind me. More stones hit the house. She jumped each time.

Back in our places with tea, I continued. "Two level-headed women armed with those forks over there just might discourage him from whatever he's about."

Once more I walked to the kitchen––this time, Dovie stayed put––and returned with a cookie sheet and a muffin tin. "We'll use these for shields and the forks for spears." I made fencing motions in the air trying to lighten Dovie's mood. She smiled wanly.

"What say we put fear and our weapons behind us," I said. "Let's open the front door and walk out together onto the lighted porch." Oddly enough, I wasn't scared. "I could say to Bird, in a sensible, rational tone, 'Now Brother Bird, er Briley, back off and be a good fellow. You know what happens to folks who commit a crime.'

"Or I could say, 'Do you want something, Mr. Briley? It's getting cold out here. Could we meet somewhere tomorrow––say Tom's Boardinghouse––and talk this thing out?'"

Dovie wasn't ready for the strong woman thing. She shook her head and said in a raspy, almost inaudible voice, "I can't, Liddy. I can't."

"Well, I'll have to try it myself then." After six weeks of beating down insecurity and guilt, I came home determined to be different. If I cower now, all those days of retraining will be for nothing. I moved closer to Dovie. "I've already stood up to two men today––and they were dear friends. Guess I'll have to make it three."

Dovie stood up suddenly and dashed to the kitchen. Instantly, she returned with the pie she'd brought. "This!" she whispered. "This may get him out of our hair." Thrusting it into my hands, she said, "Go on, go on. I'll be right behind you."

And so we went. We opened the door. We walked out. My legs were shaky, even after all my 'be strong' sermons from Doctor Jacobi and myself.

"Here, Brother Briley," I shouted with as much gusto as I could manage. "You must be cold standing out there all this time. Take this pecan pie up to Tom's." I held it out to him. "He'll give you a fork and some hot coffee. You can sit in the warm dining room and enjoy it."

Like a cautious but hungry cat, he peered around a cedar and stepped onto the walk. He licked his lips and kept his eyes on the pie as he guardedly shuffled to the steps. He seized the dish with both hands.

"If you want to talk, tell Tom what time you'll be at the boardinghouse tomorrow, and I'll meet you. Whatever's between us, we can work it out. Peacefully, I hope."

Never taking his eyes off me, he backed down the path. At the cedars, the deranged man turned and disappeared. "Dovie, hear that? It sounds like our old Liberty Coaster wagon crunching in the gravel."

She and I stood statue-still until the sound faded out. Then, both weak with relief, we fell into each other's arms.

— Chapter Fifty —

DOC

"Still fragile, my foot!" I said to Tom and Quinn, while pulling out my chair from the dining table. "Doctor Jacobi told me to go easy––that Liddy was still fragile. It doesn't sound that way from what you've just described." I poured sugar from the table shaker into my coffee. "If the new Liddy holds––if she doesn't revert to her old ways, we could have a bitch kitty on our hands."

"What on earth do you mean?" Quinn asked.

"Oh, you know, these single women––some married, too. Once they don't have anyone to answer to––they get a little too free––independent, unbridled. You know, uppity."

"Uncontrollable, do you mean?" Quinn's eyes widened, and he flushed. "I can't imagine that happening."

"Tom," I said, "you remember when we hogtied Heth––God rest his soul––" I nodded in Quinn's direction"––back when we were afraid he'd run out on Liddy?"

"Yes," Tom said, almost inaudibly, rubbing at a stain on his saucer.

"We may have to kidnap Liddy now––for her own safety."

"I'd be against that, Doc, same as I was against you seizing Heth," Quinn said. "If anybody needs capturing, it's Bird Briley! What can we do about him?"

Tom refilled the cups. "Shall I brew another pot?"

I shook my head. "Not for me, Tom. Thanks." *Did I detect a bit of feistiness in Quinn's comments?* "You generally can't arrest a man for threats, Quinn."

"I pray to God he hasn't found another weapon," Quinn said. "Surely the sheriff didn't give him back his gun."

Tom wasn't saying much. "A penny for your thoughts, old boy," I said. Quinn and I both fixed our eyes on him. In the silence, I could hear the wind rustling the rosebushes that surrounded the boardinghouse porch. Suddenly, there was another sound––like wheels on gravel.

"That must be Dovie coming back from Liddy's," I said, pushing my cup to the center of the table. "Now where were we?"

But Tom jumped up and stumbled from his chair. He turned on the porch light and pulled up the window shade. "Oh, my lord! Look here!" He jerked open the door and ran out. "That looks like my Liberty Coaster."

Quinn and I followed him. All I saw was a child's wagon with steel wheels. Tom pointed toward his shed.

"Yep, mine's gone," Tom said. "I set it right there with rose bushes still in their packages. See, there's the bushes on the ground."

Quinn sprinted down the steps and held up a white and pink pie plate from the wagon.

Seeing that empty plate sent shivers down my spine. "That's Dovie's favorite pie dish! She won't even let me touch it," I said, and ran back inside to call Liddy.

"Tom! Quinn!" I yelled as I slammed the front door behind me. "Liddy's phone's dead. Let's get down there! Quick!"

But they were already running.

— Chapter Fifty-One —

LIDDY

Friday after work, I made my usual stop at the post office. "Any news today?" I asked Mrs. Jake. All I knew was that she was Jake-the-postmaster's wife.

"By the way, there is, Miss Liddy." *Does she call every woman 'miss' just like Jake always answers my questions with 'Yes, ma'am.'?* "You got a letter. And not from your mother this time. Or your sisters. But there's no return address."

I took the letter from the nosy woman without looking at it, thanked her, pushed the door open and skipped down the steps like a schoolgirl. *Who would be writing me?* On the street, I paused to look at the envelope. The postmark was 'Bower, Mo.' I didn't know anyone in Bower.

At the first street-side bench, I sat, stalling, savoring the possibilities as well as soaking up the spring afternoon sun at my back. The address read, "Miss Liddy Underhill, Depot Street, St. Luke, Missouri." Written in broad thick strokes, the script was measured, the letters erect—not slanted like mine. And I haven't been Liddy Underhill in seven years.

St. Lukans passed, spoke or nodded. The men doffed their hats and smiled. No one stopped to strike up a conversation. Were they skittish because of my time at the sanitarium? Perhaps they didn't know how to express sympathy for Heth's death.

I opened the letter, a folded sheet with the words *Missouri Pacific: Bower Depot, Bower, Missouri* on the letterhead. The lined white paper was yellow with age. After the salutation, *"Dear Liddy,"* two lines appeared in the middle of the page.

We knew each other long ago,
but one day we lost touch.

A lady and her child walked by. The girl stared at me a second, then said, "Mama, there's that woman who had the fit when we were caroling last year." They hurried on. *Nothing like a child to get to the heart of things.*

The closing of the letter contained two more lines.

Ever since I found out where you are,
My thoughts of you are never far.

It was signed, *Anonymous For Now.* A postscript read, *I would like to hear how your doing.* (Whoever it is forgot his grammar and spelling rules.) *Write to Mr. A. F. Now, c/o Bower Depot, Bower, Missouri.*

I *had* to show this to Dovie.

As I reached for the door knob at Doc Everett's office, it opened as if by magic. "Dovie" I yelped. "Just the person I need to see. Can we go to the diner for coffee?"

After Dovie read the letter, she looked hard at me. "Oh, m'love, you have a secret admirer! Have you any idea who?––" The fair skin around her eyes crinkled as she grinned.

"Not unless it was someone in Lock Rivers School. I can't remember farther back than that."

Dovie teased. "Some boy liked you and was too shy to let you know."

"Oh, surely not."

"Why not? You were probably the prettiest girl in the class. Or in the school. And the smartest. Think back."

"Well, I did find Arnie Howard's school picture wrapped in tablet paper and stuck in my history book during fourth grade."

"Aha! See? Even that young, you had––"

"And at an eighth grade party when Homer Neldon closed his eyes, extended his arms and caught me in––" I pointed to my chest.

Dovie laughed. "Didn't you ever have a beau?" she asked, as old Mrs. Haynie refilled our cups.

"No time," I answered. "We all had jobs after school. At least all the ones I knew." Here, as on the street, townspeople who entered and left, smiled at us, or nodded.

"Think! Think!" Dovie cajoled.

"Well––after graduation, pudgy little Turner Ball did admit to liking me. He was amazed that I hadn't realized it. But he married Ollie Fields soon after high school. It's not him."

"It *could* be," she said. "Maybe he's no longer married. Maybe his wife died. Maybe he is still married, but doesn't care."

Dovie was having fun at my expense, but I didn't mind. I paid the bill and walked her to the office. "Do you think I should answer him?"

"Lord, girl, yes! You're a widow now. *And* a newspaperwoman. No telling what kind of story this might turn out to be." She unpinned her nurse's hat, flung her blond hair back and forth, running one hand through it. "Ask Editor Redd if you can go to Bower. I'll bet even that miserly old lass will be glad to pay your ten dollar train fare."

Dovie tucked and pinned her hair back under her cap, secured it, and ran up the steps like a teenager instead of the middle-aged nurse she was. "See you soon. Oh, and thanks for the coffee. You've made my day worthwhile, m'love." She blew a kiss and disappeared into the office.

Walking home, I thought back to the interview techniques I'd learned from Editor Redd. *Don't ask questions that can be answered with a 'yes' or 'no.'* That lets out, 'Are you Turner Ball?' Or, 'You wouldn't happen to be Arnie Howard, would you?' Or, 'Homer Neldon, is that you?'

Never set out cold on an interview. This will take some doing. All I know is his script, that he has access to stationery in the Bower train depot. Might he be the manager? I could call the depot and ask his name, how long he'd worked there, and if he knew Mr. Mashburn in Lock Rivers. No, that would be a 'yes or no' question. Perhaps *how well* he knew Mr. Mashburn at Lock Rivers.

If the manager seemed puzzled by my questions, I might ask him who else has access to the letterhead stationery.

Try to meet your subject on his own turf. Monday, I'll show Editor Redd the letter and ask if I can do an investigative piece on this.

* * * *

"Investigative piece on a four-line letter from a stranger?" she asked, when I proposed the assignment at our weekly meeting. "Why would St. Lukans have any interest in that?" Her sternness had ceased to deter me.

Over the weekend, I had done my homework. Just because I'd spent six weeks in a sanitarium didn't mean I had no ideas. "A human-interest story, then," I countered. "Perhaps it is a cry for help from a homeless person who lost everything in the stock market crash."

"Go on," Editor Redd said. "I'm listening."

"Perhaps it was a janitor, or the manager, a burglar, a––"

"Oh, come now. Don't get melodramatic." The bulky woman shifted in her rolling chair.

I plowed on. "It's someone who knows me. Whether or not he wrote me as a reporter, I do not know. He knew my address and my maiden name and that's scary."

She lit a Marlboro with a paper match from a small cardboard folder on her desk. No gaudy table lighter for this mountain town editor. "Have you had dealings with anyone in Bower? Have you even *been* to Bower?"

"The train stopped there on the way home from––from Rakestraw." Surely she knew where I'd been. I decided to be straight with her. "From the Jacobi H*aus*."

She clacked the lid on the silver and aqua ashtray a time or two and shuffled some papers. "But did you have any contact with anyone? Did anyone get on the train there, or get off?"

"Tom Grindle, Quinn Coursey and I got off and ate in the diner across the street." Just then the image of the peddler man and his cart flashed into memory. "A mountaineer peddler nodded as we walked from the train, but he was gone when we finished eating."

"Tell you what, Liddy," my boss said. "You call the depot from your desk and see what you can find out. If you're still set on this trip by next Monday, I'll reconsider. Is that all?"

This was as good a time as any to ask what I had been wondering since returning to St. Luke. "I do have one question," I dared to say. "Why is Wrennetta Fincher no longer working here?"

The buxom woman who came to this town when she inherited the newspaper seemed almost flustered. She cleared her throat, rose from her chair and swallowed. "Ask me again next week when we talk about your story. I'll tell you then."

Obviously dismissed, I gathered my things and stood. She threw her cigarette butt into the lidded ashtray and disappeared into the restroom. The typesetter walked by and answered my look with a shrug and a palms-up. He wasn't telling either––even if he knew.

— Chapter Fifty-Two —

LIDDY

The second letter from the mysterious person came Monday afternoon. If I hadn't already received one, I might have considered it an April Fool's joke. It read,

Our eyes connected in a flash
when you came through that day.

Tuesday morning, I ran to Editor Redd waving the envelope like a child with a birthday card. "Here's another one! It came yesterday."

Her bushy brows furrowed. "Did you call the depot in Bower yet?"

"No ma'am." Today, her question extinguished my excitement. I felt worse than if she'd thrown a glass of water at me. Sighing, I stepped around the corner to my desk and looked. Nothing was on my news spike. Gathering notepad and pencil, I lifted the receiver and waited for Miz Myrt to say, 'Number please.'

When she did, I asked her to connect me with the Bower operator. This reminded me of the year I came to St. Luke, when we played operator tag to get me from the Outler's. "Bower?" Miz Myrt asked. "Pardon me, but who do you know in Bower, if I may be so bold as to ask."

"That's the problem. I don't know who it is, but I've got to find out." I'd told the telephone operator my business, for heaven's sake! I heard her cough.

A different voice spoke. "Bower. Number please."

"Connect me with the railroad depot manager, please."

Soon a man answered. "Hello, Bower Depot. Olin French here."

"This is Liddy Coursey calling from the *St. Luke Banner*." I stopped for his response, but there was none. "May I ask you some questions, sir?" He cleared his throat but didn't stop me. "How many people have access to depot stationery and stamps?"

The man took his time to answer. "No one but me. And why does your paper want to know that?"

"I received two letters on depot stationery. One last Friday and one yesterday. The envelopes were addressed to me, not to the newspaper."

Editor Redd came to the door. She nodded and flashed as near to a smile as I ever saw.

I acknowledged her signal and continued with my call. "I am trying to find out who might be writing since I do not know anyone in Bower."

"Didn't whoever wrote sign a name?"

"That's the puzzle, sir. The signature was, 'Anonymous for now.' Do you have any ideas, Mr. French?"

"Well, it certainly wasn't me, missy. And my baggage handler never learned to write, so it's not him. The night clerk's busy tending to the passengers and freight that comes in––along with the next day's schedule."

"I have several more questions if you will allow me, sir."

"There's no train scheduled in the next hour. Shoot. I mean, go on."

"Are there hobo camps around the depot? I've read about people leaving home and heading west, but when they ran out of funds, they stopped at camps while looking for work."

"A small group down by the Creel behind the diner is all. They're no trouble. Sometimes they come inside the depot on the coldest nights since we're open all hours. And the diner gives them the leftovers."

I persisted. "When I was through Bower in mid-March, I noticed a peddler with a cart. Who––"

"Oh, he's harmless. Does odd jobs, cleans the depot, keeps the grounds––"

"So there *is* someone else who could pilfer in the stationery drawer?" I might be getting somewhere after all.

Stationmaster French hesitated. "Well, yes––I guess he could, though I have no reason to suspect him. If that's all, miss, I have work to do."

I thanked him, said goodbye and hung up. Then I ran––walked to Editor Redd's desk. She was intent on something and didn't look up for what seemed like five minutes. Finally, she waved me away.

"Too much to do today. Work on your other stories," she said, and went back to her business.

* * * *

For three days, Mrs. Jake, with a twinkle in her eye, handed over a note––each one from 'Mr. A. F. Now.' Tuesday's read,

Our eyes connected in a flash
Though mine I tried to hide.

Try as I might, I couldn't remember locking eyes with anyone on the train or in the diner. That mountaineer seemed familiar, but I didn't get close enough to see his eyes. Hmm.

Wednesday's note said,

I worked in lumber, then in lard.
I bolted from the silence.
Fondly, A. F. Now.

Is that word 'lard'? Or is it 'land'? And what does 'lard' mean? Would this be a childhood doctor––dentist––teacher?––No, no man teachers at Lock Rivers, except Mr. Schott, the county superintendent. I didn't know the janitor or the bus driver's names.

All week, I racked my brain. A customer at the store? A lumber mill worker? The milkman––iceman?

Thursday's message had increased to four lines.

If you will tell me day and hour,
I'll meet you at the train in Bower.
Bring a friend if you're afraid
Because I won't be armed.
A.F. Now

No letter came Friday. That night, my friends and I gathered for dinner at Tom's. Tom put Xann in charge of the dining room and sat with Dovie and Quinn and me. I told them about my letters.

Dovie opened the discussion. "Someone's trying to get back in touch with Liddy, and she wants to find out who it is."

Quinn scowled. "It might be Bird Briley."

"He'd be dangerous," Tom said.

They were talking all around me as if I weren't there. Dovie went on, "Maybe you two could go with her to Bower?"

Quinn turned to Tom. "Maybe it's that peddler who knew our names. Remember, Liddy?" He finally acknowledged that I was sitting among them. "You said there was something familiar about him."

"Yes, and I want to know who he is. I'll talk to Editor Redd Monday. Whenever she decides to let me pursue––if she does––"

Quinn interrupted. "If she does, don't make arrangements over the phone."

Tom added, "There's a tip-off person in St. Luke. We know that for sure." Leaning close and whispering, they said together, "Miz Myrt."

"So that's why she asked who I knew in Bower––as though it caught her by surprise." That also explained her cough.

Dovie dove back in, this time talking to me. "I strongly insist that Tom and Quinn go with you, in case this person has less than honorable intentions." She finished her glass of tea and continued. "Like Bird Briley, who's not above using a dirty trick to snare a trusting person like you."

* * * * *

Monday morning, I came to our meeting as I did every week.

"OK, Liddy. Let's hear what you've come up with," Editor Redd began. "You're like the pestiferous woman whom Jesus helped because she wouldn't go away. She wouldn't take no for an answer. No offense."

This was better than I'd hoped, so I sat on the front of my chair and started in. "First off, my father-in-law and my friend, Tom at the boardinghouse, have insisted on traveling with me––at their own expense, of course, presuming *The Banner* will pay my fare."

"You've got to convince me of the news-worthiness of this trip first. Then we'll see."

She lit a cigarette. Her graying hair was parted in the middle and pulled back in a tight bun. Deep creases, like parentheses, separated her cheeks from her nose to her turned-down mouth. Rimless glasses magnified dull eyes.

After inhaling, she rested her head on the back of the leather chair and blew smoke rings into the upper reaches of the musty room. Then she sat up and looked me in the eye. "So you ride the train to Bower shadowed by two bodyguards. How are you going to know this man when you see him?"

I was ready. "I'll write him before I go, describing my looks, telling him what train I'll be on and that I will have two––male companions, though I do like your term."

She tried to smile and blow smoke at the same time. "Go on."

"I'll ask him how we'll recognize him, and tell him what time our train arrives. I'll ask him to meet us inside the depot." Searching her eyes for any softness or hint of intent, I found none, but I continued. "I'll have his letter in my hand before I buy my ticket."

Editor Redd dropped her cigarette into the elegant ashtray and put the lid on. "Again, I ask, what is newsworthy for St. Lukans? You've worked here for nearly nine years and done very well, but I can't see where this idea is anything more than a personal goal."

I began to see the writing on the wall, but she continued, squirming in her chair, leaning her arms on the desk.

"If this man is a petty thief, a looter or chiseler, a pickpocket or a flim-flammer, that's one thing. But if he's pulled a Dillinger or is a hop fiend or an eel, you should tread carefully. I *do* want you back here."

That was good to hear. Once more I dared hope.

"However, you journeyed here from Lock Rivers, so he must be from there. Hence, I repeat, of what interest to St. Lukans?"

"But––but––" I decided to plunge ahead. "You heard about Brother Bird Briley turning into a gun-toting menace after the Methodists churched him. Why, ever since I've been back, he––"

"I know, I know," she broke in. "Do you want to possibly face him again this soon?"

"But the person who's been writing me sounds harmless. Maybe Bird repented."

"Maybe, *schlaybe*, girl! You're taking your life in your own hands––"

My voice rose to match hers. "But maybe he knows something about Heth's death that he wants to tell me."

Suddenly my boss reddened and coughed. She pulled herself out of her chair and turned to the window. Her cotton hose were rolled around her ankles above sturdy black oxfords.

I slumped, disappointed. "Is that a 'no' answer then?" I asked after a pause.

She turned to face me, composed except for red eyes. "I'll give you some time off. With pay. Preferably over a long weekend. If you can convince me the results are interesting––or newsworthy––I'll consider reimbursing you for the cost of your train ticket. Let me know what you decide. That's all." She sat down again.

"Yes ma'am, thank you ma'am." I stood, but I wasn't through. "You said you'd tell me about Wrennetta. And why Isabel Nance is working here now?"

She took off her glasses, tucked a pencil in her hair and said, "Pardon me, dear Liddy, but I see those as editor's decisions. Remember, you've been on leave since the Christmas holidays. Why don't you forget about them, and concentrate on your own work?"

— Chapter Fifty-Three —

QUINN

The details of our train trip to Bower, where Liddy discovered that her mysterious correspondent was her long-gone father, need not be told. But once we arrived––you can imagine what it was like seeing your father for the first time in what, a dozen years? She dropped her handbag, screamed and ran toward him. He caught her in his arms and lifted her off the floor. They clung to each other for what seemed like an hour.

Their reunion affected us, too. I wiped my eyes and Tom blew his nose as we watched. It was funny how Liddy tested her father further. She stood on tiptoe, grabbed him by the shoulders and said, "Open your eyes!" He obeyed like she was the parent. "Look!" She turned toward us. I told you about his eyes being two different colors." I held out her handbag that she'd dropped.

"I knew," Underhill said, "not to send a clue about eye colors. That would have given it away for sure."

After greetings were over, Liddy introduced Tom and me.

"Oh, I already know these gentlemen," her father said.

Tom spoke for the first time since we stepped off the train. To Liddy, he said, "This man called us by name when we were on our way to pick you up at Rakestraw. That's why, on the way back, when we stopped here for lunch, Quinn and I kept a tight hold on you. Remember?"

She nodded. "I need to use the washroom," she said, and left to get directions.

I had a question for the former mountaineer peddler. "Say, why did you disappear before we came out of the diner that day?"

"Lost my nerve," he answered. "I guess seeing her––seeing that she was really here––spooked me. I wasn't as ready for a meeting as I thought. But I'm ready now. I'm tired of this lonely, dead-end existence."

I continued. "By the way, you never did tell us how you knew our names. Do you have a spy in St. Luke? An informer?"

He looked around to see if Liddy were back. "Have to admit it, I do."

"Miz Myrt?" I asked, looking at Tom.

He nodded. "I'll tell you about that sometime."

When Liddy returned, father and daughter walked once around the depot lobby, arms entwined around each other's waists. Energized by their meeting after too many years, Liddy suddenly stopped when they returned to where Tom and I stood. She whirled around to face her father.

"Come home with me!" she said with more enthusiasm and eagerness that I'd ever seen from her. "With Heth gone, there's plenty of room. We can catch up; get acquainted all over again, adult to adult. Please!" Looking into her father's face with what I perceived as joy and love, she continued. "I can't believe I didn't consider that the letter writer might be you. Forgive me."

"Pshaw!" he said. "Think nothing of it. After being gone so long––"

Tom teased Liddy. "You were thinking of a possible suitor, were you?" Everyone laughed. She reddened and delivered a playful punch to his arm.

The train back to St. Luke would arrive from points west in fifteen minutes. "If you're going with us, better get your things and your ticket," I urged Webb. "This train only stops long enough to unload and load passengers and the mail."

He pulled a bill from his pants pocket and looked at Liddy. "Are you sure, child?"

"Go get your ticket," she said, shooing him in the direction of the clerk. "We have ours already since we paid the extra dollar for a round-trip ticket."

Soon, the stationmaster announced the arrival of the train in route to St. Luke "and points east." Webb spoke quietly to Olin French, who gave the rag-tag peddler––his part-time janitor–– his ticket. The men shook hands. Mr. French lugged a World War I duffle bag through his office door, and Webb dragged it behind him.

"If you're sure," he said once more to this daughter, who was barely a teen when he walked out of her life. She grabbed his other arm and pulled him along as we headed to the platform.

At dusk, our train whistled in to St. Luke. Before it had fully stopped, I smelled smoke. Hurrying from the car, I saw flames alternately billow and wane north on Depot Street. It looked like Liddy and Heth's house. Fire bells clanged, a sign for all men and boys to come running with their buckets. Voices shouted in urgency. "Over here! Get some water over here!"

Lacking a fireplug setup, the town men, as they always did during a fire, began a bucket brigade, hauling water from the town spring across the road. They carried pails past the cedars and as close to the flames as the heat would allow. A line to send the empties back was manned by the boys and circled around to the spring. Hand over hand, the buckets came and went.

A constable's deputy stood guard at the end of Depot Street, barring entrance. When he saw me, he called, "Oh, Mr. Coursey! Miz Liddy's house! They can't get close enough to tell if she got out in time," he shouted.

"Mrs. Coursey is with us," I answered. "She's been to Bower today."

"Thank God! One of the men said he saw a figure running inside the house."

I looked back. The others had detrained. I saw Liddy's hand fly to her mouth.

"Oh no!" I heard her scream. "Oh no!"

Tom moved in beside her, perhaps expecting her to faint as she did at every stressful situation. This time, however, she appeared to steel herself. I walked nearer to offer support and sympathy. In an instant, she began to shiver, and Tom held her with both arms and spoke into her thick hair.

Webb paced. Suddenly, he pulled a flannel shirt from his bag and helped Tom wrap Liddy in it. Then he ran down to the closed street. "I want to help!" he cried. "Let me by!" and soon he was lost in the crowd.

For that matter, I could help, too. "Tom, Liddy, I'm going up the street. Maybe there's something I can do." I looked back once more. Sitting on the top step of the platform, Liddy's head rested on Tom's shoulder. They rocked back and forth, back and forth. I couldn't tell if she was crying.

— Chapter Fifty-Four —

TOM

Oblivious to the tragedy unfolding just a few smoke-filled yards away, the scheduled train and its passengers chugged eastward. Liddy and I sat alone on the platform steps, she nestled in my arms sobbing. I'd dreamed of this moment—–not her sobbing, mind you, but her in my arms—–for many a year.

I thought of all the maxims and proverbs people said to me when my foot was crushed.

So I whispered into her ear, hoping she could hear me over her sobs, "An African proverb says, 'Smooth waters do not make skillful sailors.'" No response.

Dummy, that won't help! I tried again. "Liddy, my love, 'Life becomes harder'—–Schweitzer said, 'when we live for others, but it also becomes richer and happier.'"

She pulled away from my shoulder and turned to me. Her heaves of weeping gradually abated. She still didn't say anything but I sensed from her eyes that she wanted an explanation. As in, *How does that apply to me*? As in, *How can my life get any harder?*

A fresh onslaught of tears sent her back to my shoulder and I tightened my arms around her. Suddenly, an old song came to mind. In her ear, I sang quietly, *Hush, little baby, don't you cry*—–I couldn't think of the rest of the song, so I made something up. *As your friend, I'll hear your every sigh.*

She shifted in my arms; I knew she heard me. So I took a gamble and continued. *If you'll only let me, I will try*—–I had to jiggle an extra syllable in––*to comfort, love, protect you till I die.* There! I'd said it. What I'd been holding in since that day at Outler's. Talk about love at first sight.

Again, Liddy sat up and faced me. Her tear-streaked face was as beautiful as if she were dolled up for a dance. "Tom? Wha?––I don't remember those words in that song."

Again, I said, "Liddy, I have loved you since the first time I laid eyes on you. Remember? At Outler's?"

She smiled wanly and nodded.

"How hard it's been for me to keep my feelings buried all these years. Look at me, Liddy" And when she did, I took a chance and kissed her. She stiffened for an instant, and then softened into the moment. A long moment. *Dear Lord above, what bliss.*

— Chapter Fifty-Five —

DOC

The whole town of St. Luke turned out to investigate the fire. But Dovie, that sweet wife of mine, would not rest until she laid eyes and hands on her best friend, Liddy. Poor girl. As if she hasn't had enough heartbreak in her young life! Dovie and I ran down First Street, parallel to Depot. At least I could examine the girl and be sure nothing was happening that needed medicines. Her tendency to faint under stress might return.

She was in good hands with Tom and didn't require anything in my black bag. She would, however, need a goodly amount of moral support tomorrow and in the weeks ahead. I slipped Dovie two sleeping pills in case Liddy needed them later, and left the two friends holding on to each other. I kissed them both, said goodbye to Tom and made my way back to the crowd.

As I took my post across from the fire, Miz Myrt ran up beside me. I said to her, "Find Mr. Walden. Have him open up the store. Go with him and pick out enough clothes for Liddy for two or three days. All she's got is what she's wearing."

Obediently, Miz Myrt turned and moved through the townsfolk. She liked Liddy, too. Everybody did. "Bring them to the boardinghouse," I called after her. "Please."

I noticed Tom's helper at the edge of the crowd. "Xann!" I called. "Xann!" I motioned to him.

"Yes, Doc, yes?" He twisted his hands.

"Go back to the boardinghouse and prepare a room for Liddy. If you can, give her the one she lived in when she first came to town. You know, the one at the head of the stairs on the left?"

He nodded.

"Freshen it up. Heat water for a bath. Make coffee and set out something to eat. Tom's at the depot with Liddy, so it's up to you, son."

"Yes, Doc, yes sir," the young man said. He turned around and ran the few yards to Tom's. I watched him leap the steps in one bound. He continued across the screened-in porch and disappeared into the dining room.

Someone shouted, "Where's Miss Liddy? Has anyone seen Miss Liddy?"

"She's all right!" I answered.

Another voice called, "Then who was that we saw in her burning house?"

"What'll she do now?" a third person asked. "Where'll she live?"

I tried to calm folks down. "That's why we have a boardinghouse, people. She'll go back to Tom's until we can figure out what to do."

The first man persisted. "But, Doc, who was that in her house?"

"We'll have to wait for the ashes to cool," I said. "Then we'll see what turns up. Go on back home. There's always tomorrow, and it'll come soon enough. Goodnight!"

I, too, wondered. But I'd have to wait like the others. When the flames died, I followed my own advice and drove my car down First Street, turned west at the foot of Little Trot and over the makeshift bridge into the depot yard. There, I discovered a stranger.

Quinn said, "Doc, this is Webb Underhill, Liddy's father. He's the one who's been in touch with her lately."

We shook hands. I eyed him warily, and it seemed he did the same, but neither of us spoke. I finally remembered why I drove down here. "Let's get Liddy in my car," I said. "Xann's preparing a room for her at Tom's."

Dovie piped up. "I'm staying with her tonight, honey! You can go get my overnight bag and bring it to me." Then she turned back to Liddy and Tom who were heading to my De Soto.

Quinn and Webb began walking up now-opened Depot Street. "Meet you at Tom's," I called as I swung the car around and drove back up First Street, cut over to Second, and then climbed the hill to the highway. I drove into Tom's parking lot from the opposite side of the fire. I didn't want Liddy to get too close. Not yet, anyway.

After Dovie took Liddy into the boardinghouse, Quinn, Webb, Tom and I stood outside talking about how the fire might have started. Or if it might have been arson.

Suddenly, Miz Myrt came around the corner, her arms piled with clothes so that she had to look down to see where to step.

"Here, let me take those," I said, and when I did, Myrt let out a scream. We all jumped.

"Webb Underhill!" she shouted. "What are you doing in St. Luke?"

She looked like she'd seen a ghost. How did she know Liddy's father?

"If the boardinghouse dining room is open, Mr. Grindle"––he addressed Tom, then turned back to the lady––"perhaps this would be as good a time as any to tell you all over coffee." He motioned to Quinn and me. We nodded, and began moving up the steps. Webb walked to Miz Myrt and drew her arm through his. She didn't resist.

— Chapter Fifty-Six —

TOM

After Xann had prepared Liddy's former room, he brewed a small urn of coffee. "Get those cookies left over from supper," I suggested. "Is there any cake under the tin?" We might as well eat while we drink. I don't think any of us could possibly sleep now. Unless it's Liddy. Dovie will take care of her tonight and I'll think about what to do next. Doc took the armload of clothes from Walden's upstairs. "I left them with Dovie," he said, returning to sit between Quinn and myself.

Miz Myrt was as giggly as a schoolgirl. Those two surely knew each other before now. We all doctored our coffee, and engaged in a little small talk and a cookie. Then we turned to Webb, who was sitting next to Miz Myrt. We wanted a story. Here is what he told us.

Webb's journey

I walked east toward the Creel River. I had no identification, no money, and no baggage. I could be who I wanted to be. At the first port I came to, I hired on as a freight loader, a paddle man, a construction worker—anything. No one asked questions. I slept behind buildings (without dogs), in unlocked buses, and under them, if they were locked, and on porch overhangs of shacks near the river. I scavenged for cover and scraps from restaurants, begged like a hobo from a train, suffered mosquito bites, washed in the river and finally, after I'd earned enough pay, bought another set of clothes and some food. I kept traveling west, following the river and the railroad. Whenever I ran out of food and money, I stopped and hired on as a log hauler or a sawyer. Again, when I had earned enough, I continued west.

Near a rise on the river outside Bower, I found an abandoned shack that a scrawny hound still called home. One fall day during a monstrous storm, I heard a tremendous crash outside. After the rain stopped, I looked down the ravine. I could see a wagon broken to pieces and a mess of everything strowed out around it.

I began trips up and down from cabin to ravine, hauling up everything I could carry. The dog got what was edible and I got the rest. By mid-afternoon, I had picked the place clean. What a find! Now, I could have a peddler's job without buying anything. Poor unlucky sod whose wagon it was.

Later that afternoon, the dog snarled softly and loped over to the rise. I followed, but stayed hidden. Two men on small horses were in the ravine near where the wagon fell. I watched them look around and talk together. Soon, they turned and rode back the way they came.

For the rest of the week, I fashioned two good wheels out of the four broken ones, made myself a little cart, and in a few days, filled it with the dried out fabrics, sewing notions, spelling books, hats, scarves––anything I could salvage and make presentable. I picked my way through the woods to a trail that led to a clearing at the depot.

Olin French hired me to clean up around the place, unload baggage and keep the grounds picked up. He let me leave my cart in the maintenance shack each evening.

One day, while I fished close to the western shore of the Creel, from an abandoned flatboat, I came upon a scene that pulled me like a magnet. I came back to it over and over. I finally decided to climb ashore to see if I could build myself a cabin.

This is what I saw. Three old-growth hardwoods––their broad roots grown out of the ground and high into the air––looking like Greek columns side by side. That could be one entire wall. Undergrowth would fill any holes from the eyes of passing boaters.

Before I could get my mind and finances around how to finish a house in such a precarious place as the Creel River, Stationmaster French asked me to drive a Mr. Boss Lincoln from Bower to St. Luke. He had ridden the train from Springfield to Bower. He wanted to see about adding a branch of his car dealership in St. Luke.

That's when I saw Miz Myrt streetwalking. Sorry, Myrt, I mean walking on the street toward the diner. We go back a long way, in case any of you don't know, and over lunch, I also discovered that my Liddy lived here.

Well, right then, my hankering for a new home on the river vanished. Instead, I began writing Liddy these little lines that I hoped wouldn't scare her. I needed to find out how she felt about me after I'd been gone so long, so I asked her to meet me in Bower, and you know the rest.

— Chapter Fifty-Seven —

LIDDY

"Come in?" I answered to a soft rap on the door. I was still abed, still a little disoriented from all that happened yesterday.

The door opened tentatively. Editor Redd stood there, a sheaf of roses in the crook of one arm and a book in her other hand. "May I come in?" she whispered. "I know these blooms won't bring back your house and your possessions, but they will tell you how sorry I am. And here's a new journal. The pen's inside."

"How sweet of you." I motioned to the water pitcher on the table "Dunk the flowers in there. I'll ask Tom or Xann to bring a vase. Or I'll bring one back when I go to lunch. Pull up a chair––and forgive me for being so lazy this morning. It's not Monday, is it?"

"No, Liddy, it's Sunday." The bulky woman reached out and lifted a straight chair like it was made of balsa wood. She moved it close to the bed. "Besides, bless your heart," she said, sitting carefully, "you take as much time off as you need."

Apparently, she wanted to visit. This was a side of my boss I'd never experienced. I wondered if she were interviewing me for a news article. But it didn't matter. I took a deep breath, looked around the room and then back at Editor Redd.

"*Déjà vu,*" I said. "After nearly nine years, I'm back in the room I lived in when I first came to St. Luke." I smoothed the sheet and blanket around me. "Dovie made me swallow one of Doc's sleeping pills last night, and I slept soundly, even though everything I owned had gone up in flames."

Another rap on the door. "Yes?"

Xann peeked in. "Anything I can get you, Miss Liddy?"

I turned to Editor Redd. "Coffee?"

She nodded. "Hot, strong and black."

"Thank you, Xann. Two coffees, please. One strong and black and one weaker with sugar. Both hot. Thank you."

I continued where I'd left off. "When I finally awoke, Dovie was still sleeping over there." I motioned to the divan with pillows along the back. "Xann had brought extra linens when I told him she was staying overnight."

Xann knocked and brought the coffees in on a tray. He hesitated, unsure where to set it.

"At the foot of the bed will be fine," I said. "Do you know Editor Redd, Xann?" They nodded to each other. "Oh, and will you move these flowers to a vase?" I gave him the pitcher. "And draw me some fresh water, please?"

"Yes, Miss Liddy. The cup with the spoon in it is the strong one," he said, and disappeared.

Since my guest was closer to the tray, she handed me my cup and then took hers, laying the spoon back on the server.

"Umm," she said, and downed the hot liquid without a pause. She must have a lead-lined stomach. I only sipped mine and I could feel it burn going down.

"Tell me," she said, setting her cup back on the tray, and replacing the spoon, "what did you find in Bower? Was it worth the trip?" She scratched one of her thick eyebrows. "Will it be a story interesting to St. Lukans?"

"It was definitely worth the trip," I said. "I found my father!"

"Your father?" the woman repeated. "Was he your correspondent?"

I nodded and smiled. "He's in town as we speak. In fact, he is also staying at the boardinghouse. I had convinced him to live with me for the time being, but––"

My boss brightened. "Perhaps there's a story here after all. For tomorrow's paper, I'll report on the fire. It's raining right now. That will deaden any embers and leave skeletons of what is left of your furnishings. Plus reveal the remains of the one seen in your house."

I wondered what that had to do with my father. But she continued, "Then I will do a story on you and your father. St. Lukans will want to know that something positive will come from the loss of your house and belongings."

It was my turn to brighten. "Oh, thank you! That would be wonderful. My sewing machine and Gramma's trunk full of treasures will be gone. And my clothes––they don't matter." I pointed to the pile of new things Miz Myrt brought last night from Walden's. "I'll be indebted to the folks in this town forever, that's for sure."

Editor Redd leaned in closer. "Do you have any idea that it was Brother Bird who?––"

But she stopped. "We'll have to wait to find out––like everyone else." She stood, "I'd better go, my dear. You take care of yourself and come into the office when you are ready." She lifted the chair and set it where she'd found it.

"Thank you again for the flowers and the journal," I said. "And for the visit. I think I won't need Dr. Jacobi this time. I learned very well what questions to ask, and how to keep from taking the blame. And I've memorized several mantras to help keep my perspective and deal with it."

"Excellent, excellent. We'll all be rooting for you. Goodbye." And she was gone.

As soon as she'd had time to walk down the stairs, across the dining room and out the front door, Tom rapped. "I've come for the coffee things," he said.

He lifted the tray from the bed, moved it to the divan, and then came back to the side of the bed. "What I really wanted was an excuse to see you again." He drew the chair Editor Redd had so recently vacated up close.

"Have you thought about what I told you last night? I know it's too soon after––after everything that's happened––but you must know how I feel––and how long I've loved you––no matter where you were or where I was."

He reached for my hand that lay on the coverlet closest to him. I didn't pull it away.

"No," I said, "I had no idea you wanted to be more than a friend. And I'm sorry for yelling at you and Quinn the day I returned. I was ungracious. You both had my safety in mind. Forgive me." I laid my left hand over his and smiled into his eager eyes.

He leaned out of the chair and kissed me quickly, then kissed both of my hands before he placed them back on the bed. "You're safe with me, my dear, dear Liddy. I hope you can learn to love me." He stood, blew a kiss, turned and walked to the tray and picked it up. Holding it high in one hand like an experienced waiter, he opened the door with the other. "See you at lunch," he said, his eyes sparkling over a crooked grin.

I leaned back on the headboard. Things were happening so fast. I reached for my journal and pen.

— Chapter Fifty-Eight —

LIDDY

I needed a day away. A little before noon, on the middle Saturday of May 1940, I sat on the massive and well-tended lawn of Sadberry Park, near Springfield, and leaned against the trunk of a redbud. No children or animals roamed this section, thank goodness.

I drove several hours to find a place where no deadlines loomed, no printing presses clacked and no phones rang. And where I could escape the incessant chatter of Isabel Nance who acted like Keener Junior was the only baby ever born in St. Luke. She didn't know––and I wouldn't tell her––that after a miscarriage, I never had a chance to get pregnant again. I must keep smiling at her and pretending interest, even though I hurt inside to hear talk of babies.

Morning breezes soughing through the pines, birdsong near and far, the cool shade––this was my favorite kind of quiet.

Relaxing into the ambience of the open space, I opened my Jacobi *Haus* journals to look for a column idea––my only concession to the newspaper office. I turned to an entry written after a one-on-one session with Zindi––the same woman I shared a dinner table with one night.

But I wasn't quite ready to read. The expanse of the Sadberry lawn looked as large as our yard back in Lock Rivers, but this one was uncluttered. No sassafras grove with an understory of forsythia. Gramma's day-lilies that grew beside the grove had produced no blooms that I could remember. Once I freed them from encroaching privet sprouts, honeysuckle, and several years' growth of yellowbell, and enough sun got through, they finally bloomed.

That February day at the Jacobi *Haus*, I transcribed every word of Zindi's I could get down, using abbreviations and high school shorthand.

I wrote that day, so I wouldn't have to look at her. She was everything I wasn't. Jean Harlow-blond, tall and willowy, able to wear bold colors and prints, like Frona Lee wore but shouldn't have. Flashy, with nice teeth and fair skin. Vivacious. As she talked, her hands moved constantly. Her eyes and mouth dramatized any subject at hand.

She broke the rules and got away with it. If she felt bad or got her period, she'd stay in bed until mid-morning, especially on days she was to give a demonstration or a presentation. She tried to get back into Dr. Jacobi's good graces by talking long and confidently. If it worked for him, it did not work with those of us who resented her.

If we were outside during free time, she shined up to the men, even interrupting their work––the gardeners, the carpenters building a greenhouse––old, young, homely or handsome, unkempt and not. It didn't matter.

Several times, she begged the doctor for one-on-one sessions she'd missed, and he usually obliged her, even if he needed to be elsewhere.

Envy? Jealousy? Righteous indignation? Maybe. But in one thing I could top her: working at *The Banner* gave me an edge in grammar and vocabulary usage. Zindi was Mrs. Malaprop personified.

"I pride myself on having a photogenic memory," Z. began on this particular day. "I can remember every person who registered at the Rakestraw during the time I worked there. And where they lived."

"How long was that?" I asked, but she ignored me.

"From McQuiggan came the Sage Thomases and the Featherses, and a man named Mack. And Dr. Hadfield, a dentist, who I heard later, had been thrown by a runaway horse down in Arkansas."

Ants crawled from the grass onto my shoes. Thoughts of home intruded, like the tiny gnats flying around my face. In the middle of *our* yard, wisteria attached itself to the lower branches of a barren walnut tree from Mother's home place. At its base, crape myrtle suckers sprouted and leaned, searching, too, for sunlight.

I bent back to the journal entry. "The Riddles and the Motherwells, and a whole clan named Hooks, who gathered to one side and sniffed like pampered cats at whoever walked by. There were the Halls and the Blockers, or rather Mr. Hall and Mrs. Blocker, and Berry Case, whose hair, they say, fell out in clumps one Halloween."

Diagonally across this part of the park is an area that could be someone's backyard. At its center are three recovering willow oaks—–victims of last year's ice storm. Underneath, two rusty washing line posts appear to stand guard over iris beds and day-lilies––clothes of the fields. A bush hollyhock grows narrow and tall. From this distance, it resembles a Rose of Sharon, which Grandmother sometimes called Althea.

Back to Zindi. "Slate Cicero was an extinguished gentleman from Oklahoma. He came only once, wearing a white suit"––she called it suite–– "and fedora. Before he left, he fought with the stable groom over poker winnings.

"From west Missouri came the Winters and the U. B. O. Swans, and Eddy and Flay Chambers. And the Gilberts and Juice Ponder. Mr. Ponder stayed three days before he got carded off to the local jail so drunk, out on the road that Mrs. Ames-West's audio's tires ran over his left hand."

I looked up from my reading and shifted to a more comfortable position. The ground seemed harder and the tree's leafy shade had vanished. Nearby, a robin pecked for food. Quietly, I stood and backed away toward the bench by a stone wall. The bird kept to its task.

As I read, I continued to marvel at the skill of Zindi's recall.

"Cotton Leary always came with four girls. They were never the same ones but were enough alike that it seemed that they'd been here before. They never stayed long, and their names were Rose, or Blossom, or Rosebud, or Lily. Others were named April, or May, or June. A few of his girls had place names. I remember Savannah, and Dixie, and Tulsa.

"Say," she said, after stopping to get a breath. "Would you like to write my autobiography?"

I looked at my watch. It was time to head back to St. Luke. No, I *did not* want to write Zindi's biography, but this recall talent of hers might make a good newspaper column. I'll propose it to Editor Redd on Monday.

— Chapter Fifty-Nine —

This mid-June morning was typical of Missouri Ozarks weather—–it would soon be near eighty degrees after a night-time low in the mid-sixties. As I walked to *The Banner* office, rested from the weekend, I was eager to get about my work.

Editor Redd's Lincoln Zephyr was not in its usual spot, even after 9:00. If my boss was anything, she was punctual. And she is never ill enough to miss work. Hmm. I pushed open the door as usual, and as usual, there sat Isabel Archer Nance, new mother and new receptionist.

Her eyes widened when she saw me, and she suddenly stood. "Editor Redd left word that if you come in, to tell you that you can go back home today. With pay. She is—–away on business."

I didn't buy it, and I wasn't leaving. My boss had been mysterious about Wrennetta and Isabel. Something was up, and I intended to find out what it might be. "No, I have some work to do—–"

Isabel walked around the desk and blocked my way down the hall. "No, Liddy. I had instructions to keep you out of the office today—–"

I picked up an empty news spike from her desk and waved it in the air. "Get out of my way, girl, or I'll jab your—–"

She hugged the back wall and sidled to safety behind her desk. "But–-I'll get in troub—–"

"I don't care. I've worked here longer than you have. That gives me some seniority." I slammed the news spike back on her desk. "Now leave me alone." I stalked to my three-walled cubbyhole of an office that opened into the hall and the printing machines.

Suddenly, the bell on the Teletype machine sounded. Out of curiosity, I hurried over to see if the incoming story might be usable in an article or a column. I caught the last of the message: "––netta Fincher's trial this morning at Madison as an accomplice in the faked death last December of a well-known St. Luke peddler."

I screamed.

But I didn't faint.

Isabel came running. "I told you you weren't supposed to come––I don't know why folks around here have been trying so hard to keep you from knowing––I guess they thought you were not strong enough to take the news. I'm sorry." With one hand, she reached out to comfort me.

"I'm sorry, too, Isabel, for threatening you when you only did what you were told." We cried in each other's arms––she in sympathy, I suppose, and me?–– With the pain of knowing that my life was frozen again, just when I thought I could move on to other planes and places.

I gathered my things, and we walked to the office door. I hugged the young mother who was trying to be a good employee. "Tell Editor Redd whatever you need to that will keep you in her good graces. I'll figure out how to tell her that I know. Without bringing you in to it."

She sniffled. "Thank you, Liddy. Maybe someday we can be––friends. Goodbye."

I walked down the steps that I'd so lately come up. *Heth's alive! My husband's alive!* I stepped around the Reserved for Editor parking sign, and put one foot in front of the other till I reached the edge of the lot. A bench under a large oak seemed to beckon. And I needed to think. Even after such a shocking discovery, I was aware of the beautiful day. (Doctor Jacobi counseled us to find something positive for every negative.) A warm breeze surrounded me like a shawl. Day lilies and tickseed coreopsis bloomed nearby. Birds chirped. The air smelled of last night's rain. The natural world was in its prime, but mine had suffered a jolt.

Just then, as fast as a bolt of lightning, I knew what I had to do. I stood, picked up my handbag and valise, and headed toward the courthouse. This decision was non-negotiable.

Inside the Gillette County-South Clerk's office, Omega West, deputy clerk, greeted me.

"I know about Heth, Mrs. West," I said to her. "You can spread the word that folks don't have to guard their tongues any longer."

She hadn't said a word so far, but when I finished speaking, she let out a long breath. "Thank goodness! We haven't known about it too long ourselves. Then you know why Mrs. Fincher's not in this office today?"

"Yes," I said. "I saw a wire at *The Banner* telling about the trial. Now, what I want to do this morning is file for an annulment or a divorce. Can you help me?"

As a non-verbal answer, she lugged an oversized ledger from a back table, hoisted it to the counter and opened it. "As short as I am," she said, "I have to use a step stool to see the entries." She climbed up. "What year were you married?"

"Nineteen-thirty-three. In early November. On a Sunday."

"Who married you?"

"Doc Everett. Brother Briley walked off when we didn't have the money to pay him.

"Roscoe Everett? Was he a Justice of the Peace?"

"I suppose so. He took over, anyway."

"Yes, he has a bad habit of running just about everyone and everything in this town," Omega West said, as she kept turning the giant pages. "I'm not finding your marriage license, Liddy."

"We both signed it. Mrs. Fincher brought it over to the boardinghouse that day Heth returned from his trip." I leaned over to see the ledger. "Might it be in the Madison records?" I asked. "With two county seats, might documents accidentally end up in the wrong one?"

"Good idea. I'll call them. Excuse me." She walked into a side office.

While Mrs. West was on the phone, I paced the width of the waiting area, back and forth, back and forth. The dark wooden floor smelled of cleaning oil like our schoolrooms in Lock Rivers. A sun catcher with a hummingbird hung on a north window.

Omega West finally returned. "The strangest thing," she said, "Madison didn't have a record of your marriage license, either, though they'd had recent inquiries from a Genese Underhill about a legal matter."

"That's my mother! Hmm. I wonder what––Oh, well. What shall I do, then? Are we not legally married unless the license is filed?"

"Let me call the Bureau of Vital Statistics and see if they can find anything." She disappeared again.

I looked at a large map of Gillette County-South––zoning, voting, and township boundaries. *Just when I've gotten used to being a widow.* A bright new poster with "I Want You"––and a stern Uncle Sam pointing a finger at the audience. A*nd living alone.* Under the picture, "For the United States Army." In small letters at the very bottom, was "US Army Recruiting Service, June 6, 1940." A*nd loving it.*

"Nothing there, either, I'm afraid," Mrs. West said, as she came back to the counter. "Maybe you're not married after all, Liddy." She smiled wryly. "The last resort would be Doc Everett himself. Shall I call him?"

"Please do, yes. I'll wait."

Again, the woman disappeared. Again, I paced the waiting area. I finally sat in one of the heavy brown chairs. *Not married! Ever? Have all these seven years really been a lie? My unhappiness could have been avoided? Heth's, too? Oh, what wasted days and nights! Years, even.*

"Good. You're sitting down, Liddy," she said when she returned. "Doc found your marriage license in his filing cabinet. He forgot to bring it by this office and have it recorded."

"Y–You mean," I sputtered, "––we've never been married––legally?"

"It appears so," she answered. "This is the first time I can remember such a thing happening. I'll write a letter detailing all my attempts to locate a license if you wish, then when Mrs. Fincher comes back, she can notarize it. I'll make a copy for you and for our records."

I nodded. "Please do. I'll check back every day. Thank you very much."

Two monstrous discoveries in the same morning. Oh my goodness! Oh my goodness! In the years before the Jacobi *Haus*, I would have fainted dead away. But now––I'm just angry––furious, in fact. And in an odd way, relieved.

—— Chapter Sixty ——

On my way home from the courthouse, I stopped by the post office. Mrs. Jake handed me a thick letter from Mother. The postmistress must have known about the scandal, for she didn't speak, just nodded and smiled. I didn't tell her that I already knew.

No wonder Mrs. West at the courthouse heard from Madison that a Genese Underhill had filed some legal business.

It turns out that in mid-March, after courting Mother for seven years, Mr. Ferrel gave her an ultimatum: either file for divorce and marry him or he was through. Several earlier trips to Madison for this very reason had gotten balled up in red tape and Mother's ignorance of the system, she said in her letter.

Finally, she found an official who filed her papers, but told her to keep looking for her husband. After three months, she received a certificate of divorce. A notice was published in the Madison newspaper, she said. Mother and Mr. Farrel were married the next week. Mr. Ferrel hired Mrs. Bishop to care for his mother and the newlyweds lived in Genese's house.

I never thought to tell Mother that Daddy was living in St. Luke. Too late now.

But when I see Daddy at supper, I'll tell him about Mother and Mr. Farrel.

"Your mother's married again?" Daddy asked, when I told him. "That means I'm a single man?"

"Looks that way," I answered.

"Thank you very much, my dear," he said, kissing me on the cheek. "You have made me a happy man." My father breezed out the front door of the dining room and tripped down the steps like Heth did those seven long years ago. I would soon learn why.

Chapter Sixty-One

MIZ MYRT

If Mother didn't send me the Madison Gazette every week, I would have missed this trial altogether. And why is it in Madison when St. Luke is also a county seat? Perhaps the lawyers agreed on the farther courtroom because of its size. And the sensitive nature of the crime to the three families in St. Luke.

Since Liddy Coursey works for the paper, Editor Redd obviously chose not to publicize the trial in *The Banner*. Small town newspapers must have an unwritten code not to upset their customers––or their employees. Even if it means keeping the whole town in the dark.

I pulled up in front of my childhood home. I would spend the night with Mother, so I could be in the courtroom early enough to get a good seat.

I'd thought for the longest that there was something fishy about Heth Coursey's death. No one ever saw or heard what was in the note––just the little bit that came out in Editor Redd's article afterwards––that he was dumped in the Creel River. If *that* was true, just one more piece of river garbage, I'd say.

"Hello, Mother. No, I can get this case by myself. Don't come down those steps."

Poor Sula Mae. It's a good thing she didn't live to see what her last-born turned into. I don't see how Quinn stands it either, but he puts on a brave face––for a fellow with a son in jail.

"Yes, Mother, I asked Esther to work my switchboard this morning and in return, I promised I'd take detailed notes and tell her everything.

No, I won't stay the whole weekend, just tonight and part of tomorrow. I'll treat you to lunch after the trial if it ends early enough."

Mother sometimes forgets things. She asked me again why I came to see her.

"A St. Luke woman's being tried as an accomplice in a faked death. You remember Webb Underhill? His daughter's husband disappeared last July and everyone thought he was dead. They're just now catching up with him."

I spread my things on the guest bed––the one that used to be mine––and then drew a glass of water from the kitchen faucet.

"It's thought that this woman helped pull off the hoax," I explained to Mother, "but she pled 'not guilty.' That's why there's a trial."

* * * *

The bailiff strode to the front of the room. "All rise," he bellowed, then looked down at the paper in his hands. "The state of Missouri vs. Wrennetta Fincher." He also gave the name of the presiding judge, who walked in from his chambers through black curtains. The judge motioned for us to sit. I didn't get his name or those of the prosecutor and defense lawyer. They were all new since I lived in Madison.

Little ol' Wrennetta Fincher. Still pudgy at twenty-eight and wearing a gathered shirtwaist with the stripes going around. Tsk, tsk. Her wide patent belt did nothing to mask those extra pounds, either. I looked around and saw her mother Verna Lue and Mr. Fincher––I didn't even remember his name. They were staring straight ahead, poor things.

The bailiff held the Bible and swore the girl in, then motioned her to the witness chair. A head band the same color as her belt corralled her brown hair styled in a pageboy cut.

After all the preliminaries, the prosecutor got down to business.

"Miss Fincher, will you describe for the court your whereabouts from December 11 until now, six months later, this June 17?"

She didn't bat an eye. "On Monday, December 11, I had permission from Editor Redd at the *St. Luke Banner* to travel to Drury College in Springfield for their journalism week."

"And what was your assignment at Drury?"

"I thought––and Editor Redd agreed––I might be able to help the students with stories of my experience at the paper."

"And did you travel to Springfield? To Drury?" The courtroom sat as silent as a sanctuary after a funeral.

She paused for a split second. "No. No, sir."

"Will you tell the court what you did instead?"

"I drove to Brownriver Settlement." A few quiet gasps.

"What were you driving, Miss Fincher?"

"My father loaned me a Deuce 32 from his car lot."

"Will you tell the court where Brownriver Settlement is located?"

"In the boot heel on the banks of the Creel River."

"About how many miles from St. Luke, would you say?"

"The gauge was broken. It took me two days to get there."

"And what did you do after you arrived at your destination?

Silence. Wrennetta looked at her parents as if to say 'I'm sorry.'

"Did you understand my question, Miss Fincher?"

"Yes, sir. I found a room in the Settlement Hotel."

"You *found* a room? Would you explain that? Do you mean you registered for a room in your own name?"

"Uh––"

"The court can't hear you."

"I discovered that Heth Coursey was living there."

"How did you find that out? Hadn't he been gone from home since July of last year?"

" A source told me that Heth had gotten in a little trouble down at the shipyard where he worked, and that the river patrol had called the sheriff wanting to know if Heth was who he said he was." She looked right at me.

"Go on."

"The person asked me to tell Liddy Coursey so she would know where her husband was. My––informant said he had taken up with some 'dirty, rotten gypsies and that they were worse than––'"

"And did you tell Mrs. Coursey where her husband was?"

Silence.

"Shall I repeat my question?"

"No."

"Why not?"

Wrennetta exploded. "Why should I? She horned in on my territory when she moved from wherever she came from. Heth was *my* boyfriend. I set my cap for him when I was just a girl. This woman even got hired by Editor Redd. Can you imagine how hard it is to work with someone who stole your man?" She slumped back in her chair.

The judge spoke up. "Just answer the question, Miss Fincher. No need to go into hysterics."

"Let's go back to your trip to Brownriver. Did Heth Coursey know you were coming to the Settlement?"

Silence. Before the man could chastise her, Wrennetta answered. "I wrote him a letter addressed and sealed in a second envelope. I sent it in care of the river patrol with a note of explanation."

"Would you tell the court what was in the note to the river patrol?"

"I said that he was my uncle, and I needed to tell him about a family emergency."

"Did you receive an answer from Mr. Coursey?"

"I object," shouted the defense lawyer.

The judge straightened up in his chair. "Is Mrs. Coursey in the courtroom? Are any of Mrs. Coursey's immediate family in the courtroom?"

There was no answer.

"Overruled. Continue with the prosecution. But can you wrap it up?" He looked at the prosecutor and then at his watch.

"Yes, sir. The contents of the letter, Miss Fincher?"

"He said to come on down. That he would tell the desk clerk his niece would be arriving soon and would be staying for a few days."

"Thank you. Let me remind you of the charges against you, Miss Fincher. Aiding and abetting the false accusation of death; causing city, county and river patrol expenditures for searching the Creel River; anguish and eventual hospitalization of Mrs. Coursey after her husband's said demise; the cost of said treatment; the anguish of Mr. Coursey's father and siblings; the theft of Mr. Coursey's affections––Shall I go on?"

"Stop! Stop! All right, I admit it. Heth and I worked out the details of his death together. He said he never wanted to go back to St. Luke again."

— Chapter Sixty-Two —

LIDDY

On September first, two years after discovering I was never officially married, I was cleaning my room in the boardinghouse, where I continued to live after my home burned. I changed the linens, dusted and swept, trying to stay in front of the old wire fan that blew air in from the north window. A hickory tree stood close to the building and provided shade during most of the day.

Tom had offered more than once for me to move into his suite of rooms, and he would take mine. When I refused, he countered––his glittering eyes and crooked grin teased me––that I could move in with him. Again, I refused. He courted me as gallantly as any of Jane Austen's heroes ever courted her heroines. I loved that. It's nice to trust someone like I trusted Tom. And I was beginning to believe that I loved him.

Suddenly, a sharp double rap on the door startled me. "Tom! What a surprise! Come in. I was––"

He interrupted me with a quick hard kiss on the mouth. "Liddy," he said in a voice desperate with urgency. "I need you to go up to the Ponders on Little Trot as fast as you can. Mrs. Ponder's in labor for the fifth time and Dovie's not answering her phone. I'm not sure this woman can go through childbirth again by herself––"

"Tom, I don't know anything about––"

"She'll tell you what to do. Just get her in bed and ask her to lead you. She's done this before. I imagine she's got it down to a––Xann will take you in my pickup. He's delivered meals up there. He knows the way."

"But––Give me fifteen minutes."

"Thanks, love." He kissed me again. "The Ponder boys showed up at the boardinghouse just now. I'll try to keep them busy doing something today—raking leaves, straightening my shop, working in the kitchen."

On the drive up the mountain, Xann repeated what the oldest boy said his mama's warnings were before they started their trip down. *Keep to the path and don't kill any toad frogs or Belle'll give bloody milk—and we'll need good milk for this new mouth. And keep your eyes 'n ears open—rattlers is sheddin'. This time of year, they go blind, and'll strike out at any swish. Maybe Tom'll walk you halfway back by dark. By then, you'll have a new brother. Or sister. Lord God, where'll we stash this 'un in this crowded house—guess a drawer's good a place as any.*

When we arrived, Xann walked ahead of me, but he turned and said, "This lady's got superstitions you've never heard of, so don't be surprised. Do what she asks." He pushed open the door. "Miz Ponder? It's Xann. From the boardinghouse? I've brought you some help."

Just then, the opposite door opened and my mental picture of a mountain woman appeared there. She was dragging a wooden washtub behind her. When she saw Xann, she let out a sigh of relief.

"I've brought you some help, Miz Ponder. This here's Miss Liddy. You just take it easy and tell the lady what needs doing. Nurse Dovie will be here later." I saw Xann cross his fingers behind his back. Turning to me, he whispered, "She's all yours," and left, closing the door quietly behind him.

"Liddy, did Xann say? Nice name. Xann's a nice boy." The woman's shapeless housedress was as thin as the slippers she wore. Her graying hair that had not seen a brush in several mornings fell to her shoulders.

"Yes, ma'am," I said. "I'm new at this, so please tell me what I can do to help."

"You can set the kettle a'boil—an' I'll bring in that sack of rags 'afore the pain puts me down. Lay out the scissors—I drug this washtub in to catch the blood. God knows I won't have the strength to scrub out these ol' planks again—I learn't that when Weems came. Now where's that chair with the cane missin'?"

She pointed into a dark corner behind me. I brought the chair over. "Put it right over the tub. That's turned out to be the perfect birthin' chair. When Sharp—he's my third boy—found it in a trash pile in the loggin' ditch, he lugged it home like he'd found a goldmine."

"When the water boils—pour it in the reservoir and—ohmigod—heat another one. Thank goodness, Weems brought up two bucketsful this time. Don't think I could man––" She bent over in pain until the contraction subsided.

"And that old' shuck mattress––daren't pollute it and have to make another'n. Liddy, I'm thinkin' there's a rubber raincoat hanging in the back hall. It could go next to the mattress. There's sheets and blankets in the bureau––" She pointed and I hurried, though I had to raise a window shade to find the dresser.

"Ouch. Stop kickin', you little devil. Gotta set by a window––don't want the little booger to grow up lovin' the dark ––Oh, Lord, the hurtin's gettin' worse and worse and closer and closer. While I can still think straight––Miss Liddy, hand me that there dried foxglove and that bottle of wine under the sink. Both me and the bairn'll need strong heartbeats to get through this. Bring me that mandrake root in the window. With the wine it'll ease the pain––"

Hurry, Dovie, hurry, I prayed. I didn't know whether to lift her to the bed that I'd spread an inch deep with washable coverings, or wait till she gave the word.

"Please Lord, don't let the pain be too strong this time," the woman prayed aloud, like she was used to talking to God everyday. "Thank you for sending this angel. Help us get through this, Lord, and I'll kill––ooh!––where's the chair––that man of mine if he ever comes near me again. I promise you, Lord." She was panting and sweating. "You done give me four boys, and so help me if they foller in his no-good, boot-leggin' footsteps, I'll––"

I decided it must be time, so I lifted her tiny frame to the bed. "Breathe, Miz Ponder, breathe, breathe, oh––"

Light flooded the room as the door opened. "Oh, Lord, did another angel just walk in?––"

Dovie moved into action. "Mrs. Ponder? I'm Dovie Everett, remember? The mid-wife? I came as fast as I could." Her black bag was open when she ran in. "Liddy, bring me a pan of hot water. Pull that table over and set the pan on it. Then––Oh my goodness, I see its head. Push, Miz Ponder, push. Liddy, go hold her hands. Be careful her fingernails don't break the skin of your arms. These country women are strong. They have to be."

"Blankets in the chest––mmmmmm."

"She's out. Those herbs and that wine finally kicked in. Happens every time. Just when she thinks she can't stand it any longer, she goes to sleep. She'll be fine. This baby's nearly here."

All night, all day, angels watchin' over me, my Lord. All night, all day, angels watching over me. I couldn't believe my ears. This frail little woman was singing through her pain. Soon, we joined her ––three voices blending throughout this pitiful hovel. In an instant, the cry of a newborn took over.

"Lord, what's that sound––a bairn's cry?––My eyes––so heavy––Angels, are you still here?––A boy, you say?––Can I hold 'im?––Name?––Angel––Angelo? That'll be 'is name–– Angelo. For you two angels. You wanna hold him?"

"You can wash him off, Liddy," Dovie held the towel-wrapped infant toward me. "Use those rags over there. They look clean. And this water's cooled off enough." Dovie brought the pan of water to the counter. "Here, lay him here."

Such a powerful feeling came over me at that instant, I didn't know if I'd be able to stand. Finally, to hold a baby after all these years. *Hush little baby, don't you cry––* I couldn't remember the words, and I couldn't see the child under my hands. My eyes were so full of pent-up tears that I stood there and sobbed through my humming. Somehow, I cleaned the little thing, and Dovie weighed and measured him. Could that thin, tired woman manufacture milk for this tiny creature? I gave him to Dovie and she nestled him in his mother's arms.

"Th' Lord, be praised! Hallelujah––for helpin' me get through––this––soft bed––"

They both slept.

Dovie and I wept.

— Chapter Sixty-Three —

TOM

Dovie dropped by the boardinghouse to see Liddy three or four days after they delivered Angelo Ponder. I hurried out of the kitchen and asked her how things had gone that day. But before she could answer, I told her how proud I was of Liddy for helping Miz Ponder, especially with no experience in birthing babies.

"You should have seen Liddy cry while bathing that newborn," Dovie said about her friend. "With all those tears in her eyes, I don't see how she could have seen him. It's a wonder she didn't drop him. That girl wants a baby more than anyone I've seen in a long time," she said. I hope one day she finds a way––" she nudged me playfully––"to get one."

"I'm trying," I said, "to get up enough nerve to ask her to marry me. Sometimes, I think she loves me back, but other times, she seems distracted and far away. Do you think she still loves Heth?"

"I doubt it, Tom. In fact, I'm not sure she ever loved him in the traditional way."

"I don't think he ever loved her in the traditional way, either," I said. "Not what I could see of things. So why did they marry at all?"

"Gotta go see Liddy, Tom, and then get on home," Dovie said, sliding out of my presence without answering. "Doc'll be wondering where I am. I promised him a pecan pie for supper. You know, like the one we bribed Bird Briley with that time?"

I nodded and sighed.

"Are you glad he died in the fire, Tom?" Dovie asked me on her way to the stairs.

"If he set it, yes. If he didn't, well––We'll never know, will we? The authorities couldn't find any sign of kerosene or other flammables. Some folks say the house was haunted, and wondered if the haint set the fire to help protect Liddy."

Dovie was gone for a few minutes. Then, as the two friends walked down the stairs and crossed the dining room, Dovie caught my eye, winked and said, "Liddy, why don't you and Tom come over later tonight for pie and coffee? How about nine."

"Depends on what Tom has planned for supper," Liddy said, smiling, as she came to stand by me. I took her hand and she didn't resist.

"Sounds good to me," I answered, looking at my adored one. "We'll be there."

We walked with Dovie to the door. I opened it, and saw the four Ponder boys at the foot of the front steps. One was holding the baby wrapped in a blanket.

Dovie hurried across the porch, pushed open the screen and asked them, "What's wrong? Is he sick?" She ran down the steps and grabbed Angelo from Sharp Ponder. The nurse sat on the third step and turned the edge of the blanket down from his face. Liddy and I stood on the porch and watched. Liddy gripped my arm with what I took to be alarm.

"No," the eldest boy said. "It's Mama. She's too weak to take care of him. She told us to ask the lady who came to help her if she would take him. Mama thought she remembered Middy or––"

Liddy let out a muffled scream behind her hands. I instinctively put my arms around her to keep her from trembling out of control. Or to hold her, if she fainted. Or just to hold her.

One of the other boys––Weems, maybe––held out an ancient paper bag. "Mama sent these clothes, too." Dovie reached for the sack. "Mama knew Tom could get good milk for him," the third boy said.

Liddy finally found her voice, and I dropped my arms when she began to speak. "Oh, thank you, thank you!" she said to the band of boys who had traipsed down from Little Trot to give their baby brother a new home. "I'm speechless!" She wiped her eyes. "I accept! I accept!" She walked down to the boys and enveloped them with her arms. "You tell your Mama she's made me the happiest woman in the Ozarks." The boys reddened and hung their heads, each with a shy smile that couldn't be hidden.

I followed Liddy down into the yard and spoke to the boys, "I'll drive you back home. Dovie, anything you want to ask them? Any message for Mrs. Ponder?"

Dovie stood and handed Angelo to Liddy. "Tom, why don't I drive up with you and check on her? Let me get my nurse's kit from the car." On her way, she called back to Liddy. "Call Walden's and Moody's and order baby things. Here, check what's in this bag first. You'll need bottles, evaporated milk, diapers, a crib and crib sheets. Call Xann and see if he can deliver them."

The boys climbed into the back of the Green Queen pickup and were 'oohing' and 'ahhing' over the upholstery and the chrome.

Liddy walked over to the porch, cradling Angelo in one arm and holding on to the railing with her other hand, as if she were afraid she might trip with her precious bundle. She didn't look at us and wave, but continued into the dining room completely engrossed.

I hated to leave her alone, but what else could I do?

— Chapter Sixty-Four —

LIDDY

September 30, 1942

Dear Mother,

I finally have a baby! No husband yet, but I believe Tom will ask me soon. I may ask him first!

Dovie examined Mrs. Ponder who was too weak and malnourished to take care of her fifth baby. Mother, she gave him to me! Since I'd helped Mrs. Ponder through her labor, she wanted me to have him.

Angelo is a month old and growing like a bunny rabbit. He drinks evaporated milk, which is cheaper than the commercial baby formula, and he sleeps a lot. Tom keeps him while I'm at The Banner. *We have two cribs, one in the kitchen and one upstairs in my room.*

I'm happier now than I've ever been. But there's sadness, too. When President Roosevelt signed the Selective Training Service Act the middle of this month, many St. Lukans decided to leave here to help the war effort––among them my best friends, Dovie, and Doc Everett. All the young men––Keener Nance and Xann Price and Landers Beane––have already left. Papa Quinn took an officer's position in the Army. Before he left, he told me Heth was given the choice of jail or conscription. He took the draft.

Daddy is managing Boss Lincoln's car dealership. He and Miz Myrt are courting, but I seldom see them except when they come to the boardinghouse to eat.

On top of all this, Editor Redd has decided to retire. Guess what? She asked me to become the editor of the newspaper. See what I mean? Nothing but good is happening now. I'm nearly afraid to crow too loudly for fear things will come crashing down again.

Mother, thank you for everything. I feel like my journey is over.

I've made my choice: I'm home.

The End

LaVergne, TN USA
22 March 2011
221223LV00001B/5/P

9 781450 254175